Readers love TEMPESTE O'RILEY

Caged Sanctuary

"…this is a wonderfully sweet story… Suffice to say the author takes her readers on a gentle rollercoaster of emotions in this book, and I really enjoyed the journey."

—Sinfully… Addicted to All Male Romance

"…a sincere, well thought out story that the author handled very much appropriately giving two men their happy ever after."

—MM Good Book Reviews

"These men will quickly drag you in, especially Kaden who will steal your heart in his own earnest and shy way."

—Prism Book Alliance

Truth in Lace

"It was amazing!"

—The Blogger Girls

Temptations of Desire

"The writer did an excellent job with the characters, they are likable and perfect. Not perfect in the way that they have no flaws, but in a way that they grab you and complement each other."

—Love Bytes

"I love this series!"

—Fallen Angels Reviews

By TEMPESTE O'RILEY

Caged Sanctuary
Grand Adventures
Whiskers of a Chance

DESIRES ENTWINED
Designs of Desire
Bound by Desire
Desires' Guardian
Temptations of Desire
Truth in Lace

Published by DREAMSPINNER PRESS
www.dreamspinnerpress.com

WHISKERS *of a* CHANCE

TEMPESTE O'RILEY

DREAMSPINNER PRESS

Published by

DREAMSPINNER PRESS

5032 Capital Circle SW, Suite 2, PMB# 279, Tallahassee, FL 32305-7886 USA
www.dreamspinnerpress.com

Whiskers of a Chance
© 2015 Tempeste O'Riley.

Cover Art
© 2015 Catt Ford.
Cover content is for illustrative purposes only and any person depicted on the cover is a model.

ISBN: 978-1-63476-524-4
Digital ISBN: 978-1-63476-525-1
Library of Congress Control Number: 2015942997
First Edition September 2015

Printed in the United States of America
∞
This paper meets the requirements of
ANSI/NISO Z39.48-1992 (Permanence of Paper).

To those who only want to be loved as they are and all those seeking to find acceptance in their skin.

I want to give a special thanks to Katy, for without her, Keith would never have found his strength and Jason would never have found his heart.

CHAPTER ONE

KEITH SKYLER sat in the hard, high-back wooden chair across from his father, Adam, fighting the desire to scowl at the ignorant male. It was bad enough to be called into his office like a recalcitrant child, but to have to sit in the uncomfortable chair while Adam sat in the plush office chair irked him even further. The positioning was deliberate, to remind Keith that his father had the power, as if he didn't know that already.

"What part of 'Taylor and I are moving to one of the outer areas of town' don't you understand? You insist that since Taylor is without a mate, she needs me to live with her. You also demand it so Zeke can have a male figure in his life, at least until Taylor or I mate. She wishes to move closer to her work, as do I."

Adam Skyler's expression was stoic, as always, but the energy pouring off him was bordering on violent. Keith waited for his father to respond, knowing Keith would get what he wanted, though not certain what the cost would be yet. One did not simply do things without the great and mighty Adam Skyler, Alpha of the Glacier Rim Tribe, giving his approval… except when he and Taylor did.

"Why are you only bringing this to me now, Keith? You know how I feel about your sister's wild ideas of living with the humans. It's dangerous!"

"Other tribes live—"

"Chain." Adam closed his eyes as he pinched the bridge of his nose. "A 'tribe' of lynx is called a chain, and you know it."

"That's a human term, one that isn't even agreed upon by the inter-tribal council. Other lynx call their groupings *tribes*, not *chains*." He hated the term *chain*. It made them sound like a stupid fence instead of the extended family and friends that make up a tribe. Well, that's what tribes ought to be. Theirs failed on many points to be that, mostly thanks to his father's extreme patriarchal methods. When he took over, if he ever did, he swore to make their tribe more egalitarian—though Adam did not know that yet.

"I will not debate this with you, nor do I approve of Taylor and you moving away from our area."

"Father, the house is already bought. We signed the papers yesterday and picked up the keys." Yeah, he knew their method of gaining a little independence was inappropriate, willful, and could easily backfire, but he was determined to give his sister all the freedom he could and hopefully teach Zeke to be a good man, as well as a good lynx.

"You already did *what*?" Adam bellowed, his stoic demeanor finally cracking.

"We bought the house."

"On whose authority?"

"Mine. I am the prince and heir, and well over the age of adulthood. I need room to live and breathe. Taylor needs room to raise Zeke without the other females in her space. I know they mean well, but Zeke is *her* son, not theirs."

"They are only trying to help your sister. She's all alone and trying to raise her child."

"No, she's not. She has me. I know her mate died, leaving her single and with kit, but I am there for both of them. Besides, with both of us working in town, this arrangement makes the most sense. And don't worry, the house abuts the woods, giving us plenty of room to hunt, roam, and live in both our skins."

"And if I forbid this move?" Adam asked, his tone dropping to one of resigned irritation—a sound Keith was well used to.

"We are locked into the mortgage, Father." Adam Skyler was never one to waste money, a fact Keith was exceptionally glad of right then. "We will have to pay for it either way, and it would be foolish to own a home and not use it."

The growl from his father was not unexpected. Still, were he in his feline skin rather than his human skin now, his fur would want to stand on end.

"Since you have made it difficult to argue against this nonsense, you and Taylor may move, *but* I will visit shortly after you are settled. If the residence does not meet with my wishes and standards, you will come home and find a way to sell the house."

Thank you! "Give it a chance, Father. You know Taylor's tastes. She wouldn't live anywhere unsuitable."

"Anywhere among humans is already unacceptable, but we shall see."

"Thank you, Father. I need to make sure things are ready for our move." Keith waited, hoping Adam would allow him his leave and not push further.

"You are excused, Keith. However, I do not appreciate being managed this way. Until you come of age, I am still the alpha of this chain."

Tribe, dammit! "Understood, Father."

Keith quickly stood and exited the room, then maneuvered through the house to find Taylor. He was itching to shift and go for a run. His lynx always wanted to be outside, in his fur, after he was called before his father—or the council for that matter. By the time he found Taylor, outside playing with Zeke, he was bordering on screaming. Seeing them playing in their lynx forms helped calm him, allowing him to breathe easier.

"Taylor?" He couldn't help the smile that tugged at his lips when she turned, her tufted ears swiveling before her gaze met his. "When you're ready, I need to pick up the U-Haul and get things loaded."

They had been packing, but as their father never came to their part of the house, even though it was just one floor up from his own suite, he hadn't noticed all the boxes or layout plans. Their father's home was more akin to two houses stacked one atop another. He and Taylor had their own kitchen, living room, dining space, and bedrooms, but they didn't have any freedom or real space to be themselves. Not with their father and his advisers always underfoot and snooping into their lives.

Taylor hurried to where Keith stood, shifting as soon as she stopped in front of him—luckily her nudity no longer fazed him. When he was younger, her doing that had bothered him a great deal, but only because she was his sister. "He said yes?" she asked, her voice cracking on the last word.

Damn, she must have been more worried than she'd let on. "Of course. He insists upon checking on us once we've moved in, but that is to be expected," he explained, shrugging one shoulder. He didn't want to make a big thing about their move while they were outside. He never knew who might be within hearing range, after all.

Taylor grinned as she launched herself at Keith. "Thank you!" Without letting him go, she turned her head and called to Zeke, "Go make sure all your things are packed for Uncle Keith to take with him. I don't want you upset that something special left with him instead of being in your travel bag."

Laughing, Keith unwound his sister from around his body. "Go put something on, would ya? Like I want your girly bits on me."

Taylor swatted Keith's chest as she took off after Zeke—who had opted to stay in lynx form as he hurried inside and up the stairs.

By the time he'd caught up to them, Zeke was in his room, going through the special travel bag Keith had bought him the week prior. He'd been so proud of Zeke for not saying anything about their packing, not even to the other kittens in their tribe. Keith had been so careful when bringing boxes in and out of the house, making certain that neither his father nor his advisers were around to see what they were doing.

"Can't believe you managed to get his approval so quickly," Taylor said from behind him as he stood staring at the stacks of boxes ready to move.

"Hey, playing the money card usually works with him. Why do you think I wanted us to have signed the mortgage papers and all *before* I said anything to him? I'm not stupid, and moving away is the only way either of us will have any freedom to be who we are, instead of who he thinks we should be."

She sighed contentedly. "I know, and I can't wait to get going. Are you sure you want to do the move yourself? Zeke and I could help, instead of us only getting there after you have the house all set up?"

"Taylor, I know how you want everything set up. We've gone over the pictures and floor plan dozens of times already. This is safer for Zeke and will give me a chance to scope out the woods a little more before he gets there and wants to go run or climb."

"Yeah, I just hate for you to do all the work like this."

Her pout was adorable, but he had reasons, personal ones that he didn't want to tell her yet, for wanting to go ahead of them. When they'd gone over to view the house the second time—which was when they'd put in the bid—he'd caught a scent he never thought to find. The pull had been almost painful, and now he just needed to find out who it belonged to. Even though he needed more information, his mind kept yelling *mate*. Being gay, he hadn't believed he would have a mate, but he couldn't think of any other reason for the insta-hard-on, the driving need to mate, or the way his cat paced just under the skin after he refused to go back to the house early and find who the luscious scent belonged. Hell, he wasn't really certain he wanted to find the person. He didn't want a female! And though only Taylor knew that his heart and body only craved others of the same sex, he feared finding who Baast had chosen for him.

"I've got some friends that are going to help me unload in exchange for pizza and beer." He chuckled. "Seems that works for humans as well as cats."

"All right, Keith. But if you need help, you'll call me, right?" Her little upturned face always reminded him of her cat with its wide hazel eyes and tiny button nose, which she tended to wrinkle when annoyed. "Please."

"Of course, but it'll be fine. I promise. This time next week, you'll be in our new home and won't have anyone but me nosing into your business."

"Won't that be wonderful?" she chirped, bouncing on her toes. "Okay, go make sure you have your immediate-needs bag ready. When do you leave?"

"A little after lunch tomorrow. The cats helping on this end of the move will be here in the morning. The humans are, of course, meeting me at the house. It's all going to work out, sissy, I promise."

By the time Keith made it to bed that night, he was so anxious he barely managed to get any sleep. He wondered about the scent he'd caught, and the future, and hoped for freedom from his father's keen gaze and bigoted mouth.

THE DRIVE to their new home wasn't long, but loading everything into the U-Haul while his father looked on, scowling and making unhelpful comments, had Keith's nerves frayed and his temper short. The hope-slash-fear of finding his mate added extra layers to his stress. By the time he arrived at the Wendy's where he would meet the guys, he was in serious need of a drink—or three. Since that wasn't an option yet, he pigged out on Spicy Asiago Ranch Chicken Club sandwiches and Frosty treats. Carbs instead of booze....

"Dude," Dale groused. "How can you eat all that and still be as thin as you are?"

His eating habits drove his human friends crazy. If they ate like he did, they'd all be too big to get through the door. "Good genes," he quipped, same as always.

"So not fair," Ryan pouted. He struggled with his weight, wanting to be thin to attract guys at the club, but his body wanted to be slightly chubby no matter what he did.

Personally, Keith thought his friend needed to stop worrying about what shallow club-boys thought and focus instead on being happy and healthy for himself. "Sorry, didn't mean to make you feel bad, Ryan."

"You don't. Just wish I had your metabolism. Seriously, I can't figure out where you put it all."

If he just told them he was a lynx shifter and they even knew what that meant, they would know why—all shifters had overdeveloped metabolisms, a side effect of all the shifting they did. However, he was forbidden to reveal his species, and as often as he hated not being able to share that part of himself with his friends, he knew it was too dangerous for humans to know of their kind... or of any kind of shifter, for that matter.

Well, a few humans knew, but it was exceedingly rare and considered dangerous to their kind as a whole. What if the government or scientists wanted to collect them and experiment? A shiver tore through him at the thought. He pushed the morbid thought away and focused on his friends again.

"Ready to head out?" he asked. He didn't like depressing Ryan, so he usually didn't eat around him.

"Yeah, let's get this party started!" Dale crowed.

An hour later they were at his new home, with the U-Haul, and various cars filled with human and a few of his cat friends—the ones who didn't look down on humans—parked along the driveway and curb. As soon as he opened the truck door, the scent of his mate slammed into him, stealing his breath for a moment. Conscious of the other cats close by, he schooled his face and took a few slow breaths, trying to force down his desire and need. No way did he want others to know what was going on before he found the woman. *Woman*, he groaned internally. Why did he have to have a mate? Being gay was hard enough and not something he could let others know about, as it just wasn't done—not with how his father would react—and being mated on top of that would just be cruel.

By the time they were done with all the unloading, Keith decided that the Gods hated him. The scent of his mate constantly called to him—burning wood mixed with sandalwood and grass—teasing him mercilessly, and worse, he'd caught one of his neighbors watching him and his friends moving their things inside. The man pushed all his buttons—well, what of him he could see, thanks to the man being on the other side of a window from him—making him both thrilled that he'd moved and regretting it. His neighbor hadn't come out to meet him yet, but if the man didn't stop by soon, Keith decided he would just have to go over and say hello—if this whole *mate* thing didn't interfere. If he mated, he'd be screwed... or rather, he'd never be screwed again. That depressing thought wound through him, helping him keep his hormones in check and his focus off sex.

Once all the unloading was done, they broke out the beers and called for pizza. That done, Keith cranked up his stereo so it could be heard outside, though not too loudly, not wanting the cops called, then joined his friends for food, booze, and relaxing. Though it would have been more relaxing if the two couples—both gay couples, no less—hadn't been determined to dirty-dance and make out so much. Jealousy was ugly, he knew that, but right then it was a hard fact to remember.

Going to sleep the first night in his home, one that his father had nothing to do with, should have been an exciting and freeing event. Instead he tossed and turned, dreading the next day more than he had anything since his mother's passing when he was a boy. He had nowhere to be, and the house was mostly put together. He'd been up half the night after his friends finally left, putting books on shelves, dishes in cupboards, and trying to convince himself that his mystery mate would be a male. The last item was his only failure of the night.

CHAPTER TWO

JASON GRANT looked out his office window for the fifth time, desperate to catch another glimpse of his new neighbor. The adorable man had moved in the day before, but there had been so many people around at his place that Jason had felt too nervous to go over and introduce himself. Today, however, he'd made a casserole to take over as an excuse to say hello. Jason knew most men would think his offering odd, but if it was a good enough excuse for nosy women all over the world, he figured he could use it too.

He'd also showered, shaved, dressed, and redressed three times while waiting for the sexy neighbor-man to show signs of being up and about inside his new home. Jason wasn't surprised he hadn't seen anyone yet, not with the man's friends staying to party until nearly three a.m. after they'd unloaded the U-Haul for the second time. Nevertheless, Jason hoped he'd see him soon, or he'd have to go shower and change again due to nerves alone.

As he sat in his office chair, he thought back to the previous evening and his first glimpse of the new man. Given what he could compare him to as he moved around and unloaded things, different objects in the yard, and the vehicles he'd seen, Jason figured his new neighbor was a little over six feet tall. He had spiky, light brown hair that appeared soft and had golden tips when the light hit him just right. He was both lithe and strong, Jason noted, remembering seeing the man lift an overstuffed love seat by himself before sauntering back inside the bungalow-like house.

Jason chastised himself for his obsession, unsure if his new neighbor even batted for the same team. He knew some of the man's friends did; he'd seen two of the couples making out in the backyard. Between watching the strangers groping and grinding on each other and his immediate infatuation with a man he hadn't even met yet, Jason had stroked off three times the previous night before he'd been able to get to sleep.

He dropped his hand into his lap to caress his hardening length when he saw the face that had haunted his dreams the night before and his waking hours since. There in the small kitchen window stood his desire. The man had a serious case of bed-head, and as no curtains were up yet, Jason could see the other man wore nothing but a pair of baggy shorts, low on his lean, tapered hips. His chest and abs were so defined Jason could see the contouring even from his office. And damn did he love a man with a little hair. He squeezed his throbbing member through his slacks and imagined running his fingers through the light brown fuzz on those well-defined pecs. He continued to rub up and down his length as his gaze followed the thin trail down past the shallow dent of a belly button before disappearing inside those sinfully low shorts.

Jason's gut cramped as his neighbor bent to pick something up, and he decided watching from afar simply wasn't his thing. He closed his eyes and pulled his hand away from his groin, determined to behave and take the man food instead of jacking off. Again.

Jason stood there for another moment, admiring and planning before he turned and headed to the bathroom to splash some cold water on his face and tidy up before he entered his kitchen. He checked on the food one last time before he gathered the cut-glass casserole dish from the oven and set it carefully in the wire scrollwork carrying tray his best friend, Sasha, had given him as a housewarming gift. He checked himself in the mirror one last time, took a deep breath, and stepped out the front door.

Gathering his courage, Jason walked down the sidewalk as he scolded the acrobatic butterflies assaulting his stomach and then took the three stairs up to the front door. He pushed the doorbell with his elbow and waited, praying this wasn't another huge mistake. He was never impulsive, usually taking his time to get to know someone long before doing anything to reveal his interest. This time, though, he didn't care, or rather, Jason was determined not to let his past influence his chances with the new man. If he ever opened the door, that is.

Frowning, he hit the doorbell again. A minute later, he heard sounds from the other side and pasted on his best smile. The door swung open, revealing a confused-looking but adorably mussed man standing there. He still wore nothing but the shorts, though his hair was a bit calmer.

"Hello?" The deep voice had a slight lilt, but he couldn't place it just then.

Jason met the man's gaze and almost lost his grip on the dish holder. He had never seen such vivid blue eyes before; so bright and piercing in the man's pale, beatific face, they made him seem almost otherworldly. "H-hi," he stuttered. "I'm Jason Grant."

"Hello, Jason." A soft smile spread across the man's face as he looked Jason over. The slow perusal had Jason's cock instantly hard again and his pulse racing so loud he was certain the Adonis before him could tell. "I'm Keith Skyler."

"Hi, Keith." Jason liked how the name felt on his tongue. "I brought you a 'welcome to the neighborhood' dish," he said, holding the casserole out a little.

"Thank you. Why don't you bring that inside?" Keith led him into his home and to the kitchen. Jason was surprised to see that most of the unpacking seemed to already be done. Or, at least most of the boxes were broken down, the furniture in place, and some knickknacks and books were on the various shelves.

He set the dish down on the counter next to the stove and smiled at Keith. "I hope you like cheese?" he said and gestured to his offering. When Keith raised his right brow and looked down at the dish, he hurried to explain. "It's a five-cheese broccoli-noodle casserole."

"Is that a fancy way of saying really cheesy mac 'n cheese?" Keith laughed when he nodded. The deep, happy rumble raced up Jason's spine, making him shiver. "I happen to love all forms of cheese, and seriously, who doesn't like macaroni?" Keith moved around his kitchen as if he'd lived there for years instead of less than twenty-four hours. He took down two plates and turned to face Jason. "Join me?"

Yes!

"DAMN, YOU'RE a good cook." Keith worked to scoop another bit of the cheesy noodles onto his plate, a smile playing at the edges of his lips.

"Thanks. I've never had it with wine before, but you were right, they do pair quite nicely." Of course, they were both a bit tipsy by then, but Jason didn't care. Spending the time with Keith was well worth the extra running time this indulgence would require.

"Mmm...." Keith moaned around another bite. "I could get used to this." He swallowed and then cleaned the tip of his fork with slow, deliberate licks of his pink, and rather dexterous, tongue.

Jason groaned as he sat transfixed, watching every little flick and curl of the appendage he wanted to suck on and devour—well, one of them at least. He'd been half-hard all through lunch, but now his pants were too tight, as all his blood rushed below his belt. If the man didn't stop teasing him, he'd have to excuse himself and go take care of things in the restroom. "More wine?" he asked, hoping to redirect his thoughts.

"Please," Keith said, his voice dropping to a low rumble, but shook his head no as he looked up. "Actually, I think I'm about done with this course."

Course? "Uh, I only brought the one dish."

"Oh, I know, but what's dinner without a little dessert?"

Jason nodded, mentally scrambling as he tried to think of where he could run quickly for a sweet treat. "I can go get us something. What do you like?"

Keith chuckled, his eyes half-lidded as he smiled at Jason. "Help me clean up here, and I'll provide everything we'll need."

A small whimper escaped before Jason could control himself. "S-sure." He hated when he stuttered. He'd been so happy he hadn't done so, aside from that first time. Damn, the man had his brain fried and his dick weeping already!

They finished the little left on their plates and set about clearing the table and rinsing the dishes. Keith took every chance, or so it seemed to Jason, to brush against him, driving him to the edge of his control and keeping him teetering there. As he placed the last dish in the dishwasher, Jason felt large, strong hands slip down his back before coming to rest on his hips.

He stilled, hoping Keith wouldn't pull away, fearing he'd simply misinterpreted the gesture. "K-K-Keith?" *Stupid stutter.*

"You know, I saw you watching me last night."

"Y-you did? I was j-just curious about who was m-moving in." He hadn't thought anyone paid any attention to him as he sat in his office the night before. He wasn't memorable, as he'd been told many times.

"Mmm-hmm," Keith hummed against Jason's ear as he took a step forward.

A second later, the heat of Keith's body pressed against his back. Without thinking, he leaned back into the warmth and strength now surrounding him. He'd caught a whiff of the man's earthy scent before, but now it seemed as though it poured off him, seeping into every nerve and thought Jason had.

"Why?" Jason breathed, unsure what to do next. He knew what he looked like, and at just a touch under six feet tall, with somewhat dirty blond hair cut in a conservative, business look, and lackluster hazel eyes, he couldn't believe a man with Keith's rugged, model-worthy looks could really want him.

"I think it was the serious look on your face as you watched us unload." He felt a shrug against his back. "Or maybe the activity you got up to later was what caught my eye. But either way, I was hoping you'd come over soon."

Keith traced his ear with the tip of his tongue, sending shivers through Jason's suddenly superheated body. "A-act-tivity?" Jason asked. He hadn't thought anyone could see him.

Keith pressed against him tight, letting Jason feel how hard he was—and how big. Damn! "Oh yeah. I dreamed about you, about taking you in this very kitchen."

This couldn't be happening. Keith wanted him too? "And what did you p-picture us doing?"

"I'd rather show you," Keith whispered into his ear before sucking the lobe into his hot, wet mouth and biting gently.

Jason nearly came just from that little action. "Oh God." He whimpered, pushing back and rubbing his butt against Keith's rigid cock. "You—I—Oh, please," he choked out. He never did things like this, but right then, all he could think about was how perfect Keith would feel deep inside him, filling him, taking him right there on the counter.

Keith spun him around to face him so fast Jason got dizzy. He looked up, confused, before Keith took his mouth in a rough, demanding kiss that stole his breath and what was left of his thoughts. His world condensed down to the sweet bite of teeth and the wet slide of Keith's searching tongue as he mapped and ate at Jason's mouth. He was vaguely aware of moans and pleading whimpers, but he couldn't focus on anything but the man currently devouring his very soul.

Keith's fingers dug into his hip, hard enough he knew he'd have bruises later—a thought that brought more heat to his passion and joy to his battered heart. He snaked his other hand up to Jason's head, his fingers threading through Jason's short hair, and tugged enough to drive his want and need higher. Keith used his grip on Jason's hair to tilt his head to the side and back, eliciting more breathy sounds from Jason. Keith kissed down his neck, nipping as he went. He rubbed his cheek against Jason's and demanded roughly, "Tell me I can have you. Right here. Right now."

Before he could make his mouth work, Keith bit him, sinking his teeth into the flesh where his neck and shoulder met. Instead of saying yes, as he'd intended, Jason keened high and loud, the sound echoing through the kitchen. Keith swiped his tongue over the now-tender skin before kissing his way back up his neck. "I need to hear you say it. And as much as I love the sounds you're making, you have to answer me. Now."

The deep, rumbling words edged him closer to oblivion. God, but he loved a man who knew what he wanted during sex. "Y-yes," he panted and rocked his trapped dick against Keith's. "Please, yes."

The possibility for any more words was cut off when Keith plunged his tongue back inside Jason's mouth, grinding their cocks together as he thrust in a way Jason hoped Keith would soon be doing a bit lower.

CHAPTER THREE

KEITH'S FINGERS released their tight hold on his hair. Moments later, his hands dropped down and roughly cupped Jason's butt, adding a delicious pressure and friction to their grinding. Jason's lips were tender as he drowned in Keith's dominance and taste. Jason clutched at Keith's back, digging his fingers in and reveling in the strength of the muscles there, in how they moved beneath his fingers.

An eternity later, Keith tore his mouth away, licked his lips, and panted against Jason's mouth. "I have to have this," he murmured as he squeezed Jason's cheeks in his hands and lifted, pulling him off his feet.

Jason was suddenly facing the counter again just as Keith's hands moved to the button and zipper of his trousers. In moments, his pants were down around his knees. Keith caressed up and down Jason's lower back and across his backside, before he dipped his fingers inside Jason's boxer briefs. "I love how these fit you. They hug your ass so perfectly." Keith groaned before sinking his teeth into Jason's shoulder again and tugging the briefs down.

Jason shivered as the cool air moved across his now-exposed, weeping cock. The bite added the perfect contrast while pushing his need higher. Rough and demanding were his favorite traits in a lover, but only in the bedroom, or kitchen as the case may be. "C-condom?" he moaned, desperate for more.

"In a minute. Right now, I'm going to taste this ass of yours. When I'm ready, I'm going to take you right here where you stand."

"T-taste?" He groaned. He'd never had a lover willing to rim him. He'd done it, and knew it felt good—his previous lovers' sounds and actions had proven that—but now he hoped he could hold out long enough to get Keith in him before he shot.

"Mmm-hmm, until you come for me."

"But," he said, trying to find the words to say he wanted more even as he thought he should be thankful for what he was already receiving. "Want...."

"Oh, I didn't say I'd stop then. I plan to make you scream before I fill you." Keith punctuated his words by dropping to his knees behind Jason and nipping his left cheek. "And then I'll make you scream again."

Jason shoved back into Keith's face, his entire world now only his need and the overwhelming sensations as they shot up his spine. "P-please...."

Keith caressed and massaged his ass with his hands and lips, exposing Jason's hungry hole to the cool air repeatedly. He jumped when a steady stream of warm air hit him there and drew a groan from so deep within him, he was certain it came from his soul. The first swipe of Keith's tongue forced him to stretch across the counter and hold on tight or risk hitting the floor. At first, the licks went from the base of his balls to the top of his crack, but after a few swipes, Keith focused in on his pulsing, needy entrance, nibbling and stabbing at the tight muscles with his teeth, lips, and tongue.

Jason had never felt anything like it before and was quickly pushed to the edge as he writhed against the granite counter, drowning in Keith's ministrations. Just as he thought he would lose it, a finger pushed against him, the pressure both welcome and needed. The tongue didn't stop licking around the digit as it slowly penetrated him.

Moments later, Keith's other hand massaged and tugged on Jason's sac, driving his pleasure and need higher. Keith thrust one finger inside as he continued his oral assault, the slide and friction wonderful. Keith kept filling him only to retreat over and over again.

"More, please," Jason begged, not caring how he sounded. He needed to come!

Keith withdrew his finger, but before Jason could form a protest, it returned, joined by a second. The stretch and slight burn pulled him back from the edge, but only for a few moments. The licking and probing tongue again added to the pleasure coiling at the base of his cock. Keith thrust his fingers in, stretching and twisting, preparing Jason for what he hoped would come soon. Very soon.

When Keith's fingers twisted hard and curled, tagging his happy spot inside, Jason screamed, arching back into Keith, desperate for more. The hard press of teeth to his ass jolted him, but instead of distracting him, as he was certain it should have, he groaned and reveled in the delicious sensations.

"Like that, huh?" Keith's deep voice growled. "God, I wanna eat you whole."

Jason whimpered at the thought of his cock slipping between Keith's full, wide lips. If Keith was as talented on the front side as he was the back, Jason wasn't sure he'd survive the onslaught but wasn't about to complain. "I want," he panted.

"Don't tempt me, Jay. You have no idea how much I want to taste all of you, inside and out." Keith punctuated his words by sinking his teeth into Jason's hip before bathing the area with his tongue. "Come for me, now!"

The tone, coupled with Keith zeroing in on his prostate, hard, sent him over the edge. Jason keened as his world turned white, pleasure rocketing up and out of his cock as he shot against the counter and floor.

At some point, his knees failed him completely. He wasn't certain how long he was out, but when he managed to focus his eyes again, he was sprawled across Keith's lap as he sat on the floor, Jason's head against the man's chest. The steady thump of his heart and the gentle caressing up and down his back and side helped to bring Jason's world back to center.

"Mmm... there you are." Keith lifted his chin, gazing down into his eyes with a focus Jason had never felt before. "You always pass out like that?"

Jason shook his head. "No." In truth, he had never had an orgasm that hard or all-encompassing, but he didn't want to think about those that had come before, not right then.

"Open your eyes." The rough voice startled him—he hadn't realized he'd even closed them. Then he thought about how he was sitting.

"Sorry," he mumbled, forcing his eyes open and up to meet Keith's gaze. "Didn't mean to squash you like that."

Keith laughed, a rumbling, happy sound that made Jason smile. "You aren't near big enough to do that," he said, ruffling his hand through Jason's hair. "I simply wanted to make sure you were okay before I continued."

The leer and tone shot straight to Jason's groin, and if he hadn't just had the best and longest orgasm of his life, he knew he'd be hard again. "Continued?"

"Told you I'd make you scream before I fucked you, didn't I?"

Jason nodded.

Keith leaned down and pressed his lips to Jason's, but where the kiss had been bruising and violent before, it was soft and sensual now. He slid his tongue along the seam of Jason's mouth, but when Jason opened to receive Keith's, his lower lip was suckled and nipped instead. He squirmed around until he straddled Keith's lap and ground his ass down against Keith's hard dick, reveling in the sounds his motions elicited.

Keith grabbed his hips moments before his world flipped again. After a second, he realized he was the one who was suddenly upside down, not the world. Jason was now flat on his back, looking up into the deepest azure eyes he had ever seen. "I am only going to ask this once. Are you positive you want me to continue? If you don't stop me now, I will devour you from the inside out."

Who talked like that? "I'm…. P-p-please take whatever you w-want."

"Damn, I love how you can't even get the words out, you want me so bad." Keith sealed his mouth over Jason's again, plundering as he mapped every inch.

Jason reached down, then tugged on Keith's shorts, determined not to be the only one naked—or near naked, as his pants were still tangled around one of his ankles. Keith only pulled back long enough to trap Jason's hands, pinning them to the floor, before again taking his lips in a devouring assault that had Jason panting and dizzy.

Several minutes later, Jason ripped his mouth away and gasped for breath. Instead of pausing, though, Keith moved to kiss down his neck, licking and nuzzling the flesh there before biting and nipping his way down to the juncture between shoulder and neck. Jason jolted, the pain mixing with the pleasure in a way he'd never felt before. "Keith," he moaned, desperate for more.

Without releasing Jason, Keith reached up, opened a drawer, and rummaged around inside. When he pulled his hand back, he held a small bottle of K-Y liquid. That was great, but he wasn't doing anything without a raincoat! Keith chuckled against his neck. "Don't worry, baby, I've got a condom around here too. I know someone left a couple," he whispered against Jason's ear before tracing it with the tip of his tongue. Keith groaned. "Gods, you taste good."

Keith pulled away, then sat up a moment and riffled through two other drawers before shouting and presenting a circular condom wrapper for Jason's inspection. "Now come here," he growled.

Jason lost himself in the kiss this time. The world was nothing but Keith's hands, tongue, and lips. Eventually he found himself on his knees with Keith behind him. Keith stroked up and down his back, going from his nape to where his butt met his thighs. "So pretty," he purred. "Gonna love feeling you tight around me."

"Then take me, dammit," Jason snapped, his patience long gone. He needed Keith to fill him. He trembled, tears stinging his eyes, as he pushed back, begging for Keith as he never had with anyone before.

A chuckle behind him sounded moments before a wet finger prodded at his entrance again.

"I don't need more prepping! I need you in me."

"I know what you need, Jay. But I won't mistreat you or this gorgeous ass of yours. Now," he added, and smacked Jason's right cheek hard, "behave."

The shock and heat from the slap rushed through his body, stole his breath, and lit his skin on fire. Before he knew what he was doing, Jason pushed back against the invading digit, begging. "Again. P-please."

The groan behind him was telling, and moments later Keith rained a series of sharp swats against his butt, alternating which side he hit. Jason heard whimpers and cries and was only vaguely aware that his own voice was making the sounds. When the spanking stopped, Keith caressed the stinging cheeks as his other hand continued to plunge, two, then three, then four fingers into Jason's throbbing channel. Jason felt so full and hot he could no longer form words.

Keith slowly pulled his fingers out, leaving Jason feeling so empty he nearly wept at the loss. Then he heard the sound of the wrapper ripping, and the flip cap of the lube clicked again. Jason trembled when Keith lined his sheathed rod up to his pulsing hole. Keith thrust in in short, stabbing jabs—not enough to penetrate, just tease. Jason timed Keith's movements for a moment and then on the next thrust forward, he slammed back, his body swallowing Keith's huge cock. Mostly. He froze at the fiery pain that shot through him. He hadn't taken into account how long he'd gone without sex or the size of the member between Keith's legs.

"Shh…," Keith crooned, smoothing a hand down Jason's lower back, hips, and thighs. "Give it a minute. You need me to—"

"No, d-don't move. Just, g-give me a minute." He fought with his body, forcing his muscles to relax and accept Keith. The man was going to fuck him, dammit. He wasn't about to let things end now. After a few moments of focus and caressing, his body relaxed and opened to Keith's invasion. "O-okay," he moaned, pushing slowly this time to take more of Keith inside.

"You're so perfect," Keith murmured. He draped himself over Jason's back and kissed Jason's nape as he carefully pushed all the way in. He stopped when he was fully seated, which thrilled Jason. He loved how full Keith made him feel. How he would go without this feeling, this man, on a daily basis, he wasn't certain, but he forced the morose thoughts away, focusing instead on the slow drag and push as Keith started thrusting inside him.

Jason lowered his chest to the floor, loving how the change of angle made the sensations that much more electric.

Keith picked up his pace as he slammed into Jason, the growls and moans from Keith more animal than man. Jason loved hearing them.

White-hot pain sliced through Jason when something pierced one hip where Keith held him. The pace never faltered, even when he screamed, and the pain mingled with the overwhelming pleasure, sending him over the precipice again. His body convulsed as his muscles clamped down on Keith's member, squeezing and milking it as he emptied his bliss through the tip of his cock. Keith hammered him through the orgasm, roaring out his release moments later.

They stayed that way for a time, Keith panting, draped across Jason's back. Eventually Keith moved and separated from him slowly, before helping Jason onto his side. Keith curled around him as he lay in the middle of the kitchen floor, panting. He felt delirious yet sated in a way he never had been before.

"Jason?" Keith asked after a few minutes of lying there quietly, holding Jason around his waist.

"Hmm?"

"I'm sorry," Keith mumbled into his shoulder.

Sorry? "What for?"

"I've never lost control like that. I didn't mean to hurt you," he continued. "Be still and I'll clean you up."

Jason lay there, trying to figure out what Keith was referring to, but his mind drew a blank. All he could think about was how wonderful and perfect being with Keith felt. When Keith returned with a warm cloth and a towel, he wiped the spend and lube off Jason from his navel to the top of his butt. He then produced another cloth and dabbed carefully along Jason's hip.

"Ow!" Jason snapped and pulled away. Confused, he looked down and noted not only the marks he knew would be finger-shaped bruises shortly but also four puncture marks just above his hipbone. "What the hell?"

"I, um…. Be still and close your eyes for a moment," Keith murmured, not meeting his gaze. "Please."

Even with the evidence that Keith could, and had, hurt him, Jason still felt safe with Keith. He nodded and closed his eyes, unsure why he did so. He gasped a moment later when Keith's tongue ran up his hip, slowly tracing the small cuts. Every time Keith licked him, he moaned as a flash of heat ran up and down his spine in a way he'd never felt before. The logical part of his brain wanted to push Keith away, knowing that human mouths and wounds didn't mix; the rest of him told that part to shut the hell up and enjoy the moment.

"All better." Keith's voice was soft and tentative, which it hadn't been since they'd met.

Jason opened his eyes and met Keith's, again falling into the depths of the oceans within. "What?"

"I've waited for you, waited for so long to find someone like you, and when I do, I go off and hurt you the first time we're together." Keith whispered as if he were talking to himself, not Jason, which confused him even more.

"I don't understand, Keith."

"I know, just please believe me when I say it wasn't intentional."

Jason thought about it before he nodded. "It's just a scratch, Keith. I'm the one who pushed you to be rougher. Now," he added, looking around the room, "you think we could find a more comfortable place to cuddle than the floor?"

He didn't want to move, but the cold tile wasn't doing anything good for him. Keith helped Jason pull off the stubborn pants still clinging to one ankle. Jason then let out a yelp when Keith fluidly stood and proceeded to scoop him off the floor and carry him to the couch. Keith sat and pulled Jason between his thighs so Jason's back rested against his chest and loosely wrapped his arms around Jason's waist.

"Um, you have no drapes and we're both still naked."

"The only window with a view to where we're sitting now is yours, so unless you have someone at home," Keith rumbled, his tone turning possessive, "I don't see the problem."

Knowing Keith couldn't see him, Jason smiled, pleased at the words and tone. "No, no one lives there but me. Not even a pet, unless you count my laptops," he mumbled, post-sex lethargy claiming him quickly.

"Good—now rest, Jay. We can talk later."

The last thing Jason felt and heard before sleep claimed him was Keith's warmth and what he could have sworn was a cat purring.

CHAPTER FOUR

KEITH PACED the length of his living room and into the kitchen, then made the trip in reverse, again, as he talked to Taylor on his cell. He'd had to wait to tell her about Jason until she'd gotten away from anyone who might overhear. "He's human, Tay. What the hell am I gonna do?"

"You want him, though, even though he's not a cat. Right?"

"Yes!" He didn't mean to snap, but seriously, that had to be the mother of all stupid questions. "He's beautiful, makes me feel… I don't know how to describe it. I want him so bad I burn with it, and having had him but not completing the mate-bond is making me crazy. I want to go over and live in his house, curl up in his bed, be a part of his life, but humans don't feel the mating pull. They don't mate!"

"You're so cute when agitated. Take a couple of deep breaths for me and then try to think this through logically. You can use logic, Keith. I know you can." Her voice grated on his nerves. *Of course I can think logically!* "Now what makes you so freaked about him? Is it his being human?"

"Let me think…. Oh yes, the fact he's a he. He's a human. He won't feel the mate-bond. Which one would you like me to stress out about first? Or maybe I should freak about how Father will take it if he finds out?" Not that he could hide their bond, if Jason accepted him, from any cat once it was complete. Jason's scent would be on him, just as his scent would forever be on Jason. The thought of what his father might do to Jason had him leaning over the sink in the kitchen, fighting hard not to be ill.

"Keith, you seriously need to calm down. Father wouldn't kill your mate." Taylor's voice cut through his impending panic, but so did the lack of confidence in what she said.

"He would if he thought he could get away with it. He'll never believe our mating is true. Jason's not only human, but as I said before, he's male. You know he doesn't believe cats can be gay, and mating with humans isn't done. It's not against intertribal law, but still…." How would he protect his mate from his father? From his own tribe? He groaned as his thoughts continued to spiral.

"Do I need to come down there early?" Taylor asked, her voice softer but somehow laced with steel. That was one of the things he loved about his little sister: she was one of the strongest shifters he knew.

"No, I have to go back to where you are shortly anyway. No need to move your plans around." He didn't want to return, not right then, but when they had their monthly gathering, the heir had to make an appearance whether he wanted to or not.

Taylor's soft giggle made him smile, even as worry still rode him. Gods! Jason was so perfect for him. Intelligent, kind, able to handle his more dominant side. What wasn't to like?

"Instead of fixating on what he isn't, why don't you work out how to win your boy's heart? Humans, as well as most shifters, don't mate by destiny, but rather by choice." Taylor had been mated by choice, but her mate had died, leaving her a single mom. Somehow she'd survived the loss and managed to be an amazing mom to Zeke. "How do you think us mere mortals find love? Date your Jason. Woo him. Take him out to dinner, to the clubs you like to go to. Find things you both like to do and enjoy getting to know him better."

He knew she was right. Keith had watched his friends date, not just hook up. He could do that! "Thanks, Sis. I'll try asking him out for a normal, human date. I'm not sure how to explain that I'm not human to him, but I'll let him get to know me first, and then let him know about more. Right?"

"Right. Now, try to get some rest, or go hunt, or something. You need to be the calm, clear-headed prince by the time you get back here. If Father smells all this stress on you, he'll try to force you back, and you know it."

Yeah, he did know. The micromanaging asshat had called a dozen times to "talk" about this or that, to worry, to ask a million stupid questions, to try to make Keith second-guess himself and come home before Taylor and Zeke left to live with him. "I will. Promise."

Twenty minutes later, Keith opened his back door, frowning at the lack of easy access he would need in his lynx form to enter and exit. Making a mental note to see about having a small door put in that they could work as their cats, he turned out the lights, then shifted into his pale tan fur with the black-tufted ears, neck ruff, and tail. He took a moment to stretch out his legs and back before he peeked out to check for humans and possible predators.

Once satisfied he was alone, he darted across his backyard to the woods behind. He wanted to check out the area before Taylor and Zeke arrived, plus he needed to be in his fur for a while. Things were easier to manage as a cat. Eat, drink, hunt, find shelter. As the worries of his human form lessened and slipped away, he let himself enjoy being a lynx for a time.

THANKS TO having to drive back to the tribe's land, Keith wasn't able to take as long as he'd like to explore and hunt, but as he'd told Jason he'd be leaving that night, leaving his car in the driveway overnight wouldn't make things go too well between them.

Fighting the urge to play hooky from their monthly gathering, Keith reentered his home before shifting. He'd left the lights off, not needing them thanks to his extraordinary eyesight. A normal lynx's vision was nothing to sneer at, and he'd always been thankful that sight and hearing for lynx shifters was almost the same as for the cat, instead of the muted and shortsighted senses humans had. After a long shower, where he nearly scrubbed his skin off, hoping to mute Jason's scent on it, Keith dried off quickly before redressing.

After making two trips around the house, making sure all the locks were flipped and doors closed tight, he grabbed his wallet and keys and then hopped into the car. He spent a few minutes staring at Jason's house, wanting to go over and see him before he left, but knew that wasn't a good idea. He'd never leave if he did that. Besides, he didn't want to make Jason worry about his possessiveness so early. Humans didn't take to that too well, from what he understood.

Keith started the car, setting his radio to his favorite indie rock station, then pulled out and pointed the car toward his father's home. A place that, hopefully, he would never have to spend much time in again. Even when he became alpha, he wouldn't move in there. He knew Taylor didn't intend to, either, though she had mentioned maybe moving back to the tribe lands once their father was no longer in charge.

About halfway back, Keith's phone rang, startling him out of his car singing—like singing in the shower, but his father couldn't yell about it in the car. When he checked the ID, he groaned. *A. Skyler*.

"Hey, Father," he said once he clicked Accept.

"It's almost time for the gathering to start and you're not here. I knew you moving wasn't a good idea."

No *hello, how is your drive*. Nope. Nada. Just bitch, bitch, bitch.

"Hello to you too, Father. Why yes, it is a lovely night for a drive."

"Don't be smart with me!"

Wouldn't dream of it. "I'm returning tonight, as you requested, but the gathering doesn't start until tomorrow night. So why are you upset already?"

"I have some people here for you to meet, but you're not here to meet them." Keith could hear what sounded like a woman's voice in the background, but it could have been the TV just as easily. "When will you arrive?" It was a demand, not an actual question.

"Thirty minutes, tops. I told you when I'd be there when you called me earlier." *Wait, people? What people?* "What people, Father?"

"Just a few visiting fems that might be interested in staying here."

"As in, wishing to move to our tribe and become members?"

"Yes, for the right reason."

Gods, he hated when his father tried to word-play things. "You mean, you invited some single women over to meet me in hopes I'd pick one and settle down." Why couldn't the man leave well enough alone! "I'm not up for being pimped out."

"Such crassness is unbecoming, son. I expect you to hurry up and make an effort to mingle and mix with the lovely females here. Surely one of them will meet whatever exacting specifications you have in that head of yours." His father's tone was becoming more and more condescending as he continued to speak. "I made sure there's a good mix of shapes and sizes to choose from."

Gritting his teeth, Keith fought the urge to turn around and go right back to Jason. He knew twenty-seven was old for a shifter not to have mated, but he would never mate a woman. And now that he'd found Jason, even the idea of putting up with a night of fawning females, each of them hoping to catch the attention of the next alpha, made him nauseous. No one but his mate should ever touch him. And no one but him should ever touch Jason that way!

Taking a deep breath, in the hope of sounding calmer than he felt, he thought about possible actions. He couldn't refuse to appear, not when his father, his alpha, demanded it. He'd already promised to be there, and his father knew he wasn't scheduled to work during gatherings. He'd had a hell of a time making sure his job never overlapped tribe gatherings, but they'd caved because he always worked harder than they asked him to.

"It's wonderful you thought to schedule a slumber party for Taylor—" He just hoped she didn't kill him for his comment. "—maybe I should call one of the guys and crash over at their place for the night?" Or three.

The sputtering on the other end of the line made Keith smile. His father hated when he didn't do as he was told, but being in his father's home as Adam threw women at him was not his idea of fun. "You will be here as soon as you arrive back home. You will present yourself with a smile on, clean, neat, and as close to happy as you can manage. You only have a few years before you take over as alpha, yet you still haven't settled down. Don't have an heir. Aren't even seeing anyone." Well, the man was wrong on the last two. He had an heir, through his sister: Zeke. And he was dating; Jason had agreed to start seeing him. They planned to spend the whole weekend together, in fact.

"Father—"

"Now," his father demanded.

"I'm always charming and polite when you do this to me, but throwing big-boobed airheads at me is not the way to endear me to your wishes. I have no interest in mating until I find the other half of my soul. You know that." *And it will be a male that completes me, but we won't mention that part yet....*

"Such a childish attitude, Keith. Most shifters do not have fated mates, as you know, so waiting for someone who most likely doesn't exist is asinine. Besides, as the heir, you are responsible for having children. You must have an heir! The Skyler line will not die out because you want to be too picky."

"I will attend. I will talk to the women you picked out. However, I will not take any but my mate home with me. See you shortly, Father."

Not waiting for a response, he clicked off the call and tossed his cell onto the seat beside him. Keith had to pull over a few minutes later when he realized he was shaking. He didn't want the police to notice his weaving or distraction, nor did he enjoy the idea of wrecking his car. He loved his Shelby GT. He'd restored it from the junkyard he'd found it in back in high school. If it were up to him, it would be the only car he would ever drive. Eh, that or Taylor's truck. His father's heavy-handed manipulations were driving him crazy. He'd hated when his alpha tried to fix him up, but now that he'd found Jason, the idea made him ill to even consider.

It took him a little while, but he got himself under control   not that his cat was helping. No, he wanted to go back to Jason and claim his mate properly. *He* didn't see why they had to wait. Once he was calmer, Keith entered the roadway again, and too soon for his liking, he pulled up in front of his father's house. Before he'd so much as gotten the car door open, Taylor was there, waiting with her open arms and loving personality ready to wrap around him.

"I didn't know about the fems ambush until just a little bit ago. I'm so sorry, Keith," she whispered as she hugged him. "This batch has a few that aren't the vapid, big-boobed wonders he usually finds you, at least."

He knew she was trying to make him feel better, but the thought of any female, especially now, made his skin crawl and his cat want out. "Vapid or not, they aren't my mate, Tay. It feels disloyal to even go in and pretend."

"I get that, but unless you want to explain *who* your mate is tonight, which I don't advise, then playing nice is the right choice. It's not like you have to make out with them or anything. Just chat, be dull and boring, and escape as soon as possible."

"I wish it were that easy. But I'll be good, no matter how much I don't want to."

"I know, but you won't have to put up with this very long tonight, and the gathering is tomorrow night, then you can escape. I can't leave 'til this weekend," she added, her bottom lip puffed out far enough to make many five-year-olds green with envy—especially hers.

"You're going to love living there, Taylor. The trees are great, and I've already found areas that are flush with hares to hunt. I can't wait to show you and Zeke."

"Can't wait to get there too," she squealed. "But for now, go play nice prince and smile for the grumpy old cat in there."

"Yeah, that makes me want to go right in. Oh yeah, no it doesn't. But if we stay out here much longer, *he'll* come out looking for me." Swallowing hard and pasting on a smile, Keith followed Taylor into the house. The cloying scents of many perfumes attacked his nose before he'd gotten any farther than the entrance.

"How can you breathe in here?" he grumbled but made his way farther into the house to meet with his father's newest batch of ever-hopefuls. Reminding himself that he'd get to spend the entire weekend with Jason helped him make it into the living room and beyond.

CHAPTER FIVE

TWO DAYS. It had been two days since he'd left Keith's place and returned to his own. Jason's home had never felt so empty, and Keith hadn't even been there yet. The only thing to occupy his time was the same thing as always: work. Later during the same night they'd met, Keith had left, saying he had more things to pick up and move, plus work to do, so he wouldn't be back until the weekend.

Jason didn't remember the days being so boring or the nights being so long before, but time dragged painfully as he waited for Keith to return. While Keith had been away, they hadn't talked as much as Jason had hoped they would, but Keith did promise to spend the weekend with him. Reminding himself of that, Jason buckled down and got back to work on the code he needed to finish if he didn't want to work while Keith was there.

When the phone rang hours later, Jason groaned, arching his back to stretch out and relieve the aches there before reaching over to answer his cell. He vaguely noted the popping-corn sound but was more focused on the relief and on answering the irritating ringing than the condition of his spine.

"Jason Grant, how may I help you?"

"You know, if you ever looked at the caller ID, you wouldn't have to say that every time," the voice of his best friend teased.

"Sasha! Sorry, I was so deep in code I didn't bother. How are you?"

"Well, aren't you the excited little thing today? I'm good. Wanted to know if you would like to come over Saturday. I hate when you stay holed up at your place all the time." Before Jason could reply, Sasha singsonged, "I'll even cook for you."

He loved Sasha, but the man had seriously crappy timing. And missing out on Sasha's cooking…. Damn! "Actually, I've got a date this weekend. So… as much as I'd love to eat dinner with you, I'm going to need a rain check this time."

The loud squeal made him pull the cell away from his ear and frown at it. Good grief, the man was loud. He waited a moment before putting it back to his ear. "Are you done trying to rupture my eardrums? Seriously, Sasha!"

"You said 'date.' You mean like a *date* date?"

"Ha-ha. Yes, like a date with a hot guy. Don't know if we'll actually go out somewhere or just hang out here, but I'm hoping for a little of one and a whole lot of the other." He couldn't wait to see Keith again, and now that he wasn't working, the craving was back just as strong as ever.

"Oh, I like the way your voice drops when you mention this guy. So who is he? Anyone I know?"

Jason chuckled, enjoying how excited Sasha sounded, and knew he was talking with his hands as much as his mouth—he always did when excited. "His name is Keith Skyler, he just moved in next door, and *he* likes my cooking."

"Oh, so you've already had him over? You naughty boy!"

"No. I took him my special mac 'n cheese as a 'welcome to the neighborhood' gift, if you must know."

Sasha gasped before he started in again, and this time his tone was harder and no longer playful. "You already put out, didn't you? Dammit, Jason. You know better than that."

Rolling his eyes, Jason sighed. "One, when have I ever done that before?" No, he was the one who demanded dates, in the plural normally, before more than kissing was allowed. Except with Keith, it seemed. "Two, he's not like anyone I've ever met. He's, I don't know how to explain it. He was possessive but in an endearing way. Not in the crazy-stalker way, I promise. And three, how the hell did you go from food to sex like that?" He never could make sense of Sasha's leaps in logic, but he was usually right, sadly.

"You've said that before, Jason," Sasha snapped, ignoring most of what Jason had asked. As usual. "So that means you *have* or have *not* been with this guy already?" The growl in Sasha's voice was adorable, not that he'd ever tell the man that. Sasha was all of five-six, with inky-black hair, light blue eyes, and swarthy skin, thanks to his Russian heritage, and was the best friend Jason had ever had, but the questions were getting on his nerves.

"That's not really anyone's business. You know I don't play kiss and tell."

Sasha grumbled a moment before saying anything understandable. "Fine. I just don't want you hurt. You know that."

"I do, but he's different. I know I sound like a sixteen-year-old girl right now, but something about him just clicked with me. And he's gorgeous! Like he could be a model or something."

"Yeah." Sasha chuckled. "You do, but if he makes you this happy, I'll lay off for now. Do you need any help getting ready for your big date? Maybe with your clothing or dinner choices?"

"Sasha!"

Sasha's giggle drew him in, and moments later they were both laughing so hard he thought he might cry. God, he loved his friend. "As if I'd ever let you do that. You'd have me making tree bark to serve for dinner and wearing all leather, or some such insanity."

"No bark, I promise."

"No bark," Jason muttered. "You're a funny man. Seriously, I need to get my work done so I don't have to work this weekend. I'm not trying to be rude, but…."

"But getting laid is more fun than hanging out with me?"

"Something like that. I'll call you later and we can get together soon. All right?"

As soon as they said their good-byes and he set the phone down, it rang again. Annoyed, he snatched it up again, but thinking of what Sasha had said, he checked the ID and smiled. "Keith?" he said as soon as he answered the call.

"Oh, I like the way you said my name," Keith drawled. "Yeah, it's me. Look, Jay, I was going to be there Friday, but things got rearranged so—"

"Oh." He'd known it was likely to happen eventually, but Jason had hoped Keith would stay interested a bit longer.

"So," Keith continued, as if he hadn't spoken. "I'll be back tomorrow night instead. I thought we could get dinner."

Oh. "Oh! I…. You still want to go out?" *Yeah, Jason, sound a little more clingy. That'll work.*

"I never say things I don't mean, and I never make a promise I don't intend to keep. Now, are you free tomorrow night? It's only one day early, but I don't want to mess up your work schedule either."

"Y-yes." *Dammit!*

"Good. I'll pick you up at six and we can get some dinner and talk. As enjoyable as last time was, I'd like to get to know you some. Maybe learn what you do for fun or what you like to watch…," Keith said, his voice soft.

Jason nodded before he realized Keith couldn't see him. "That sounds good. I'll be ready."

"Good. I can't wait to see you again, baby," Keith rumbled. His voice sent a shock of need through Jason so strong he was instantly hard and throbbing. A groan slipped out before he thought to control it. The dark chuckle on the other end of the line only served to make him harder.

"No starting without me, Jay."

"Then you better not be late tomorrow."

"Be good and I'll see you tomorrow night."

Minutes later Jason sat alone in his office, horny but determined to save it for his date. He just hoped he was on the menu again. Reminding himself of his workload and thinking about how much he wanted time with Keith, he got back to work quickly. He spent the next couple of hours coding.

By the time he finished, he was antsy and frustrated, so he gave up on having a relaxing evening. He cleaned up his area and then headed to his bedroom to change. He decided that if he wanted to actually sleep that night, he needed to wear himself out a bit.

Twenty minutes later, he stood outside his home, dressed in black running shorts, a bright blue T-shirt, and his favorite neon-blue running shoes. Once he'd stretched and warmed up, he set out to run five miles for the second time that day. He ran every day, though usually only in the mornings.

As he paced himself, ear buds in, he reveled in the warmth in his muscles and in the freedom he always felt as he flew down the sidewalk. Soon the only sound Jason heard were his footfalls on the concrete running path and the music playing softly in his ears. When he reached the corner, Jason turned and headed onto the trails behind his house. The hard-packed earth soothed his nerves more than anything else ever seemed to do. Evening was one of his favorite times of the day, though it was usually cooler in the morning. Still, the rhythm of his breathing and footfalls soon had his nerves calm and his body humming.

Shortly before he arrived back at his home, the fine hairs on the back of his neck stood up and he felt as though he was being watched. Jason looked around but didn't pause, unsure what bothered him. He didn't notice anything out of the ordinary, just a big kitty cat off in the woods and a few squirrels jumping from tree to tree. Shrugging off the weird feeling as best he could, Jason sped up. He didn't stop until he was back inside his house.

He flipped the lock, just to be sure, and paced the kitchen to cool down. He normally would have walked and stretched outside before coming in, but he still felt as though he was being watched. Once he'd done his stretches and cooled off a bit, he headed over to the fridge and grabbed a bottle of water. Jason stood at the sink, staring out into his backyard as he drank. The entire line of houses butted against the woods was one of the main reasons he'd moved to the area.

Jason frowned as he again noticed the large cat moving around, unsure why it bothered him. Of course, he wasn't certain what kind of cat it was. It was too big to be a regular house cat, but it didn't look like what he thought of as a wild cat, either. Whatever kind it was, it was both cute and impressive. Shrugging, he finished his water and headed to the shower. He was tired and sweaty, as planned, and now all he wanted was to be clean and sprawl out across his cool bed.

Half an hour later he lay across his sheets, feeling dozy and comfortable, in nothing but a pair of boxers. But try as he might, he couldn't seem to slip completely into his dreams. When he heard something rustling outside, he huffed and got up, thinking maybe some warm milk would help him rest. It usually worked.

Once in the kitchen, however, he found himself looking out the window over the sink again, wondering about his kitty visitor. Instead of just making himself the warm milk he'd planned, he made a double batch and filled a shallow, wide bowl with the second helping. Before he thought better of it, Jason pulled down a can of tuna and opened it before scooping it out onto a small plate.

Feeling a bit foolish for heating the milk first, Jason unlocked and opened his back door before carefully moving outside. He looked around but no longer saw the cat, though he hadn't really thought the animal would stay there when he walked outside. A wild animal wouldn't, at least. He bent and set the two dishes down a ways into his backyard. Just before he reentered his home, he turned back to the tree line, hoping to catch another glimpse of his visitor. "Hope you like warm milk and tuna."

Shaking his head at himself, Jason stepped back into his kitchen, relocked the door, and turned off the lights before collecting his warm drink and settling back into bed. Anticipation curled in his belly, but exhaustion, mixed with the milk, lulled him to sleep quickly, a small smile on his lips. The last thing his mind caught on was an image of how Keith had curled around him after that first time they were together.

KEITH WATCHED from the tree line as Jason moved around in his kitchen, purring as he thought about the next night. Tomorrow he would be able to spend time with his mate again. He was still uncertain how Jason would take the news of him being a lynx part of the time, or of them being mates for that matter, but the longer he was away from Jason, the more he ached inside.

He knew all the stories about mates, had seen how his parents behaved and how his sister was with her mate until he passed away, but while he had always hoped for one, he hadn't really thought he'd be so lucky. In all his years—not that he'd lived that long, though—he had never met a mated gay couple. Gay human couples, sure. Even a few committed gay vampire couples, though he knew his tribe would have a fit if they knew he associated with "bloodsuckers." But cat shifters? Never.

Keith's father had repeatedly told him that mates were always of the opposite gender and that as his eldest male child, Keith had a responsibility to take a proper mate and produce an heir—and had subjected him to events like the other night. Women were lovely, but he didn't make love to them. Ever. Groomed since birth to become the next leader, Keith knew his life path, though he'd never been certain he would actually take over from his father. Not if his father, or the council, found out about him being gay. And leading the tribe was something he both wanted and did not want to do. If he did, he could make the changes he'd dreamed of making since he was little, but at the same time, just thinking of the responsibility and adhering to the law exhausted him. He would take his place when the time came, as long as his father didn't find a loophole to keep Keith from becoming the next alpha.

The sound of Jason's back door creaking open pulled him out of his musings. Keith cocked his head, his ears twitching, as he watched Jason step out wearing nothing but a thin pair of green boxers and carrying a plate and a bowl in his hands. Sniffing, he caught the scents of milk and fish. Confused, he crept closer, trying to figure out what the man was up to, and why.

Once Jason set both items in the grass, he turned and carefully picked his way back to his doorway. Before he went inside and closed the door, he turned and murmured, "Hope you like warm milk and tuna."

Keith froze, confused as to why Jason would do such a thing, but moments later he was left alone with the snack. He listened carefully, making sure Jason wasn't hanging around to watch him through the window, before carefully stalking forward to check out Jason's offerings. He sniffed both items, but they smelled good and the milk was even warm.

With one last look at the now-dark house, Keith mentally shrugged, deciding it would be rude to waste the sweet offer his mate had left him. After testing the temperature, he quickly consumed the milk and tuna before hurrying back to the trees, pleased not only with his mate's kindness but with the thought that at least Jason wasn't against having his cat around.

He paced around the trees before climbing up, again settling on the same limb from where he'd watched Jason earlier. He took his time cleaning his whiskers, paws, and fur before curling up and taking a nap. He briefly thought about going into the house next door but dismissed the idea quickly. What if Jason saw him inside? The beautiful man already seemed skittish; Keith didn't figure making him think he was a liar would help him win his mate's trust and affection.

Tomorrow, he thought as his slightly simplified mind drifted—satisfied at having seen his mate and with the full belly he now had—before slipping into sleep.

CHAPTER SIX

JASON PACED back and forth across the length of his living room, even more nervous now than he had been when he'd first met Keith. He tried to remember the last time he'd been this worked up over a date, but couldn't. He had spent half the afternoon and early evening trying to decide what to wear on his first actual date in ages. "Stupid," he grumbled to himself, annoyed with himself for being jittery. "You've already had sex with the man, but dinner is too much for you? Just be yourself," he reminded himself, hoping it would help.

Stopping midstride, Jason forced himself to calm, smoothing his hands down his shirt and slacks in an effort to make himself presentable. He turned on his heel, then headed into the kitchen. He grabbed a cold bottle of water and took small sips. Jason took a deep breath between each one and eventually managed to calm to a reasonable level.

He tossed the now-empty bottle into the recycling bin and jumped when his doorbell buzzed. Jason checked the wall clock in the kitchen and realized it was six, exactly. Hurrying through the house to the front door, Jason held his breath for a count of five, then let it out slowly before he opened the door and smiled. His mouth went dry and his pulse raced at the vision before him. Keith stood on his small porch in black dress jeans, a green button-down dress shirt, and black Docs on his feet.

"Keith," he breathed out, unable to make his voice stronger.

"Jay," Keith replied.

The sweet smile Keith graced him with then melted Jason completely. "Did—do you want to come in for a drink or head out?"

"Relax, baby," Keith said, slipping his arm around Jason's shoulder. "We have reservations in an hour, and the restaurant is only about twenty minutes away, so we have time if you want."

"You want the nickel tour, then? My place is a little different than yours."

"Sure. Yours looks a lot bigger, from what I can tell."

Jason flashed a smile, nervous but excited. He so rarely had anyone visit that showing his place off was kind of exciting, though he figured that made him a dork. He didn't care. "This is the living room, of course. And here we have the dining and kitchen areas," he continued. A door from the dining room separated his kitchen from where he ate, though there was only an archway between the living and dining areas. He had all hardwood floors except in the kitchen—where he'd had tile laid. "Down the hall are a bathroom, the guest bedroom, the master suite, and my office."

"You'll have to show me those later," Keith purred, crowding against him.

It took Jason a minute to remember why they weren't heading to his bed, *now*. "P-please."

Keith wrapped his strong arms around Jason and pulled him back against his chest. "Come on, Jay, or we'll never make it to dinner. Not if you keep sounding like that."

"Right, dinner, eating…." Jason grumbled and stepped away from Keith's warmth. "Who said I gave a damn about eating?" he whispered. The smirk that flashed across Keith's face made him wonder if Keith had heard him, but he shook off the thought.

"Come on, I'm taking you on a proper date, whether you like it or not."

"Bossy."

"You know it," Keith teased, the smirk turning into a full-blown grin.

When they stepped outside, Jason noticed the pristine white Shelby with dusky blue racing stripes parked in his driveway. He hadn't paid attention to what Keith drove before, but he was certain he would have noticed a car like that had it been there. "When'd you get this?"

"Few years ago. She was in my garage the other day."

"It's a shame to keep a beauty like this hidden away," Jason said as he stepped over to the car and ran his fingers along the glossy paint. He'd always wanted an old-school muscle car but had gone conservative, as he did with everything. He glanced over to his tan Toyota Corolla, wishing everything about his life wasn't so safe. *Of course, being with Keith is a lot different, so maybe….*

"I tend to ride my bike more than drive the car, but come, let's go eat." Keith opened the passenger door and held it while Jason settled, before closing it, walking around the front, and getting in.

KEITH ENJOYED getting to know his mate, watching as Jason ate and laughed. He still hadn't figured out how to explain he was a shifter to the very human Jason but figured he had time. No one would expose the truth of his existence to a human. Humans were never told the truth unless there was a great need and the human was special for some reason. Well, unless the shifter was trying to rescue a human from a vampire or other monster. Then it was kind of necessary—if not downright obvious.

By the time they returned to his home—Keith's not Jason's—Keith had trouble focusing on anything but the need to take his mate again and again and again. He'd always curbed his appetite for men, knowing how his father and the others in his tribe would react. No one in his tribe knew he was gay, except his sister. If they did, Keith knew that some would insist he was only "like that" to hurt their alpha. Others would accept him, he was certain, but he'd never wanted to test that hope. The idea that shifters couldn't be gay was ridiculous. He was gay, he was a lynx shifter; therefore, shifters *could*, in fact, be gay.

However, he seriously could have done without the way they were woken up the next morning. Keith bolted upright in bed when he heard the bedroom door open, and his heart slammed against his ribs hard as he fought to focus his eyes. When he did, he was even more confused. Taylor stood in his doorway, her hands balled up on her curvy hips as she scowled down at him.

"Aren't you two cute," she cooed.

"Shh, Taylor. Don't wake him," he hissed, trying not to wake his mate.

She pointed at Keith, then back to the living room. The sudden grimace on her face was all the information he needed right then. "Now," she hissed before turning and stepping away.

Keith carefully extricated himself from his octopus of a bed partner, thankful not to wake him in the process. He then tossed on his briefs and a pair of sweats before he slipped out of the room, closing the door softly behind him. Taking a moment to focus and calm his racing heart, Keith then hurried to where his sister paced next to the couch.

Keith opened his mouth to address her odd agitation when he realized his nephew, Zeke, was curled up on the couch, sleeping. "Why don't I put him in his bed and then we can talk?" he asked, not wanting to wake Zeke any more than he did Jason.

"I'll put him in his new room, but you have to get that human out of here, quickly," she snapped. "Father will be here this evening, and the longer he's here, the more likely we won't be able to get his scent out enough for Father not to freak out."

"There were multiple humans here when I moved us in. Father knows that. What difference does Jason's scent being here make?" He didn't see what her problem was. One human or twenty, why care?

"Oh, let me think…. You had sex with him here. He came. I can smell it, and if I can, so can Father. Besides, there's no other female scent but mine, so you can't even claim it was some woman you were with."

"Dammit!" She was right and he knew it, though why his father was visiting so soon was beyond him. The whole point of her not coming until Saturday was so Keith could have everything done *before* she brought Zeke to his new home. Beyond that issue, though, was how much he hated the idea that he had to wake Jason up.

He watched as Taylor carefully scooped up her son before returning to his room. When he opened the door, he found Jason up and hurriedly throwing on his clothes from the previous night. Before he could speak, Jason's head snapped up, and his enchanting hazel eyes fired with anger and hurt as they locked on his.

"You have a wife and kid!" Jason yelled.

"I don't. Taylor's not my—"

"Shut it, Keith! I won't be some dirty little secret, and I won't be lied to," he continued as he barreled past Keith and sprinted out the door, shoes still clutched in his hands.

Confused and hurt by the anger in Jason's voice and eyes, he stood there staring at where his mate had been, unsure of what to do. Go talk to his sister or chase down his mate? Neither choice sounded good, not if his father was really on his way.

He was startled out of his shock when a small but strong hand cuffed him across the back of his head. "What the hell, Taylor!" He rubbed the spot, more insulted than sore, but still pissed off.

"That's what I'd like to know. What were you thinking, having a human here?"

"But I told you about him. You've never cared before that I was gay." He couldn't understand her ire. She'd always been on his side before, just as he always was on hers.

"I don't care that it's a guy, but you failed to mention that you were having sex with him in our home, Keith. And with Father insisting on visiting, on checking out where we're to live, bringing your boy here is beyond stupid."

"But…. Father's not supposed to be coming here, not yet. That's the whole official reason for me moving with you, so you'd be protected and provided for and Father wouldn't need to worry." He knew they'd agreed to a visit, but only once they were settled. Being Taylor and Zeke had only just arrived, that didn't count!

Taylor sagged and rubbed her neck with one hand. "I only found out a little bit ago and hurried over to make sure things were ready before he arrives. I knew you'd said you'd met your mate, so I wanted to make sure your Jason wouldn't be around when Father arrived. Besides, your mate being human would make him hard to pass off as my boyfriend, because he would clearly have been there without me."

"Goddess! I didn't think of that. I was just so happy to find my mate was a male...." He didn't know how to explain away his lapse in judgment or how to cover it before their father arrived.

"Look, we need to talk, more than I thought obviously, but I need to clean up after your playtime with your mate and you need to go do something about your boy."

"He's not my boy or my friend; he's my mate, Tay."

"I know, but he's not a lynx. He's not even a shifter. He's a—"

"Human. The word you're looking for is *human*. And yes, I realize that, but his shape and species are irrelevant. He *is* my *mate*."

Taylor's shoulders drooped, her gaze darting around the room a moment before landing on Keith again. "I didn't mean it that way. You know I don't have an issue with humans. But, um, you need to go fix this with him while I do what I can to clean up the house. I heard what he said, and you being an idiot is one thing; making your mate think you're a lying, cheating, closet case is a whole other. Go talk with your mate and I'll fix things here."

"Thank you," Keith said and hugged her tight before he turned and hurried out the door.

He got as far as the stoop of Jason's house before he froze, his senses suddenly alert. His muscles coiled beneath his skin on instinct. He sniffed and swore under his breath. *Vampire!* Not taking the time to knock, Keith grasped the doorknob and turned it, thrilled that it easily moved. When he threw the door open, he froze, confused at the bizarre scene before him.

Jason was sitting on the couch, his beautiful face streaked with tears. Next to his mate sat a small male vampire. The vampire was wrapped around Jason, holding him tight, and running one of his long, slender hands up and down Jason's back. The vampire turned his head, then met Keith's gaze and bared his fangs as he growled and clutched Jason tighter.

"Get your filthy hands off him," Keith bellowed, fury and pain lancing his heart, and lunged toward the creature still holding his mate.

The small vampire crashed into him before he reached the couch or Jason. Keith fought for dominance and purchase against the damned creature that dared to touch what belonged to him. The logical part of his brain knew this was more than stupid; vampires should never be fought one on one. They were usually stronger than shifters, especially if they were more than a few centuries old, but he didn't care right then. The only thing he could think of was killing the creature before it could take his mate from him.

He shifted into his lynx, biting and clawing, stronger in his shifted form than his human skin. He tasted the spicy-penny taste of vampire blood when he finally managed to sink his teeth into the creature's shoulder, having again missed his throat. Shifters were taught that vampires were toxic to them and that vampire blood would poison them if they ingested it, but he knew the truth was much different from what they were all told as kits. Their blood was no more dangerous to shifters than shifters' was to a vampire. No, they weren't poisonous, but their blood did tend to incite bloodlust on both sides. Right then, that was fine with him. He wanted to shred the pretty little monster before he truly destroyed it.

Keith felt fangs dig into his fur and flesh just above his shoulder at the same time he heard Jason's voice screaming over the sound of snarling and hissing. "Stop! Oh my God, stop! P-please, someone help!"

He froze at the same time the vampire did. But neither released their holds or fangs from the other. Jason continued to yell about some cat attacking someone named Sasha, confusing him even more. That was the name of his mate's best friend. Before he could figure out what was happening, Jason leaped and landed on Keith's furry back, hitting him, continuing to wail about his friend.

Allowing himself to be pulled away from the vampire was physically and mentally painful, but he was too confused about why Jason would protect the vampire. Besides, he didn't want to fight Jason. Keith moved back, hissing at the vampire, his hackles still up. He wanted to be between Jason and the creature, but Jason wasn't cooperating.

The petite male wiped the back of one hand across his mouth, clearing part of the blood away, but his fangs were still out and his eyes were still black, ringed in bloodred. "I'll kill you before I let you hurt him again," the vampire growled. It was almost comical considering how tiny the guy was—well, if you didn't know he was a damn vampire, that is.

Keith shifted, still crouched on the floor, eyes never leaving the vampire's. "He's mine, bloodsucker. You can't have him."

"He's not *yours*," the vampire retorted, snorting softly. "He's a human, not one of your damn kittens for you to lord over."

"K-K-Keith? Sasha?" Jason asked, his voice brittle as his gaze bounced back and forth between them. "Wh-what's going on?"

"That's what I'd love to know," Keith spat out. "You run out of the house, and when I find you, you're curled up with one of *them*!"

"One of w-what? I don't...." Before Jason finished his sentence, his eyes rolled up so only the whites were visible, and then he collapsed. Keith barely beat the vampire in his bid to catch his mate before he hit the floor.

"Way to go, asshole," the vampire—Sasha?—snapped. "Break his heart and expose him to what we are. I'm sure your tribe will be thrilled with you."

"I did no such thing, and who the hell are you? Why was he protecting you?"

"I don't need protection, *cat*. But as it looks like I'll have to put up with you for now, my name is Sasha Tolstoi." He sounded bored and put-upon, which only served to piss off Keith more. "And you would be the infamous idiot Keith, yes?"

Keith stood, cradling Jason to his chest, never taking his eyes off the vampire who had returned to looking human again. All five and a half feet of him. Seriously? *How can anyone take someone that tiny seriously?* "I'm Keith, his mate."

He almost chuckled at the way Sasha's eyes widened and his mouth hung open in obvious shock. "Mate? But-but Jason's human. Shifters don't mate with humans, much less with the same gender in this backwards area, no matter how asinine those rules are." The last part sounded more like he was talking to himself than to Keith, so Keith held his tongue. However, he wasn't thrilled with standing there, nude, in front of a vamp while Jason was unconscious.

"Wait, what about your mate next door? You can't claim them both!"

"She's not my mate, fang boy, she's my sister. He'd have known that if he hadn't run out so fast. But how the hell did you get here already?"

Sasha waved off his question with one slender hand. "Shouldn't you get dressed before he comes to? You'll have no chance of explaining any of this away if you're still bloody and naked."

"I'm not going to lie to Jay," Keith snapped. "Besides, can't you just edit his memory if you want? That is your thing, isn't it?"

Narrowing his pale blue eyes, Sasha snorted. "I have never messed with Jason's mind and have no intention of starting now. Especially not to help a two-timing kitty."

"Not a kitty."

"Lynx, yes?" Sasha tilted his head to the side as he continued to stare. "Last time I heard, that's a type of cat. But seriously, get dressed and I'll bring him out of his swoon."

Keith tore his gaze from Sasha to inspect Jason's neck. He didn't see any marks, but he knew vampires could heal the holes easily. "You didn't *bite* him, did you?" he asked as he laid Jason out on the couch.

"No! Now stop pawing at him and go put something on."

Shaking his head, Keith refused to move away. "I'm not about to leave my mate with you," he growled, not willing to let any male, much less a vampire, near his mate.

Sasha rolled his eyes and sighed. "Damn territorial shifters. Wolves get the rep for it, but you're all that bad. Fine, here." He disappeared down the hall and in mere moments returned with a pair of sweatpants. "They'll be a little short probably, but not too much."

Keith sniffed the offering, but all he could smell on them was soap and Jason. Satisfied, he stood, keeping himself between Jason and Sasha, and slipped the pants on. They weren't bad, just a little snug. "Better?"

"Much, thank you. Now please move so I can wake him up. I have no clue how you're going to talk your way out of this."

CHAPTER SEVEN

UNCOMFORTABLE WITH the idea of stepping away from Jason, Keith scooped him up again and settled on the couch, this time with Jason in his lap. "Does he know what you are?" Keith grumbled, wondering about how easily Sasha seemed to be taking the whole situation in front of them.

"Looks like he's about to find out. Are you sure he's your mate? I mean like your *mate* mate?"

"Yeah, I am. Not that I know how I'm going to make my father understand that, but he's mine and I won't let him go." Keith knew his fur would be standing up if he were still in his other form. As it was, he wanted to take Jason and run.

"Can't you just appeal to your... to the alpha of your tribe or whatever?"

Keith gave a bitter little laugh. "My father is Adam Skyler." Sasha gasped and Keith knew why—even the vampires in the area knew who Adam Skyler was and knew not to mess with him or his. "He won't be amused with my *choices* and *issues* with men—that's how he refers to homosexuality in humans—when he finds out. No way is he going to be okay with me having a human male as a mate. We won't even get into how pissed he'd be if he caught me talking to one of you on top of all that."

"You're the Skyler heir?" Sasha inquired, his gaze tracking him with a mixture of pity and compassion as Keith held Jason, who was still out cold. "How can you mate him? A human can't take your bite."

Ignoring the question about his status in the tribe, Keith asked, "Like your bite would be better?" He tightened his hold on Jason, the thought of anyone else's teeth touching his mate—cat, vampire, human, it didn't matter to him—pushed him to put himself between Jason and anyone who dared to come near. Instead of fighting again, he swallowed down his building rage and hissed, "I don't want to feed on him!"

"We don't have to bite through anything but a little skin to bind our chosen ones, unlike shifters. Well, if they're our true mate, that is."

Keith rubbed his eyes with one hand, not thrilled with the entire conversation. Sharing information with a vampire, sexual or otherwise? What was the world coming to? "I really don't like discussing this with you, but seeing as you're important to Jason…. Our saliva heals wounds similar to how yours does, so it's not an issue."

"There's a little more to a shifter, of any kind, bonding their mate than a little bite. It's a big bite, with all the animal teeth out, into their shoulder. Jason's a little weaker than you shifters—and I can't believe I'm saying any of that out loud."

"I'll figure it out, thank you very much. I would never hurt my mate! Now, if you know how to wake him…," Keith said, swallowing his pride. "Please."

"Yes, you will, as I won't allow you to hurt him. Honestly, it's too bad you can't be the next alpha," Sasha mused.

Keith wasn't sure he wanted to point out that that's exactly who and what he was to be. "Um, I *am* the heir to the Glacier Rim Tribe."

"Oh, good. You're exactly what they need," Sasha said, confusing Keith even more.

Sasha moved closer, then bent down slightly and brushed his lips across Jason's forehead. "Awake, little one," he whispered before stepping back.

Jason gasped and sat bolt upright in Keith's lap. "Don't!"

"Jay?" Keith murmured as he rubbed his hand up and down Jason's back, hoping to sooth his mate. "Jason?"

After a moment, Jason finally focused on Keith again. "You…." He looked around, confusion clear in his beautiful hazel eyes. "Sasha? You had f-fangs and blood on your face." He turned back to Keith. "And y-you, uh…."

"Turned into a cat? Yeah, I know."

"Wow, you have even less tact than I thought," Sasha grumbled.

"Sorry, but what did you want me say?" There was no easy way to say, "Hey, dude, I'm a cat part of the time." Not to a human, at least.

"Stop it, you two," Jason snapped, drawing their attention back to him. "Now, does someone want to explain to me why my best f-friend and my b-boyfriend attacked each other, and then we can get to the issue of what the hell ever you both did to look like…." He turned his beseeching gaze up at Keith. "Oh, and where's your w-wife?"

Sasha chuckled, making Keith want to smack the vampire upside the head. "Taylor isn't my wife, Jay. She's my sister. And as for why we were fighting, I thought he was a danger to you, and I think he thought the same about me."

Jason blinked hard a few times and then looked over to Sasha. "You were fighting over me?" Returning his gaze to Keith's, he scrunched up his face slightly. "And why the hell would you think Sasha was d-dangerous?"

"Hey now, I can be plenty dangerous," Sasha grumbled, his bottom lip thrust out. Even Keith had to admit the male had a pretty pout, not that he'd ever say that aloud. "And he'd just hurt you, so of course I thought he was a threat to you."

"You never fought with anyone I've ever gone out with before." Jason squirmed before pushing off Keith's lap and settling on the seat beside him. "And that still doesn't explain the blood and fighting and the, um, fur?"

Keith looked over at Sasha, who just shrugged, before meeting Jason's eyes again. "He's a bit more dangerous than you'd think or there wouldn't have been a fight, Jay. He held his own," he explained, hating the need to say the last part.

"Oh good grief. Your boyfriend is a lynx, as you saw, and I'm not exactly your average human, either. But that's neither here nor there. There's a bigger issue."

Keith gaped at Sasha. "That wasn't a very smooth explanation there, either, fang boy. And you say I'm the one that needs more tact?"

Jason folded his arms over his chest, drawing Keith's eyes there and reminding him of how Jason's flesh had tasted the night before: salty, sweet, and completely addictive.

"Yeah, Sasha, I kinda got that something isn't quite normal with you two, but how could you not tell me? You're my best friend. How could you hide this from me, and just exactly *what* are you?"

"Um, Jason, hon, why aren't you more shocked or disbelieving or something?" Sasha asked instead of answering him. Truthfully, though, Keith wanted to know the same thing. Since when did humans not freak out about supernaturals being real instead of things from myths and stories?

"You remember me telling you about Mr. Sanchez, my first boss while I was still in college?" Sasha nodded, but neither he nor Keith spoke, both waiting for Jason to continue. "He wasn't human, Sasha."

"And you know this how?" Keith asked, incredulous. "And he let you get away with knowing?" Most supers didn't let humans know what they were.

"Because I saw him shift when he was hurt, though I suppose I shouldn't have told you his name. I promised not to reveal what he was. But, well, you're my family. You are my family still?" Jason asked, staring at Sasha.

"Of course I am. I've watched over you since you were a small child, though you wouldn't know that."

"You did, er, have? But—"

"I just didn't know you knew about your old boss. You never said anything. Well, if you could deal with and hide the fact you knew of wolf shifters this long, I suppose you shouldn't have that much trouble with being the mate of a lynx."

"Mate?" Jason gaped at Sasha. He turned to face Keith. "What does he mean 'mate'?"

"Mate, as in the life partner of a shifter." Keith didn't really want to get into a more detailed discussion with a vampire there, even if vamps had their own version of mating. Still, fangs and fur just didn't share.

"You haven't known me long enough to decide about such things as forever," Jason countered. An odd look, one Keith couldn't place, flitted across his dark features.

"We don't decide, Jay. A mate is born to us, not chosen. They are our perfect complement, though I've never heard of a male having a male mate, much less a human one."

"You don't choose? And what do you mean no male mate?" Jason asked, shifting across the couch to the opposite corner. "I am quite certain that I'm male. Just because I'm mostly a bottom doesn't mean I'm a girl." The glare he sent made Keith shiver, and for once, it wasn't with excitement or lust.

"I, uh, I know you're a guy, Jason. Nothing would have happened between us otherwise. I just never thought I'd have a mate, not with me being gay. Mating is done between males and females, always, or so I was taught. Now I wonder what else I might have been misinformed about." Keith reached out, hoping to hold Jason again, or at least his hand. The need to be near him was bordering on painful, and the gut reaction to another male—vampire or no—being near his unclaimed mate, was getting progressively harder to control. The only saving grace in this situation was that Sasha was staying in his chair and not trying to touch Jay.

"But you *are* gay, right? My gender wasn't a surprise too, was it?" Jason's voice was flat, his hands fisted at his sides, and he no longer made any attempt at eye contact.

"Look at me. Please," Keith added when the frown on Jason's face deepened.

Instead of complying, Jason repeated his questions.

Keith sighed, wishing he knew what was upsetting Jason so much. "No, your gender isn't a surprise to me. I've known I was gay since I was about ten or eleven. Well, when I knew that there was a word for it. Before that, I thought I was the only one like me. Gay and shifter don't go together, or so says our council and leaders."

"At least you knew that much. And the choice? I don't like how you're making mates sound."

The knot in the pit of his stomach twisted. Keith had a bad feeling about giving an honest answer but didn't see a way around it. Not while he had a witness, especially a blood drinker.

"As I said, a mate is chosen by the divine, the universe, or fate; however you want to put it. It is said that Baast gifts some of us with a mate. Not everyone finds their true mate, though that doesn't mean they can never find joy or love, they just don't find the completion of their soul." Keith was still having trouble wrapping his head around the fact he had a mate, especially one so sexy and sweet, but this was not how he'd wanted this conversation to go. "Actually, very few have true mates," he added.

Jason's brows raised as he flicked his gaze over to Sasha. "What do you think about all this, Sasha?"

Sasha looked at them with sad eyes. "What I think?"

"Yes. You always have an opinion about anyone I'm interested in, but not now. Now you're just sitting there staring blankly. What gives?"

"I think you're damn lucky to have found someone that will be as loyal to you as he will," Sasha explained, flicking one delicate hand toward Keith. "Once mated, shifters can't cheat, even if they want to. It's one of the few things I like about his kind."

The odd tone coupled with the sadness in the creature's eyes made Keith wonder who'd hurt Sasha in the past. He had a couple of friends that were fanged, so he knew vampires were still people—mostly. He didn't want to feel for the vamp, but damned if he didn't. Pushing that issue aside, Keith focused on Jason again.

"I'm the same guy you went out with last night and woke up with. The only difference is I'm a little furrier than you thought." Keith cracked a small smile, trying to get Jason to relax and let him back into his space.

"Were you planning to ever tell me the truth, either of you?" Jason snapped instead of responding to either man's comments.

Sasha sighed, pinching the bridge of his nose. "I had no reason or need to tell you what I am. If you knew about your boss, then you know humans aren't usually told these things. Humans that aren't feeders definitely aren't told about ones like me."

"Like you?" Keith asked at the same time Jason did. What was so special about the little vamp?

"Ugh!" Sasha barked, his gaze snapping over to meet Keith's. "My name is Sasha Tolstoi, cat. *Tolstoi*. Think on it a moment, you'll figure it out."

"It's Keith, not *cat*. Even a vamp can remem…. Wait!" he yelled. "Sasha, as in Aleksandr 'Sasha' Tolstoi, Prince of the Konstantin Coven?" No, no, no! His mate was not the best friend of the local vampire coven's prince! "You can't be that Sasha."

Jason stared at Sasha as if he hadn't ever seen his friend before, making Keith even antsier—as if being in the same room as the bloodsucker's prince wasn't enough of a reason.

"P-prince? What t-the hell, Sasha?" Jason seemed to choke on his words as his stutter made its appearance again.

Sasha waved his delicate hand through the air as if to shoo away both men's questions and worry. "I am still the man you've known since you were a teen, Jason. And yes, Keith, I am that Sasha. I'm curious why you're taking this so well. Shifters don't usually manage this part without either running or attacking."

"But you k-kill people?" Jason looked as though he might pass out again. Instead he yelled, "I've seen you eat and it's light outside! You can't be a v-v-vampire."

Keith rolled his eyes. "Gods, I hate how people actually believe all the crap they read in books and see in movies."

"Agreed, though some of the inaccuracies are useful, at times." Sasha smiled at Keith before addressing Jason again. "We do not burst into flame, like Hollywood would have you believe, hon. And no, I do *not* kill humans," he continued, his voice dripping with disdain. "I never have and have no interest in starting now. I also punish any of my people that practice such habits."

"You don't?" Jason asked, the hope so clear in his voice and face it hurt Keith to witness.

"No. Your friend here can verify that," Sasha added, his penetrating gaze shifting to meet Keith's again.

Keith nodded, knowing enough about vampires in the area to know the ins and outs of their feeding. "They don't, that I know of. Grace swears their prince—your friend here, I guess—doesn't allow it. Kane, another vamp I know, says the same thing. No killing in his—" he continued, gesturing to Sasha "—coven's territory. They feed on humans, though."

"O-kay."

"What about your boyfriend being furry?" Sasha asked after a long pause in the conversation.

"I… I don't know how I f-feel about that. The woman really is your sister?" Jason asked, not meeting Keith's gaze.

He wanted Jason's eyes back on him—not his hands, his friend, or the floor. "Taylor is my little sister. Zeke is her five-year-old son, who will also live in the house with me. She wasn't supposed to be here yet, but I did tell you about my having a sister last night, Jay. I wasn't hiding her from you or you from her."

"I didn't know that! I wake up to some strange woman snapping at you about me being in her house, what was I supposed to think?" Jason yelled, finally looking at Keith again. "I won't be the piece on the side again!"

Keith filed that bit of trauma away for later and tried to think through what had happened that morning so he could figure out how best to calm his upset mate. "Had I known she would be here today, I would have told you. She didn't call me to tell me, she just appeared. I'm so sorry, Jay, but you knew it was her home too. You said last night you were excited to meet her."

"I… I wasn't thinking, but…."

"Baby, she was just trying to get to me before our father arrived. I wasn't hiding you from her."

"Shit!" Sasha groaned. "Alpha Skyler is coming to your house? Now?"

He nodded, not amused any more than Sasha seemed to be. "Yeah, that's why she came early. She wanted to make sure things were set up right and to warn me before he arrived."

"I'm surprised he allowed you to move off your tribe lands outside the city."

"It wasn't his choice," Keith explained, trying hard to play nice with the vamp as he figured Jason wouldn't be giving up his closest friend any time soon. "Trust me, he's not happy with either of us. Right now she's trying to make it so Father doesn't freak and try to force us home."

"I don't get why it matters. You're an adult." Jason's brows drew together, his frown deepening. "You *are* an adult, right? I mean, you look like one, but then you don't look like a cat…."

"I'm twenty-seven. Grown, but if the alpha orders us to return, it's going to be damn hard to defy him. One just does not defy an order from their alpha." Not if one wishes to live a long, happy, free life, that is. "But it'll work out. We'll get him out of here as fast as we can. Your friend here will play nice and not make an appearance while Father's here. Then we can continue our plans for the weekend."

"I don't know," Jason countered. "I…I'm not sure what I want right now, but I'm nobody's 'mate.' I don't w-want anything to do with that concept—like I don't want you to only want me like that. Only because you have to," he added, so softly Keith figured Jason probably didn't realize his enhanced ears could hear him.

"It's not like that—"

"I need t-time, end of discussion." He turned to Sasha again. "I'm not happy with you hiding things from me, either, Sasha. You're my best friend, my chosen family, but I don't really even know you. Not really." Jason stood, not meeting either man's gaze. "I'd like you both to leave for now. I n-need to th-think."

"But—"

"No, Keith, I n-need time. My best friend is a vampire, and my hoped-for boyfriend is a cat and thinks he has to mate me, whatever the hell that means. Now please, b-both of you, just go."

"I'll call you later, hon. If his father is coming, he's right, it would be best for me not to be here." Sasha flitted over to Jason and hugged him tight for a moment before he left. He didn't say good-bye, but Keith barely noticed.

"Please," Jason said again, stepping farther away from Keith.

"I don't want to leave, but I'll respect your wishes. I'll come over once Father is gone."

"No, I need time. I'll… talk to you when I'm r-ready." Jason sighed but stepped close enough to put his hand on Keith's shoulder. "I need to think and figure this out. I will call you, but I need to think without im-impending visits from an alpha cat, vampire p-princes, or notions of mate-bonds. T-text me when he leaves and maybe we can talk a little more. Okay?"

"I will, Jay. I'll text as soon as he's gone."

"Thank y-you."

Turning away from Jason and walking out the door hurt more than Keith expected, but he told himself it was only for a little while. Jason would be okay and they would move forward. He just hoped he wasn't lying as he kept repeating it to his human and his lynx.

CHAPTER EIGHT

JASON COULDN'T settle, no matter what he tried. He'd made warm milk, gone for a run, paced a hole in his living room, but nothing seemed to make the events of the morning make sense. His lover was a lynx. He'd had sex with a were-cat! His thoughts flashed back to their first time, when Keith had scratched his hip. The purring as they fell asleep. Keith licking the little cuts he'd made. It all made sense finally, but that didn't help his peace of mind much.

And Sasha was a vampire, a vampire prince no less. Yeah, he'd be hard pressed to say which revelation shocked him more. Sasha had always seemed sophisticated, but not pompous like he'd expect a vampire prince to be. They'd had popcorn fights while arguing during movies. How did that say "prince"?

Blood and fur…. How did he end up in situations like this?

He wandered into his kitchen, needing another drink, what with all the pacing he was doing. Standing at the sink as he drank a glass of water, he stared out the little window at the trees he loved. He wondered if Keith knew the cat he'd fed the other night. For all he knew, Keith might have been the cat, but if he were, why would he hang out outside instead of having their date that night?

Nothing made sense to him. Not Sasha. Not Keith. Not the talk of alphas, princes, or mates.

Definitely not the true-mates thing. Jason wanted to be wanted and loved for himself, not because some stupid pull *made* Keith want him. Why was that so hard to understand? He knew he wasn't much to look at, was forgettable, and had been cheated on—more than once—but that didn't make him wish for love any less.

Taking a deep breath once he was done with his drink, Jason wandered to his office, intending to get ahead on some work, but found himself staring over at Keith's home. As much as Jason didn't want to admit it, he'd been painfully aware of the elder Skyler's arrival. The fancy extended-cab, extended-bed truck that looked as though it had never been used for any real work was hard to miss. As was the imposing man who had walked from it to the front door. He didn't look old enough to be Keith's father, unless the man had started having kids really young.

He'd watched as Keith and the woman he now knew was Taylor stepped out of the house, each one nodding to the alpha—he still was torn between worry and wanting to roll his eyes at the word—instead of embracing him as he would have expected. Jason thought cats were big on touch. The ones he'd had as a boy were always rubbing on furniture and his pants, especially if they were black, and while fussy about when he did it, they'd definitely liked being petted. The fact he'd wanted to go over and comfort Keith after watching just that one interaction hadn't helped his mood any.

What he really needed was someone to talk to who knew about shifters and mates and such. The animosity he'd seen between Sasha and Keith worried him as well. Normally, he'd call Sasha and talk with him, but one of the few things he was certain of was that Sasha would be biased, if the way he'd fought with Keith was any indication. Of course, he was still freaked about his friend having fangs. Fangs! How had he not known?

Jason had been raised by his grandy—grandfather—after his parents died in a car wreck when he was a baby, but he didn't even have him now. His grandfather had passed away while Jason was in college. Now all he had was Sasha, his best friend since the day they'd met. But when he remembered meeting Sasha wasn't when Sasha had first met him, obviously.

Tired of thinking in circles as he watched the sun set, the pinks and purples completely lost on him, he turned away from the window and picked up his cell. *Why have you been watching me since I was a boy?* He hit Send, wondering if Sasha would tell him the truth, something he'd never thought to worry about before.

Almost immediately, his cell chimed. *As a favor to your grandfather. He was afraid of losing you after his son, your father, died. But I became your friend, hon.*

He stared at the words, confused. Grandy had asked? *He knew what you are? Why didn't he say anything?*

Yeah, probably stupid questions, but he wanted to know.

Is your friendly kitty sans father yet? I would really rather have these discussions in person, hon.

Uh.... Jason looked out his window again, noting that yes, Keith's father seemed to still be over there, or at least he'd left his truck, which didn't seem too likely to him. *No, the man's truck is still in the drive. Call?*

Hon, you want to risk the alpha cat overhearing you talk to me? Just wait to ask the complicated stuff until the man is gone.

Almost immediately, another text came in. *Or you come over.*

Over where? To the house he'd been to a million times, or was that even Sasha's home? In all the stories and movies he'd read and seen, the heads of vampire groups always lived in some kind of fancy estate or fanged frat house. Besides, he wasn't really up for driving. Everything distracted him, but not from the worries and confusion his friend and his lover had created.

Not yet. Where do you live?

Do vampires live? Are they dead, undead? He wanted to ask, sort of, but not via text. Even he wasn't that bratty.

Sigh. You've been to my house in town, hon. But you mean my "castle," right? I'll show you sometime. You'll like it! I hate that we're texting instead of talking.

*I know, but.... This morning was too much. You know, I had to clean blood out of my carpet! *blushes* I had to freakin' Google how to remove blood!!!*

You could have just asked. I'm quite adept at such things. ;)

Not funny, Sasha! Fine. I'll call when the truck leaves. K?

Okay. Just think on this: your Grandy asked me to watch over you, he never intended us to become friends. That happened because I care about you, my friend.

I... know.

He wanted to say more, but couldn't make his fingers type it all. He knew deep down that Sasha saw him as a friend, not just some responsibility. Why else would he still be around? Why introduce himself in the first place? But at the same time, he was getting sick and tired of everyone else making decisions for him, hiding things from him.

Ta-ta, then. Let me know when the grumpy old cat leaves. Oh, and go easy on Keith. I've already inquired with Grace and Kane about your boy, and they swear he's a good man, fur aside.

I'll try. Gonna go eat.

Well, he was going to try. He'd failed to eat much for lunch. His nerves were still too wound up from earlier.

"WOULD YOU please stop pacing?" Taylor sat perched on the couch, her gaze flicking between his pacing and Zeke playing on the floor. He had LEGOs spread out around him as he plotted and planned how to build his latest creation. Keith swore the kid was going to grow up to be an engineer of some kind, probably designing "green buildings" for a better tomorrow or something.

"No."

"Keith, Father will be here soon, and if you're this keyed up beforehand, he's going to be suspicious. We don't need him poking his whiskers into our lives any more than he already will. Besides, there's no need to worry," she added, pointedly staring down at Zeke.

Yeah, he did need to cool it before Zeke caught on and got upset too. "Sorry."

One thin shoulder lifted and she smiled. "Is okay, big brother. By the way, once Father's on his way home, do I get to meet our new neighbor?"

Damn! He'd told her everything about his earlier talk with Jason and Sasha, so why would she push? "Don't know yet. He was really upset with both his friend and me. Well, more with me, I think. Something about the concept of true mates freaks him out, but I don't know why. I'm half tempted to try to talk to his *friend*," he emphasized the last word, not wanting to have little ears grab on to the fact he was discussing a vampire. "But one, his friend isn't likely to be willing, and two, talking to him if he isn't would likely just make the situation worse."

He had no idea how to make his mate understand, and with humans not feeling the mating pull, he knew he had to win Jason's heart the old-fashioned way.

"Yeah, I know I'd be less than amused if it was me and my mate did that." Taylor checked her watch again and frowned. "Zeke, honey, why don't you move this to the table? Grandpa will be here soon, and you know how much he hates LEGOs on the floor."

Zeke pouted as only a small child could, lip out, eyes sad. "But Mom, I've got all the parts in order."

"And if your grandpa steps on one?" she asked, brows raised.

His nephew's little shoulders sagged. "He'll say a bunch of bad words and yell. Sorry, Mommy."

By the time Keith heard his father's truck pull up outside, Zeke was happily continuing his construction project at the dining room table after Taylor and Keith had both checked to make sure there weren't any stray land mines—LEGOs—anywhere. As much as Keith agreed that those little bits of plastic were evil if stepped on, he wasn't about to forbid Zeke from playing like a normal child. Yes, he would be Keith's heir one day, but he wanted the kid to have a real childhood, not just endless lessons on how to be a leader.

"You ready?" Keith asked his sister, knowing she was just as nervous about this visit as he was; she just hid it better.

"As I'm going to be. Let's meet him out front."

Keith walked to the front door. He opened it, letting Taylor go through, then pulled it mostly closed. This was their home now, and he didn't want his father to feel as if it was merely an extension of his home across the city.

Even though he'd seen his father a couple of days before, he still couldn't help but notice how he moved as if he owned the world, merely allowing others to inhabit it. "Hello, Father," Keith said, tipping his head slightly. It grated on his nerves more each time he had to show deference to his alpha—one he had lost respect for years ago. "Hope you had a pleasant drive."

Adam nodded to him, then shook Keith's hand before acknowledging Taylor. His father hadn't been bad about his treatment of females when their mother had still been alive, but since her death, no woman was worth much to him. Taylor deserved better.

"It was long. I see no reason to have to trek across Seattle like this." Words dripping with disdain left no question how unamused he was with their move. "Now, may we go in, or do you plan to keep me on your stoop like some beggar?"

Gritting his teeth, Keith bit back the nasty retort he wanted to reply with, choosing instead to open the door and allow their father and alpha into their den. He'd done most of the unpacking and arranging before Taylor arrived, and she'd finished off the rest; the curtains and pictures were even hung. *Jason would be happy to hear that.* The thought of Jason's modesty their first day together made him smile, even as he knew his father wouldn't approve.

"It's a bit small and simple, but clean enough, I suppose."

Keith staunchly kept his lips closed, not wanting to get into a fight with his father.

"But I still don't see why you need to live away from the chain or our land or why you feel called upon to move Zeke out to this human-infested area."

Keith had already explained that this location would put him closer to the hospital where he cared for injured wildlife as part of his job with the National Park Service. "It's easier to get to my patients, if I'm closer. The clinic Taylor works for is on this side of town as well. Besides, our yard abuts the forest, so Zeke has plenty of space to run and play."

"And if the humans notice the sudden increase in cats in the area? What then? What if someone calls animal control on my poor grandson?" their father thundered. "You both could get jobs closer to home and make things safer for Taylor's kit."

"I like my job," Keith countered, refusing to raise his voice. He would be the bigger cat, even if he needed to invest in TUMS by the end of the night. "They count on me to be there, to do my job, and Zeke *is* safe. We would never leave him at the mercy of humans that didn't understand. Taylor or I always go with him when he plays or hunts. This is a good area for us, and we like our new house."

The next couple of hours, they all suffered through endless nonsense from Adam. Everything from the human houses being too close to there not being enough prey—hares to be exact—to how poorly made the human-constructed houses were in the area. He even took a walk through their backyard, making comments about the quality of grass. If it could be used as a complaint, Adam Skyler did.

Keith had had to come to Zeke's rescue more than once as well, defending his nephew, his new school, even the child's ability to understand danger from the humans in the area. Taylor was ready to strangle their father, but Keith was determined to kill with kindness. He'd made a rule long ago never to raise his voice, lash out, or belittle anyone, no matter their species. One he tried hard to always follow.

About the time he thought they would be able to set Adam on his way, his father caught the scent of vampire in the area. Honestly, it reflected poorly on the alpha that it took him so long to notice, as Sasha had been next door just that morning.

Adam turned, his eyes wild as he scented the air. "There's a bloodsucker nearby!"

"There was. Keith chased it off already," Taylor soothed. "You know they live in the city proper, not out this far, so it was alone."

"Would have to be for him to be able to scare it off alone." The snort from their father did nothing to pacify Keith. He wanted the arrogant, prejudiced ass to go home so he could get back to his mate. Truthfully, shifters didn't fight with vampires alone, that was usually suicide, but still, the man didn't have to sound so condescending.

"I have no intention of allowing any danger near Taylor or Zeke, don't worry."

"I'm just surprised you aren't injured. Must have been a young one."

"Didn't stop to ask. We fought, it left. End of the problem. Now we need to get Zeke into bed, and he won't go to sleep if we're all out here gabbing."

"But—"

"It's his first day at the new school. He needs his rest," Taylor said calmly. "I'll be sure to send you pictures, like mom took of Keith and me."

Oh, smooth, sis! "I'll walk you out while she gets Zeke his bath." Keith just hoped it didn't dawn on their father that Zeke's first day couldn't be the next day, as he wasn't supposed to be there yet.

Adam grumbled but agreed. Using the Zeke card was cheating, but they'd use it as long as they could. By the time Keith made it back to the house, he felt as though his cat might climb right out of his skin and go find Jason without the rest of him. He watched his father pull away, waiting until the taillights faded into the distance to reenter the home.

An explosive breath escaped him as he sagged against the now-closed door. He rubbed his face with the heels of both hands, eyes closed as he worked to get his muscles to relax some. Keith could hear Taylor and Zeke in Zeke's new room. She was reading him a bedtime story, as she did most nights. Once in a while, he wanted the story from Keith, but he was still young enough to mainly want his mom.

Smiling at the calm sound of his sister's voice, Keith pushed away from his door, then retrieved his cell. He pulled up Jason's number and sent him a quick text. *Finally free of the father-beast. Are you up for talking?*

The response wasn't fast but wasn't so slow he feared his mate was ignoring the text, either. *Saw him leave. Hope it wasn't too bad.*

Not as bad as he'd feared. *Not horrible. Missed you.*

Again, the wait seemed long, though it couldn't have be more than a minute or so. *Have to call Sasha. Will call you after?*

Thank you.

Hopeful again for the first time since Jason had bolted from the house that morning, Keith settled in to wait. He just hoped his mate didn't spend all night on the phone with the vampire.

CHAPTER NINE

IT TOOK an hour after Keith's father pulled away from the house next door for Jason to call Sasha. He'd never been afraid to talk to his friend before. In fact, if something was wrong, Jason counted on Sasha to be there for him, just as he'd always been there for Sasha. The thought that Sasha was a vampire was hard to swallow, but the thought that Sasha was only in his life because Grandy had asked him to hurt more than anything. Part of him wondered, but the other part was certain Sasha was really his friend.

Tired of the doubting and worry, Jason picked up his phone again and hit One on his speed dial.

Sasha's smooth voice came through after only one ring. "Hi, hon. Feeling any better now?"

"Ha-ha. Not really. Keith wants to talk to me. You… aren't who I thought. Oh, and I don't think I like Keith's father." Actually, he was certain he didn't. Jason had watched Keith's father arrive and leave and Keith's edginess when in his father's presence—not that Jason completely understood why Keith's father and Keith didn't get along—made Jason worried for Keith.

A soft sigh sounded through the cell before Sasha said, "It's sweet you're worried about Keith."

"Can't help it. I don't like that he's convinced I'm this fated-mate thing. Or that he's a cat and didn't tell me." Jason could excuse him not saying anything before they had sex the first time. But after Keith had asked him out on a real date? Slept with him again? No.

"You're looking at the situation with your kitty all wrong. Shifters are loyal if nothing else. And with true mates, they truly can't stray. It's not possible. Besides, I can't imagine he'd have fought like he did for you if he didn't truly care for you. No shifter would do that, alone, without a damn good reason, hon."

Neither point was as comforting as Sasha seemed to think it should be. "I don't want anyone fighting over me! And stop with all this 'true' business. It's annoying." The memory of blood and their clashing forms sent a shiver through Jason, making him jittery and nauseous all over again.

"You can't tell him not to protect you from a known and obvious threat—"

"You are *not* a threat."

Even after witnessing the short fight, he still had a hard time picturing Sasha as actually dangerous.

Sasha's light laugh was unwelcome. "Don't go telling people that. I'll be up to my fangs in challenges if you do, though it's sweet of you to think that."

"Sasha," Jason ground out through his teeth, not appreciating the attitude or humor at his expense.

"Look, your grandfather didn't want you to know what I am. I don't think Drew ever thought we'd meet, honestly. However, he also knew that no one, no vampire or one that knows of our kind, would ever dare lay a finger on you as long as you were under my protection. As you got older, you reminded me so much of Drew when he was a kid that I decided to introduce myself."

"I am? He was?" His grandy had been like him? "In what ways? Grandy was straight, confident, and a bit of a rebel for a grandfather."

"You have no idea how much of a wild child Drew was when he was younger. It is true he married your gran and was annoyingly happy with her 'til the day he died, but he was also serious, loyal, sweet, and just as cute as you are now. Oh, and he had just as bad taste in partners as you until he found Lily."

"I don't remember any stories of evil exes."

"Well, of course not. Would you tell your grandchild that you'd dated and been dropped by a priest's daughter, the son of the werewolf pack's beta, or a woman he later found out was already married?"

Son? "Son! But... he was straight!"

Ignoring his outburst, Sasha continued. "No, you'd have forgotten to mention all those befores and focused on how you'd found the love of your life, as he always called Lily."

"You said son. What do you mean son? When did he do that?" *And why didn't he tell me? All that worrying about coming out....*

"You know there's more than gay and straight, right?"

"Of course I do!" He knew, he'd just never thought of bi and his grandy as belonging in the same sentence. Of course, Grandy and sex in the same conversation was not high on his list, either. "But I really don't want to think of him with anyone, male, female, or anything else. Just no. Hell no."

"Funny. Not the point, though. You wanted to talk about Keith or about me? Since Drew dating a wolf is off-limits."

"Grandy dating anyone is off-limits," Jason grumbled. "And I'm not sure which topic would be less horrible. How about, how is a twenty-five-year-old man really a vampire prince? What does 'prince' mean, anyway?"

"If I knew Drew when he was young, do you really think I'm only twenty-five? I haven't been that in nigh on two centuries. 'Prince' means the coven leader, the one that has to deal with all the political crap and maintain proper relations with humans, shifters, etcetera. It's a right pain, honestly, but I took over when my parents were killed over a century ago. It's old-world ideals that don't translate well to current concepts, but it's how our society works."

"You work for one of the hospitals," Jason accused. "How can you be a vampire and one of the hospital board members?"

"Cute. Actually, I'm the head of the company that owns the hospital, hon. It's what I chose to put some of my money into. Being nobility is like being a CEO; it's a bunch of bureaucracy and political know-how. But why not have a vampire run a hospital? I've had plenty of time to learn how."

"I guess. Still seems weird. A vampire trying to make humans live longer…. Still, no more lying to me. I'd rather know all the creepy stuff than be lied to."

"I know, hon. I do." Sasha sighed. "But none of this helps you with your dating issue. What are you going to do about Keith?"

Good question. "Not sure what I should do."

"How about this, then: what do you want to do about cat boy?"

The way Sasha's voice deepened conjured all kinds of naughty things he'd love to do with Keith. "Make this morning not have happened?" That sounded good. Make it go back to before all the cat, vampire, mate things happened. "I liked how things were going until his sister walked in."

"Nice idea, but no. You can't unlearn the truth, nor do I believe you honestly would choose ignorance. But as much as I love you, as much as I enjoy talking with you, hon, it's Keith you need to talk to. He needs to understand why you're scared. Why are you against mating, by the way? That I don't understand. If you were a vampire, I would understand being upset about being a shifter's mate, but you're human. It is rare but done."

"I don't want to be wanted just because he has to." Being an obligation didn't sound like a good life plan, nor did it sound like a happy relationship. "And stop with the laughing! What's so funny about what I said?"

"Sorry, hon," Sasha managed as his giggles died down. "Just the idea that a shifter would be with you out of obligation. They aren't like that. Honestly, if it weren't for all the bad blood between our races, I'd have them as allies at the very least. However, you need to call your boyfriend over and tell him these things. He can't show you your fears are wrong if he doesn't know about them. I will say this, though—from what I saw of him, he's smitten. A smitten kitten," he singsonged before laughing again.

Jason couldn't help himself; he joined right in, laughing 'til he cried. "You're evil."

"That's what the stories all say," Sasha continued in that light, teasing voice. "Well," he added, suddenly sounding sober, "and my exes. But that's neither here nor there. For now, go put your boyfriend out of his misery and call him. I'll come over tomorrow and we can spend some time talking about anything you like, or the next day if you're too busy having makeup sex."

"Brat! Fine, I'll go call him, if he's not in bed already. And you can come over, just, um… no more fighting. Please."

"I promise not to fight with Keith. His father is another story. Can't stand the cat. Thankfully, Keith doesn't seem to take after him. Night."

Yeah, having a cat father-in-law that hates humans doesn't sound like such a great plan. "Night, Sasha."

One call down, one more to go. One he wanted to make, yet was afraid to make. What if Keith took his need for space as a reason not to be with him? What if Keith only wanted to be with him because of the mate thing? Trying to push all his rambling worries away, Jason took a deep breath and called Keith.

HE SHOULD have known better. Really. He was certain that telling Keith to come over for breakfast, instead of when they'd talked the night before, was a good idea. Let his mind have a chance to calm down, let things settle— like the fact his lover was a lynx. But no, it only gave him hours more to fret, question, and not sleep.

By the time the knock sounded at his front door, Jason was about ready to come apart. Closing his eyes, he took a couple of slow, controlled breaths to calm his heart and breathing down. He set the pan he was cooking bacon in on the back burner, then made his way to the front door. When he opened it, there stood Keith. Damn, the man looked amazing. He looked like sex personified, wrapped in jeans and a tight cobalt-blue T-shirt that showed off his defined chest muscles. Jason was so distracted by the man's body he took a moment to register that Keith held a pot with flowers and a small bag in his hands.

"Uh, wh-what's that for?"

Keith flashed that same killer smile that had melted Jason when they first met. "It's for you, sweetheart. You said you liked orchids," he explained as he stepped closer.

Realizing he was blocking the doorway, Jason stepped back, the heat on his cheeks annoying him more than his stutter. "Come in."

"Thanks." Keith moved through the house as if he'd been coming there forever instead of only having visited once before. "It smells wonderful in here."

"Thanks. I said I'd m-make us breakfast." Jason didn't know what to say but was frustrated that he only seemed to be able to get out the obvious. "Hungry?"

"Always." Keith extended first the plant and then the bag to Jason.

Jason looked around before deciding to put the plant on his coffee table. He moved it three times on the table until he liked how the cascade of flowers draped against the backdrop of the wood. When he looked up, Keith was watching him with a soft look on his face. "I.... Thank you."

"You don't have to open the bag yet. It's all the stuff you might need for the plant. Food and such," Keith added and shrugged one shoulder.

"Thanks. I love orchids, and purple is my favorite color, so it's perfect." They stood there, staring at each other for a moment before Jason cleared his throat. "You ready to eat? I just need a minute to finish." Without waiting for Keith to answer, he stuffed his hands into his pockets and hurried back to the kitchen.

After checking the bacon on the stovetop and deciding it was ready after all, he put it on the paper towels he had ready. While that settled, he opened the oven and pulled out pancakes he'd put in already to keep warm. Pancakes were one of the first things he remembered learning to make with his gram and were still one of his favorite meals.

Without looking at Keith he said, "I can make e-eggs too, if you like. I didn't know how m-much you might want to eat or how much meat. I mean, I know you a-ate a normal meal when we went out, b-but...," he said, unsure how to finish his thought without sounding stupid. Stupider, anyway.

Keith chuckled and stepped closer, his body heat wrapping around Jason as it did every time the man was near. With the heat came Keith's woodsy, smoky scent. He nearly groaned at how fast his cock hardened. "I do tend to eat more than a human. Shifting burns a lot of calories, but you don't have to make me anything extra. This looks wonderful."

"N-no. It'll only take me a moment. It's not fair to offer to feed you and then make you go hungry," Jason countered. He set the covered dish down on the table and then hurried over to the fridge. He pulled out a half carton of eggs and looked back to where Keith stood. Instead of taking one or two out, he brought all six to the counter, pulled a bowl out from under the sink, and started cracking eggs into it. "Scrambled or fried? Or, er, omelet? I can do an omelet with stuff in it if you want."

"Really, it's okay, but since you already broke the eggs, just scrambled is fine. I'm not that picky."

The clear humor in Keith's voice did nothing to cool Jason's nerves, though it did serve to annoy him more. He was trying so hard and failing to be a good host. "You could pour us drinks," he suggested, hoping to distract Keith from watching him. "C-coffee, juice?"

Instead of watching Keith watch him, Jason focused on beating the hell out of the eggs and scrambling them. He jumped, banging into the stove when he felt Keith's lips and breath ghost across his nape. Goose bumps spread across his body, and he shivered as he fought not to push back into Keith's body behind him.

"I'll get us coffee, Jay," Keith husked before stepping away, taking his heat and scent with him. The sudden loss made Jason ache even more. *Dammit, how did the man get to me so damn fast?*

Pushing his body's wants to the side, Jason quickly plated their breakfast, and before he knew it, the food was gone and he had nothing left to hide behind. A fact he was painfully aware of. Before he could think up another reason to stall, Keith stood, then took their dishes to the sink and rinsed them off before sliding them into the dishwasher.

"We've eaten, and the dishes are done. Are you ready to talk? I know I am. I'm about to go crazy wondering what's going on in that head of yours, Jay. Please," Keith implored, one hand held out. "Come sit and talk to me, baby."

"Yeah, I am. I think," he added as he took Keith's hand. He allowed himself to be pulled into the living room and down onto the couch. Honestly, he wasn't certain he was ready, but seeing as Keith was there, at his request, he couldn't figure out any other way to manage things.

Jason sat and shifted around until they were facing each other, though he couldn't manage to actually meet Keith's gaze. "Um, you want a drink?"

"No, baby." Keith's hand flashed out and wrapped around Jason's wrist as he went to stand again. "Sit and talk to me. I know you must have a million questions for me, and I'll answer each one as best I can. Okay?"

"I do, but I'm not sure I'm going to like the answers."

"Jason." Keith didn't speak again until Jason lifted his eyes to meet Keith's. "I'm a shifter, not the bogeyman. It'll be all right, just tell me what you need to and ask whatever you want."

"'Kay. Sorry, it's not that I didn't know about shifters, so this shouldn't be so hard." He took a couple of deep breaths. "You turned into a cat yesterday—you said a lynx, right? Do you know the cat that's been watching me?"

Keith's deep rumble of a laugh startled him. *What's so damn funny?*

"Sorry, I know it's not funny to you, but I really did think it was sweet of you to leave the tuna and warm milk out."

Jason thought Keith's words through, not liking the way they fit together. "You're the cat that was outside the other night? But then…. Why didn't you just have our date then? That night, I mean. Why wait if you were already here?" He didn't want to acknowledge that he'd fed his boyfriend, thinking he was a stray. "And how do you fit into a cat-sized body? You're a big man." *In more ways than one.*

"Yes, that was me out there." Keith smiled, his eyes unfocused for a moment. "It was a bit late to call and ask you to go out, and, well, I honestly wanted time to see how you acted when I wasn't around. Also, I needed to get a good feel for the woods here, for Zeke's sake if nothing else. He's too young not to be overly cautious with, especially in a human area."

"Human area?" Jason asked, curious why that mattered more than a nonhuman area. "Wouldn't wild animals be more dangerous than a few bored housewives and their workaholic husbands?"

"No. Animals recognize us as animals but more, so they tend to not fight with us. They will play and even cohabitate with us, but they still know we're more than just animals. Humans tend to fear, revile, and attack anything they don't understand. Well, or dissect it in a lab to find out how it works. Both are bad ideas for us, but Taylor and I don't want Zeke raised to hate humans like his grandfather wants."

"Yeah, that's another thing I'm not thrilled with."

"What? That I don't want Zeke to hate humans?"

CHAPTER TEN

"NO, YOUR father's a-attitude about humans. Last I checked, *I'm* human."

Keith couldn't figure out why he needed to be told Jason was human. He knew that! "Yes, I know. What does he have to do with anything?"

Jason sighed loud enough for ten people. "If we d-date, at some point he's going to have to deal with the fact I'm human." He paused, chewed on his bottom lip. "Unless you p-plan to keep me a secret forever."

Shaking his head, Keith was frustrated he even needed to say it. He took a moment to think through his words, wanting Jason to truly hear him. "No, baby. I haven't told him about me being gay before, but you're my mate. As soon as I claim you, complete the bond, I wouldn't be able to hide you even if I wanted. Which I do not want to do. He's going to.... Actually, I'm not positive what he'll try, but he won't be happy with me. But I would never hide my mate."

"Not happy means what? He won't try to h-hurt you, will he?" Jason reached out and clutched Keith's hand, and the fact Jason had instigated the touch that time—the first time really, since he'd sent Keith home the morning before—sent shivers up his spine.

The worried glare Jason pointed toward the front door made Keith happier than ever.

"Maybe. I hope not, but I'm defying him and what he considers our truth by being gay, much less by mating with a human. But he doesn't get to decide who my mate is, though Baast knows he's tried."

The worried and pinched look Jason gave him melted Keith a little more. How could his mate be so protective of him and not be falling for him? The concern gave Keith hope that his mate would love him, accept him, even if it took time. He had time. He'd wait forever, if that's what it took—he just hoped it wouldn't require that long.

"He won't hurt you, Jay. Attacking humans is strictly forbidden."

"Yeah, but from what you say, being g-gay and being with a human are forbidden too, so forgive me if your reassurances aren't very. However, I don't want you attacked f-for being with me, either. I'm not w-worth getting hurt over," Jason added softly, too soft for a human to hear probably, but not too soft for Keith.

"Baby, why would you say that?" Keith didn't like how Jason seemed to think he wasn't attractive or worth fighting for. *What kind of stupid fucks has he been dating?* He very seriously considered trying to find Prince Sasha's phone number and asking him why he didn't take better care of Jason. The moment he thought of it, he flinched. Maybe waiting until the little vamp prince visited Jason again would be better.

Jason stared at him, head cocked to one side, and scrunched his nose. If it hadn't been for the fact he knew Jason was human, he'd think Jason was a shifter with how he acted at times, like then. "You heard that?"

"Of course."

"Huh. Be that as it may, I still don't like this whole mate thing, nor do I like the idea that your father will not only disapprove but may try to hurt you over seeing me. Why would you want to r-risk him doing that? You b-barely know me."

If Jason were a shifter, he'd get it, but as a human, he didn't, which annoyed and frustrated Keith to no end. "I'll get to know you better as we spend more time together, but what do you have against mating? It's like a marriage for humans, only more permanent."

Running his fingers through his short hair, Jason huffed. "You haven't known me long enough to talk about marriage. You... I.... Look, I get that this is a big th-thing to you, but I don't want to be in a relationship where the other partner is there because he has to be. Only if he truly desires me for me. I'd rather be alone than an obligation or whatever," Jason added, flicking one hand in the air as if to wipe away the idea of the words. "You're only here because of this fate-drive thing, not because you want me. Not really."

Keith had been afraid that was part of Jason's concerns, and again cursed the fact humans didn't feel the mating pull. "That's not how mating works. Are we certain that we want to be in the relationship? Yes, though not because we 'have to' but because the other half of the mating is our perfect match. Fate wouldn't give us a mate that wasn't everything to us. It simply doesn't work that way. Besides—" Keith smirked at Jason, remembering back to the first time he'd caught a glimpse of Jason when he was unloading the U-Haul. "Even as I felt the drive to find the owner of the delicious mating scent, I saw this really cute geek through a window and yet still hoped I had a chance with him."

"You did?" Jason squeaked, then cleared his throat, only sounding a little better on the second try. "You saw me and thought I was c-cute?"

Damn, who the hell taught him he wasn't cute or worth loving? If he found out who they were, they would rue the day they had ever hurt his mate! "Baby, I thought you were sexy as hell and hoped I'd get to meet you before this mate thing kicked in. I feared my mate would be a woman when all I wanted was to meet you. Luckily for me, fate knew the right mate for me, and you showed up on my doorstep the next day to woo me with decadent food."

Jason sputtered as he tried to speak. Finally he calmed enough to force out, "I wasn't trying to w-woo you—who even uses that word?—I just w-wanted to meet the n-new neighbor."

"Bullshit. You came over here, food in hand, reeking of want and need. You wanted me as much as I wanted you. And I wanted you *before* I knew you were my mate."

Jason didn't respond right away, which worried Keith. Did the man not believe him, or was it something else? While Keith had worked with humans for years, he had never tried to manage his way through a relationship with one. "Baby, talk to me. Why do you look like that?"

Wide hazel eyes, ones that reminded Keith of most of his kind when in their lynx skins, looked up and met his. Their wetness worried him, as did the scent of hurt from Jason. "So it's not just some pull that you have, something that could go away over time or that makes you want to be close out of need?"

"Oh, make no mistake, I want and need you, but not the way you mean. I know this may not make sense to you yet, but the mating drive only enhances my want for you. I wanted you even when I thought I was destined for another. Until just before we moved here, I honestly thought mates were for other people. I never dreamed of finding a true mate."

"Why not? Why d-didn't you think you'd have a mate?"

"Because I was always taught that shifters, at least lynx shifters, can't be gay. Wolves can, though it's rare. But that's not the point," he huffed out, not wanting to get sidetracked by the differences between lynx and wolves. "For now, I need you to understand that being mated isn't a bad thing and it isn't something that goes away. Once the bond is sealed, as your friend said, we can't stray, not that I'd want to. Mates don't separate. Ever."

"You've said th-that before, about the b-bond being sealed or something. What is that?" Jason's tone was flat even with the slight stutter, as if he didn't care about the answer, though the constant finger tapping against his leg gave the lie to the calmness.

Keith debated how to explain it to Jason, who had no point of reference. "When we seal the bond, whether with a chosen mate or a fated one, we complete the joining of our souls, not just our bodies. I'm not sure how one does that with a human yet, as I don't think the normal way would work well for human-slash-shifter matings. But I'll figure that part out later. Right now the point is that it's a bonding that's much more permanent than a human marriage. Those are broken all the time. Matings aren't."

"Huh." Jason was quiet again for a little while, but this time he seemed calm and curious as he gazed at Keith. "How is it normally done? Why can't you do that with me? And would you really want to do that if it can't be undone? What if you find you can't stand me or love me or something?"

"That's a lot of different things to ask at once, Jay. But I'll try to explain. Um, mating is usually where the dominant partner bites into the more submissive mate during sex, thus bonding their bodies and souls together. I can't do that to you as biting you that way could badly injure you. And yes, I would want that. Attraction and desire come first, but I have no doubts that we can make a true and happy mating, baby."

"I don't see how you can know that when we've only gone out once and spent the one day together, but biting?" Jason croaked out the last, his hands snapping up to cover his throat. "Being bitten by a lynx sounds like a good way for me to wind up d-d-dead."

"Jay, baby," Keith soothed, reaching out to Jason. For the first time since Jason had fled Keith's the day prior, Jason moved easily when Keith took his hand and pulled, and in moments, Jason was settled in Keith's lap. "I swear to you, I wouldn't do anything to hurt you. Ever! That's why I said I had to find out *how* to seal the bond with you, since you're human. There's a way—I just have to find it, that's all."

"But you said b-biting…."

"I did, but you liked my nibbling on you before. Hell, even though I was upset about injuring you our first time with my claws, you didn't seem to be bothered, so I'm thinking it wouldn't be as upsetting to you as you think. I just have to figure out how not to truly harm you so we can finish the bond."

"But…. Keith, as much as I l-like you," Jason said, shifting to straddle his lap, "and I do like you a lot, I'm not ready to even think about f-forever."

It was hard for Keith to focus on Jason's words as his ass settled over Keith's groin. The pressure had his mind turning from serious to carnal immediately. "No worries, baby. We can date. We have time to get to know each… other…." Keith groaned as Jason shifted, grinding down against Keith's now-hard cock. "Dammit, you keep that up," he growled, "and I'm going to be buried back inside that sweet ass of yours. Now."

Jason looked up through his long, golden lashes and smiled innocently. "Doing what?"

"I thought…." Keith struggled to get the words out as Jason continued to press down and wiggle his tight butt against him. "Thought you wanted to talk about shift…." No longer caring what they were supposed to be doing, Keith pulled Jason forward, slanting his mouth over Jason's, which immediately opened for his tongue to press inside.

As he continued devouring Jason, nipping and sucking at his sweet lips while working hard to map every inch of the inside of Jason's mouth, he grabbed Jason's hips, halting the man's motions. If he didn't, Keith was afraid he'd end up coming in his jeans instead of in his mate, something he decidedly didn't want to do.

Once Jason stilled, he moved his hands to Keith's chest, digging into the muscles there as he whimpered into Keith's mouth, driving Keith's need that much higher. He tore himself away from Jason's taste only when the need for oxygen outweighed the need for his mate, but once he had, he moved his lips down Jason's neck, nipping the tantalizing flesh there.

"I w-want…," Jason panted as he fought Keith's hold on his hips. "Let g-go a min, please."

The sweet plea was the only thing that made Keith release his mate. He didn't want to, but he could deny Jason nothing.

Jason shifted, deliberately sliding down Keith's body until he knelt between Keith's thighs. The position, the way Jason looked up and licked his lips before he shifted his gaze to Keith's groin, had Keith harder than he'd ever been. Jason ran his hands up and down Keith's thighs, sensitizing them, making him forget anything but his need for Jason. "Please." *By all the Gods, please….*

Before he could work out how to make his lips work better and beg—something he'd never done before—Jason moved, first to push up the tight T-shirt, then bending to kiss and nibble at the trail of hair beneath. The tugging had Keith arching his hips up in silent supplication. As Jason unbuttoned Keith's jeans, one button at a time, he took the time to kiss and lick every bit of flesh revealed, all except Keith's needy dick. He was certain he would die if Jason didn't hurry the hell up and swallow him!

Jason sat back on his heels, his gaze hungry, yet reverent, as he stared at Keith. "Please t-tell me I can, without a c-cover. Please," he begged, his voice wavering.

"Of course, baby. Anything you want," Keith forced out, his voice low and more feline growl than human, but Jason didn't seem to mind.

Keith shimmied at Jason's silent instructions as he guided him until Keith sat with his legs wide and his cock exposed and rising up from his body, arcing toward his navel, a constant stream of precome leaking, making a small puddle on his overheated and supersensitive skin. Keith tracked every movement of his mate as Jason bent forward and nuzzled his sac, taking a tentative lick of the skin, then groaning.

"You smell so good and taste even better," Jason managed before lifting Keith's cock. He started at the head, kissing and licking from tip to base, then doing the same on his way up the other side. He then teased his way around the head and sucked it into his mouth, sending Keith's mind into shutdown even as his body was propelled that much closer to bliss.

Jason suckled the wide flared head, stabbing the tip of his tongue into the slit before suddenly diving down and swallowing more than half of Keith's length. It was the most perfect wet heat, the way he swirled and flicked his tongue, making Keith writhe on the couch even as he fought not to thrust into Jason's mouth. He wasn't small, and he knew it. He didn't want to hurt his mate, but *damn,* it felt *so* good!

After a couple of failed attempts to deep-throat Keith's cock, Jason wrapped one hand around the base, using it to cover and tease the part he couldn't manage to swallow. The longer he stroked and sucked, the closer Keith inched to his orgasm. When Jason's other hand disappeared from sight, Keith expected Jason to take himself in hand, but instead Jason used his long, nimble fingers to alternate between stroking and tugging on Keith's sac.

Before he knew it Keith's hands were in Jason's hair. As he thrust in and out of Jason's mouth a few times, the tingle and throb in his groin made his eyes slam shut in bliss. He screamed Jason's name as he emptied himself into his mate's eager mouth.

Jason didn't release Keith until he'd gone soft, continuing to suck gently, taking every drop he could find. He even licked up the sticky trail and puddle on Keith's abs before finally sitting back and smiling up at him. The sight of his mate's puffy lips and glazed eyes was almost enough to make him take Jason then. Almost.

When Keith could get his brain and lips to work again for something other than panting, he pulled Jason back into his lap. "Come here, baby. Let me take care of you too."

The headshake confused Keith until Jason spoke. "No need. I c-came when you d-did." He moaned and licked his lips again. "Damn you taste good. Even better than I'd dreamed."

"Oh!" He had? Keith only then noticed the scent of his mate's come. "Then I definitely need to take care of you."

Not giving Jason time to stop him, Keith turned and laid him out on the couch, then pulled and unzipped Jason's jeans until his sticky member was exposed. Keith took his time, licking and nipping, until Jason was clean and half-hard again.

"S-stop." Jason squirmed away from him. "Sensitive."

"'Kay." Keith climbed up Jason's body, stalking his mate's lips, then taking them again in a deep kiss, mingling their tastes in his mouth. He'd tasted himself before—who hadn't?—but the two of them together was exquisite. "You taste so good."

"So do you."

Jason looked totally debauched as Keith wrapped his arms around him and shifted their positions 'til Jason was sprawled out on top of him. And just as he did their first time, he dozed off, Jason's hair and soft breath tickling his skin and making him purr as he rested. His last thought was of how much he hoped his mate would come to love him, and want to complete their bond.

CHAPTER ELEVEN

SOMETHING WAS different. The weight across Keith's torso and legs wasn't right, though the scent permeating his every breath was one he wanted to roll in, live with, and devour all at the same time. As his consciousness surfaced from the delicious dreams of his mate, Keith began to stretch but stopped when the weight on his body shifted and grumbled. *Grumbled? What the hell?*

Keith froze, confused as to what was on him. His thoughts were still too unfocused to manage more than forcing his eyes open. When he did, his brain finally came fully awake. Jason lay sprawled across Keith's legs and torso with his head resting on Keith's chest. The sight stole Keith's breath. Gods, he wanted his mate to be like this with him always, though he knew he had a long way to go to get Jason to trust in their future.

He carefully shifted until Jason lay beside him, though doing so meant he barely managed to stay on the couch. *Bed, definitely need to fall asleep like this in the bed. A nice* big *bed.* He was unable to do a thing about his hard-on, as all it took for him to get one was remembering the smell, taste, or sight of his mate. Hell, everything about his mate turned him on and drove him and his cat insane with want and need.

Choosing not to attack his mate was hard, but he didn't want Jason to think all he cared about was having sex with him. No, there was so much more to Jason than his tantalizing backside or his delectable cock. A soft groan slipped out as he thought about how good his mate felt and tasted. Without conscious thought, he pressed his hard cock against Jason and rutted against his hip, thrilling in the sparks that shot up his spine and tightened around his balls.

Jason stirred, then froze before his beautiful hazel eyes popped open. "Keith?" he rasped, his scent strengthening with arousal.

Keith forced his hips to still, even as his cat fought him to keep moving. "Yes, baby?"

Licking his lips, Jason lifted his head, his gaze dropping to where Keith's groin met Jason's hip. "There are much better ways to handle issues like that," he said, his voice low and still thick from sleep.

"Oh, really? What do you suggest?"

"Hmm…. A shower, a partner, and lots of slippery activity. To get clean and help your little problem there."

"Little?" Keith huffed. He knew Jason was teasing him, but still, no man wanted to be called little, especially by their mate! "I'll show you little, boy," he growled as he flipped Jason over so his front was pressed into the couch and Keith was pressed to his backside.

When Jason wiggled enough to get his arms under him, he tried to push up, but that only made Keith's cat more excited and determined to show his mate who he was. Keith bent his head and bit him where his shoulder and neck met. Not hard enough to break skin, though he wanted to. The need to complete their mating pushed at Keith, driving his need higher.

Jason stilled a moment, a soft whine slipping out. The sweet sound only managed to excite Keith more. He pressed his cock against Jason, hard, rutting against his ass, his need and want driving him hard to take his mate. Jason pushed back and rubbed his tight ass against Keith, even as Keith continued to grind against him. When Jason started to push up again and turn over, Keith's cat came out even more. He hissed as he bit into Jason's other shoulder.

Jason gasped, then let out a loud moan. "Please," he begged, though Keith couldn't understand what he might be begging for at that moment.

Unable to do anything else right then, Keith moved his lips to the back of Jason's neck and sunk his teeth in. Only the last bit of his human control allowed him to keep his teeth from shifting, so as not to make Jason bleed. He wanted to, the mating drive nearly overwhelming him.

Jason stilled at the bite as his fingers dug into the cushion, and sank back to the couch once more. "Please… I need…." He couldn't seem to get any more out, but Keith didn't need the words. The raw need in Jason's voice was enough to push him to take his mate again. However, the human in him balked at penetration, as they didn't have proper supplies and he would *not* hurt his mate that way.

Pulling back from Jason's skin was nearly impossible right then, but Keith managed it, somehow. "Turn over," he growled, his voice more cat than human. Jason did, quickly, and a thrill ran through Keith when he settled between Jason's thighs and felt how hard he was.

Not thinking, or caring, about after, Keith began thrusting against Jason, rubbing off on his mate even as Jason thrust up to meet each of Keith's motions. He dropped his head, panting, to search for Jason's skin, annoyed when he had to fight the man's shirt to get to what he desperately craved.

As their frotting became more desperate, Keith lost a little more of his control. He ripped Jason's shirt enough with his free hand that he could finally reach his neck and the skin along his collarbone. Kissing and licking everywhere he could reach, he took little nips, worrying the flesh as he did, desperation driving him.

"G-gonna come," Jason groaned, pressing his neck harder against Keith's mouth even as he thrust up harder, both men now chasing their orgasms.

When Jason arched up hard and screamed Keith's name, Keith lost it. Biting hard again where Jason's neck met his shoulder, though still with his human teeth—much to the annoyance of his lynx—Keith ground down as his balls tightened and his cock spurted inside his jeans. As bliss overtook his ragged thoughts, he was only left with the taste of his mate on his tongue and the ecstasy of what they'd just done.

Some time later, after each man took the time to calm and regain the skills needed to breathe properly, Keith managed to move off Jason and pull him into his lap again. "I, um, think that idea about a shower might be a good one, before this dries and glues us to our pants."

Jason's clear, sweet laugh rang through the room, making Keith's heart squeeze and his breath catch. "Yeah, that might be a good idea. Though," he continued with a slight frown, "I'm not sure what you're going to wear."

"If I can go clean up and get my boxer briefs off, I should be fine."

"If you must." Jason sighed. The put-upon sound made Keith smile.

"I must, baby. Now be a good boy and let me up so I can go clean up, then we can think about lunch and maybe the rest of that talk we were trying to have."

At the mention of their talk, Jason's smile fell, though he didn't seem upset and thankfully didn't smell upset or distressed, either. "Yeah, I think that would be good. I have two bathrooms, or you can share mine, but that might not get us very clean."

"Don't tease me like that, Jay." The thought of Jason wet and soapy flashed through Keith's mind, making him wish he could bounce back as quickly as he could when he was a teen.

"Oh-kaaay," Jason said, making the simple word have *way* too many syllables. He smirked, then added, "Be a grown-up about it."

A few minutes later, and with a much more comfortable body—drying spunk was itchy, after all—Keith joined Jason in his kitchen. He couldn't help but smile as he watched Jason rummaging through the fridge, grumbling about stupid foods hiding from him. Of course, the fact that

Jason's delectable ass was pushed out, thanks to him bending over to locate the various items he wanted, didn't help Keith to stay focused on noncarnal ideas. He wasn't about to say anything and make Jason stand up any sooner than necessary, though.

When Jason did stand, he sat a pile of sandwich fixings on the counter beside him. "Oh, you're back."

"Only for a couple of minutes."

"You could have said something or made a little noise. But hey, you like turkey, salami, and Black Forest ham? I have a couple of kinds of cheese too."

The happiness was rolling off Jason so much it made paying attention to his mate difficult, but he managed. Somehow. "I do, but you don't have to wait on me. I can make my own."

"No, it's fine. I need to learn what you like and what you don't if we're really going to be a couple, right? So why not start now?"

Without waiting for Keith's response, Jason pulled out a loaf of some kind of hearty nut bread, then extracted four slices, which he set on a plate. As he picked up each item—meats, cheeses, condiments—he looked up at Keith, waiting for his yes or no before using or setting aside each item. When done with Keith's sandwiches, Jason quickly made his own, adding chips and pickles on the side. Jason only had one sandwich on his plate, and it wasn't nearly as stuffed as Keith's.

"Let's eat," he said.

"It looks wonderful, Jay. But I meant what I said, you don't need to wait on me."

"I know. Just eat and be happy, okay?"

Now that the food was in front of him, Keith couldn't help but dive in. He hadn't been able to eat anything other than the breakfast a few hours ago, and that didn't make up for the lack of eating the day before. Not with his metabolism.

He did manage to slow down and actually enjoy the second sandwich, which was delicious. When he was done with his food, he smiled at Jason. "You make a mean meal. Thanks."

Before Jason could stand, Keith hopped up and tended to cleaning the plates and putting the ingredients away. He hated how some males treated their mates like servants at times, though usually only the older ones did this. He suspected that their mates had also been taught to serve them because of the time they had been raised in.

Jason watched, smiling all the while. Keith loved Jason's smile. It was wide and showed off his straight white teeth and a small dimple in his left cheek—one he wanted to lick, but then he wanted to lick all of his mate. "All done."

"Yeah, okay. You wanna try to finish that talk now?"

Jason didn't sound too thrilled, but at least he wasn't trying to distract Keith, so Keith considered it a win.

Once they were settled back on the couch again, Jason folded one leg up under himself and turned sideways to face Keith. "So what else do I n-need to know about all this lynx stuff, and are you certain your dad won't try to hurt you over me? I d-didn't like the way he was with you yesterday. You l-looked… I don't know, tense and like you were trying hard to not step away from him. I know I only saw h-him when he arrived and when he left, but he made you so…." Jason explained, rolling his right hand as if that would help him find the words he needed.

"You were watching?"

"Couldn't help it. Not even sure how I knew when to look, but I didn't like the way he obviously made you feel."

Keith wanted to crow. There was only one way he knew of for Jason to have timed looking over that well and to have picked up on his nervousness around his father. Well, only one he could think of, especially since they were so new as a couple. *Can humans feel the pull of mating as well?* He wasn't sure, but his hope for their bond strengthened with those few words from his mate.

"We don't get along very well," he explained, not wanting to point out that there was no way Jason could have picked up everything he had from that little bit of observation. "He thinks I should have mated and had an heir already. Thinks I need to stop working for humans. Thinks a lot of things that are never going to happen. But he's not the point, really. He doesn't have another heir, unless he considers Zeke, so he can't risk hurting me. Besides, I'm stronger, faster, younger, and able to do more than him. More than he ever realizes, as he's never seen me do anything unusual."

"Define 'unusual,' please. I mean, turning into a huge cat is a bit unusual, from my side of things."

"Maybe," Keith allowed. "But you knew of shifters, so it's not that weird to you. But I mean how fast I can shift or how strong I am. How fast I can run. Things I didn't want him to know when I was younger and am glad he doesn't know about now."

"That's what I mean. What's so different about you, as a shifter?"

"You've never seen a normal lynx shifter shift, so you don't have a point of reference, but usually it's a slow shift and reformation of the body from human to lynx. The same slow shift happens when one goes from lynx to human. Usually it takes a couple of minutes, but one I know of took a whole twenty minutes to finish. Mine takes mere moments. I've even done it midrun, but only Taylor knows that."

"Taylor knows a lot about you that no one else does, doesn't she? And do I get to meet her and her son?"

"Yeah, she does. But she's my sister, and I never could deny her anything, even when I tried. And yes, you will. I just wanted to work on fixing things with you before I brought over the others."

"I'm sorry for throwing you out. I just—"

"You thought I'd done something horrible and then had to watch as your boyfriend and best friend fought."

"Yeah. Are you g-going to be able to get along with Sasha? I mean, I know he said shifters and v-vampires don't usually, but he seemed to think you were different, in a g-good way."

"I have a couple of friends with fangs, as I said, and I don't hate your friend. Though thinking of Prince Sasha Tolstoi as a friend is a bit hard to process. He's thought of as being the pinnacle of vampire power here, and a bit on the cold and aloof side. But he was anything but that yesterday, so I'm not sure what to think of him. I will not attack your friend again, as long as he keeps his fangs to himself."

Jason scowled. "He would never bite me like that!"

"I don't want him to bite you in any fashion," Keith snapped, his voice more hiss than human. The thought of anyone biting his mate but him had his hackles rising, even if they were under his skin at the moment.

"You seem to like biting," Jason said, his voice oddly light for how annoyed Keith felt. He lifted one hand to touch the last bite Keith'd left during sex earlier. Keith hadn't noticed—mostly because of the button-down shirt Jason now wore—how deep and pronounced the bite to Jason's collarbone was. *Damn!*

"Oh Gods, I didn't mean to bite you that hard." Even as he tried to apologize, he was entranced with the marks he'd left on his mate. He'd tried so hard to control his cat, but Jason had tasted so good. Keith reached out and traced the marks he could see, knowing there were others he couldn't.

"I didn't mind at the time, though tearing my shirts isn't going to endear you to me any." They were quiet for a moment as Keith continued to admire the marks. "You really like seeing them on my skin, don't you?"

"You have no idea how much," Keith whispered. He swallowed hard as he pulled his thoughts from sex and claiming. "I…. Mating, we're supposed to be talking about us being mates and what your fears are, not about how much I want to finish what we started earlier."

"Right, sorry. Look, I don't know that I believe in fated mates like you do. I mean, okay, we had sex, something I never do so fast, when we first met, but that doesn't mean we're mates or whatever."

Fighting the need to yell at Jason for being so stubborn, Keith debated how to make Jason understand. He got that Jason was afraid Keith's desire and love for him would change, but he could only guess at the reason. "If you had felt as I did when I opened the door that first time, how hard it was not to react as my instincts demanded, you wouldn't have any doubts."

"But I'm not a cat. I don't understand what's going on inside you or know the history of your people, or anything." Jason sounded as frustrated as Keith felt—almost.

"History you can learn, but I can't teach you to feel as I do."

"Fine," Jason snapped. "Then t-tell me about when we first met from your perspective. What about me standing there with my mac 'n cheese was so special?"

"Hmm… I could smell you even before I opened the door, both that you were my mate and that you were human, which confused me. I was too excited to really care, though, as I opened the door. But what I saw when I looked outside nearly stopped my heart and breath. There stood this beautiful man with golden skin, lynx-like hazel eyes, and dark blond hair. Eating and being calm on the outside about drove me crazy, but was worth it in the end. You didn't run, but instead gave yourself to me, something that I will dream about and remember for as long as I live."

"You thought I was beautiful?"

"Goddess, yes! And just for the record, I wanted you before I knew you were my mate."

"You said that before. I just—"

"I never thought I'd be blessed with a mate, not one Baast herself picked for me, but I couldn't have dreamed up a better choice."

Chapter Twelve

JASON SMILED as he looked out his kitchen window and saw Keith's cat. This time he knew it was Keith, not some huge stray. Keith paced into the woods behind their homes, his cute little ears twitching as he blended into the shadows. It was getting easier to deal with the fact that his boyfriend was a lynx, though he had freaked out when Keith had changed for him the day before.

No matter what he told himself, a lynx sitting before him was not the same as a domesticated house cat. He'd wanted to show no fear, but a wild animal with huge paws standing there terrified him for a moment. He knew Keith had been able to scent his fear; he'd admitted that to Jason— begrudgingly.

Watching as Keith the lynx sat down and stared up at him had helped calm Jason. When Keith had settled down and curled up on the floor with his head resting on his paws, Jason hadn't been able to hold in his smile.

"You're a handsome cat," Jason mumbled when he caught a glimpse of Keith returning.

Keith turned and looked right at Jason, cocking his head to the side. After a moment, he turned back toward his house and let out what sounded like a muffled roar. Louder than a regular cat's meow, but not as loud or with the vicious edge he'd heard from big cats at the zoo.

Moments later, another large cat, though not as big as Keith, bounded over, followed by a small cat. Jason guessed those would be Taylor and Zeke. He chuckled when Zeke pounced at Keith, who raised one huge paw and easily pinned the big kitten to the ground. As soon as he moved his paw, Zeke was right back up and running around Keith and Taylor, making little huffing, mewling sounds.

He couldn't wait to meet them in their human forms.

Jason watched them until all three vanished into the woods. Once they were gone, he turned himself back to his task of deciding what to make for snacks. Sasha was on his way over to watch movies and talk. He was afraid that there would be more talking than movies. His biggest problem was deciding what to feed the man… vampire. He thought he knew what Sasha liked, but everything he thought he knew about his best friend seemed to have changed, and now he was no longer certain. Before he could get too lost in worry, his doorbell rang. As soon as he opened the door, Sasha's smiling face met him. "Hey, hon. You ready to watch something good?" he asked, holding a bag of black-and-white popcorn in one hand.

"Uh, s-sure?" Jason was irritated with himself. He hadn't been nervous when they'd first met, much less since then, but *now* he was. "Sorry." He stepped aside and let Sasha inside. When he closed the door and turned, he was startled to see Sasha frowning at him. "What's wrong?"

"Are you going to keep acting weird around me?" Sasha put his hands on his hips and sighed. "I'm the same man you knew before you found out about my fangs."

Jason thought about that, and yeah, in a way Sasha was right. But having fangs changed a lot. For example, did Sasha hunt humans? What did he need besides the food Jason had seen him eat? How could he be out in the sun? He had so many questions and few answers so far. "Yes and n-no. You never did explain the sun and eating issues. I mean, I'm not scared to be alone with you. That would be beyond stupid, but still, there's so much I ought to know."

"Yeah, hon, there are a few things we should discuss, but really I want you to see me as you always have—as your fabulous best friend."

"Well, yeah, you're still that, of course. Never mind. Why don't you go get settled and pick a movie off Netflix for us to watch while I go get the flavor-toppings caddy for the popcorn you brought?" He loved the caddy. It was another gift from Sasha. Yeah, Sasha might have fangs, but he'd known the man for too long to consider him as anything but his best friend.

Huge bowls of hot air-popped popcorn in hand, he joined Sasha on the pile of cushions on the floor. He noticed the frozen start to *Wolverine* on the TV and smiled. Sasha was totally gone for Hugh Jackman. Jason had been right there with him until he'd met Keith. Now all he pictured when he tried to think of the perfect male was Keith. His image always appeared front and center, even when he tried to force Keith's beautiful body out of his head.

"You know, for a man that has a thing against shifters, you sure do have a serious thing for Hugh when he has claws. Sure you don't secretly have a thing for kitty or wolfy boys?"

Sasha sputtered. "I have no such obsession! I simply love how the man seems to only be half-dressed throughout the movie. Hell, in one part he's got nothing but all that sexy-as-sin skin on. How can I not love the man in the movie?"

Jason laughed, loving how Sasha still acted like he always did, not at all how he would expect a multicenturies-old prince to act. "Relax, dear, your secret is safe with me."

"Impertinent little brat! See if I watch sexy men with you again."

They had been teasing each other about their favorite actors for years. This time was only different because of the idea of Sasha liking a shifter. Not that Jason understood why the two races had issues with each other. He refrained from asking, not wanting to disturb their fun. "Fine, fine. You may have Hugh. For now."

"You are too kind. So what had you all worried when I got here? Not more issues with Keith or his idiot father, I hope."

"No, things with Keith are going well. I watched him take his sister and her son out to play in the woods just before you arrived. It was adorable to watch Zeke—that's Taylor's son—pounce at Keith. Can't wait to meet them in person."

"Good." Sasha smiled. "But then, what was bothering you?"

"It's stupid. Don't worry about it."

"No, what was it?"

"Fine." Jason sighed, reluctant to bring up the whole fang issue. "I was wondering what you would want to snack on, and that led to wondering about if you even needed to eat. It's stupid, really, so don't worry about it."

"Jason, don't do that. Don't clam up on me like you do other people." Sasha wiggled over until he sat with his side flush against Jason's. "If you have questions or concerns, just ask. I won't get upset with you. I promise."

"I know. It just feels rude."

"So not."

"Okay, fine. I was wondering about your diet and about sunlight and vampires. I thought they weren't supposed to mix."

Sasha giggled so hard he nearly fell into Jason's lap. Jason shoved him, for once not joining in his amusement. "Sorry, sorry," Sasha managed to push out as he calmed down. "I'm not sure whose brilliant idea it was to teach humans that we can't go out in the sun, but it's crap. Too much sun can cause issues, but that's because of things like the fact our eyes are light-sensitive—you know, like why I wear shades all the time when we go out—or how I'm stronger at night. But I don't mind the incorrect info being so prevalent as it saves us a ton of issues."

Jason nodded. He could see the logic behind using misinformation to protect the vampires. "What about food?"

"I eat and drink just the same as you. You've seen me eat. I simply need blood also. At my age, I don't need much, or very often, but I would never take a life just to prolong my own like that. I know that's what the mainstream media claims, but I take from donors or animals, though the latter isn't very good. But while killing during feeding is something that happens in places, I don't allow it. Nor did my father, for that matter."

"He was the prince before you, right?"

"He was. As he was also much older than I am now, the killings in the area that have been attributed to vampires were either made up or the result of rogues in our territory. Rogues don't live long here if they can't abide by our laws, though, and no one would ever think to harm you, so don't worry."

"I'll try. So Jackman with claws tonight?"

"Yep," Sasha said, his smile flashing wide. "I have a few others of his in mind for after, too, so sit back and let the drooling begin."

KEITH SAT perched up in one of the older trees not too far from their human home, observing Taylor try to teach Zeke to hunt. It was cute to watch, though he knew his sister was frustrated. The kitten wasn't interested in learning, just in eating what either of his adults brought him. As annoying as that was, it was so like Zeke. If it was a construction project or something to read, the kit was all for it, but make him have to get messy? No way.

Taylor hissed when Zeke failed, again, to catch the hare she'd brought him to practice with. Keith didn't understand it, either. What kind of lynx didn't want to eat a nice, juicy bunny? Nothing was better than fresh hare.

She mewled up at him, demanding his attention and help.

He hopped down out of the tree and landed lightly just in front of Zeke, who startled and managed to somehow trip and roll backward. If Keith could have grinned in his lynx form, he would have. When Zeke managed to right himself, he bristled and hissed, showing how unamused he was with his uncle. Keith didn't care about the attitude, only about the kit learning to hunt and pay attention. It could mean life or death one day.

Keith batted at Zeke, smacking him in the face with his paw, to get his attention. Once Zeke was watching, Keith went through the motions of tracking and catching his quarry. The demonstration didn't take long, and at least Zeke paid attention this time. His little tummy probably spurred him to be a little more attentive. He then sat back and chuffed at Zeke, demanding that if the kitten wanted to eat, he'd have to catch his own hare. Much to Keith's amazement, his nephew immediately stopped mewling and worked hard to imitate what they had been working on teaching him all evening. Well, for a while—but then in his lynx form, time meant little. He was only impatient because he wanted to go back and check on his mate. Jason was supposed to have the vampire over, and while Keith's human claimed Sasha wasn't a threat to their mate, his lynx side wasn't so sure.

His attention was diverted from thoughts of his mate when Zeke managed to catch his first hare. It wasn't a clean catch and kill, but it was his first successful hunt, so Keith chose to ignore how sloppy it had been. When Zeke tore off two small pieces and laid them at Taylor's and Keith's paws, Keith's heart gave a little squeeze. He loved his nephew and wanted the best for him. The kit's natural impulse to care for others would serve him well when he was grown. It would make him a good hunter and father one day, Keith hoped. For now, though, Keith joined in the play Zeke sought once his prize was consumed.

Zeke didn't manage to last for long, though; kittens wore out faster than grown lynx, after all. Taylor left Keith out in the forest to take Zeke home and put him in bed as a human. The kit had a big day ahead of him, going to the human school and all. Keith, however, didn't want to return and take his human skin quite yet. He was full of hare and had drunk plenty in the small stream he and Taylor had found a ways into the woods.

Instead, Keith prowled the area, closing in on Jason's backyard sooner than he thought he would reach it. He found himself curled up in the same tree he had before, the one he'd used the day Jason left him the snack. It let him see inside Jason's human den. Keith wanted to be inside with his mate, curled up with Jason, though he wasn't sure Jason would welcome his cat in his home. When Keith had taken his cat skin for Jason, his mate had been distressed. He'd smelled and seen the fear.

Keith debated staying where he was and watching his mate, enjoying listening to his playful voice as he teased his friend, or taking his human skin again and going home. He wasn't supposed to see Jason again until after work the next day, a fact that frustrated his cat more than his human.

Taylor's voice made the decision for him a short while later when she approached the tree he rested in. "Keith, your work called. They have a hurt wolf that needs help."

Wolf? He wondered why he'd want to help a wolf but knew his human half was a healer for all animals and would want to, even if his cat side didn't like the idea. Moments later he stood beside Taylor and waited for her to open the back door again. Inside, he shifted, his thought of being human enough to make it too fast for most to track. His vision was suddenly higher and his limbs and fur had changed.

"I have got to get a cat door put in. Waiting on someone to open a door isn't my idea of fun," he grumbled as he pulled on his shorts that sat on the small table by the back door.

"Fussy, fussy." Taylor smiled up at him a moment before she sobered. "Look, I wouldn't have bothered you, but there's a message on the house phone about an injured wolf that won't let anyone near it. It can't move its back legs right. They don't want to tranq it, so you need to go in tonight."

"Not upset with you or the injured wolf. I just…. Look, Jason's friend is over and my cat isn't buying that the vampire prince isn't a threat to our mate. I know it shouldn't bother me, they're only friends and Prince Sasha wouldn't hurt him, but it still makes me a little nuts."

"I know, sweetie, but right now the human Keith is needed. The part of you that's a damn good healer needs to go to work." She pulled him into a hug. "I'm here if your mate needs anything, and he has your number, right?" He nodded, still not happy to be away from his mate. "Then go get cleaned up and get to work. You don't want something bad to happen to the poor injured wolf, do you?"

Keith hated when she used that slightly whimpery voice. As if she'd cry if he didn't go help. He would, of course, help, but he didn't have to like it. "Let me change, then I'll head out. Make sure you lock up behind me and keep your ears alert. You need to sleep, but Dad gave in far too easy for me to feel comfortable."

"Yeah, and when he finds out you're dating Jason, there will be trouble. Don't worry, though. Dad would never endanger Zeke, so go to work. We'll be fine. So will your mate."

Grumbling to himself, he stalked to his bedroom. He quickly stripped and then immediately pulled on jeans and a T-shirt before stomping into his boots. He grabbed his wallet and keys, then hurried out of the house and to his bike. The loud purr soothed his human nerves, even as his mind shifted over to thoughts about the injured wolf. He just hoped it was a normal wolf and not a shifter someone had hurt while out hunting.

That thought spurred him to hurry up. He put in his earpiece, slipped on his helmet, and sped down the road as he called in to find out where his newest patient was and what was happening to it.

CHAPTER THIRTEEN

KEITH DROVE straight over to the park, where the others waited for him. He had a reputation for being able to calm even the most aggressive animals, something he cultivated. He wasn't able to calm all wounded animals, but being as strong as he was—and regular animals reacting to shifters as they tended to do—was exceedingly helpful. It also helped that many of the most ferocious when hurt were actually shifters. Those he could always get to calm down.

It didn't take long before he stood with a couple of the park rangers and one of the other vets employed by the National Park Service there. He wasn't the only vet, but he was the only shifter vet they had.

"Anyone know what happened?"

"Denny came across the wolf. Someone shot him, but we don't know what else as we can't get near him, and knocking him out could endanger him too. You always seem so good at calming ones like this...."

Yeah, he usually was. Though the thought of working with a shifter— yeah, the wolf was a shifter—with others around wasn't high on his happy list. Still, he instructed the others to back off and let him work.

Once he had the others a ways away, Keith slowly approached the wolf, sending calm and care through the pheromones he released. Wolves and lynx didn't usually get along too well, but Keith had a couple of wolf shifter friends, so he hoped this would work. If nothing else, the wolf ought to realize that Keith was likely to be there to protect him, not hurt him.

Much to Keith's relief, the wolf did in fact calm, though he wasn't still. His back legs twitched but didn't seem to be able to let the wolf stand. There was blood, but thanks to all that had happened before he'd arrived, Keith had no idea where all the blood came from.

"Come on. Calm down, little guy. I can't help you if you don't let me near." Keith kept a string of words going, explaining what was happening in his most soothing voice as he finished getting close enough to the wolf to help. The humans wouldn't see it as odd, as he always talked to animals as if they were people. In this case, of course, the wolf was people and ought to be able to understand him. Well, unless he was in too much pain, but that didn't seem likely, considering how the wolf let him approach.

The wolf sagged back onto his side and whined but stopped trying to move. Keith held up one hand and called back to the others, "Blanket."

A moment later one of the large blankets used to wrap wounded animals to prevent shock landed beside him.

"I'm sorry, little guy, but I need to check you over before I wrap you up and take you to the hospital. Just be still, okay?"

The wolf whined softly but allowed Keith to poke and prod until he was satisfied that moving the wolf would not cause more damage than good. Keith then carefully wrapped the wolf up in the blanket before lifting him into his arms.

"Don't you want help? Or a muzzle, maybe?" one of the men yelled.

"He won't hurt me. Just get the truck ready."

There was a flurry of movement, and in no time he had the wolf in the truck and the one ranger he considered a friend there, Simon, had his keys so he didn't have to leave his bike behind.

By the time he was at the small animal center, the others had gone on with their duties. Only Simon was left as he helped Keith transfer the wolf to the table in one of the clinic's rooms.

"Thanks. He's a bit heavy, though thankfully he still seems too out of it to care about his injuries."

Simon looked at the wolf and grimaced. "Yeah. Being shot has gotta hurt. Still don't know how you always get them to calm down like that."

"It's all about attitude and tone, Si. But seriously, thanks for the help. I'm going to see what I can do for him before the others return."

"Yeah, okay. See ya." Simon nodded once, then hurried back out the doors. Having dangerous wild animals loose like that always unnerved Simon, but Keith wasn't going to cage and muzzle a shifter. Not unless he was given no other option.

Keith set about cleaning the wounds and suturing the larger ones back together. Two bullet wounds and a series of deep gouges on the wolf's side and belly. The only one truly dangerous was the bullet lodged in the wolf's lower back. It was the one causing all the problems. Shifters healed much faster than humans, but with a bullet lodged against the spine, the wolf's healing couldn't seem to compensate enough to reject the bullet and allow proper healing.

Once the more dangerous bullet was out and the wound cleaned and sutured, Keith waited, watching to see if the wolf's natural healing ability would finally kick in properly. It didn't take long to see that yes, the wolf would be fine, though it would likely take a long time to heal fully.

Two days of the little wolf recovering—unfortunately in a kennel, as Keith couldn't steal the wolf from the vet center, especially not with how badly he'd been hurt—and Keith was both certain who the wolf was and that the wolf ought to be able to shift back to his human skin finally.

After one last check of the area after most of the workers had gone home, Keith moved the wolf to his office, then closed and locked the door.

"Okay, little wolf. I need you to shift for me so I can make sure nothing more is wrong. I hope you're who I think you are. Also, I need to know what happened."

It took an inordinate amount of time, but eventually instead of the small brown wolf lying on the couch covered in a blanket, there was a young man curled up, panting, lying there instead. Keith moved the blanket to allow the wolf to keep his body covered, more for warmth than modesty, as he seemed to still be in pain.

"Little wolf? Can you understand me?"

The male, probably about sixteen to eighteen years old, Keith thought, turned his head slowly and blinked open his eyes. "What.... Where am I?"

"You're in my office at the vet center for the park you were in when hurt. I'm Keith Skyler. I introduced myself to you before, but I doubt you remember. Can you tell me your name and what happened?" Keith needed to know what happened so he could have something done about it soon. Two gunshot wounds meant poachers, probably. He hoped it was that and not someone actually trying to hunt shifters.

The strain in the little wolf's voice and face was pronounced as he replied, "Caleb Hunter, and I don't know. Dogs and men with guns, but it's all a blur now."

Caleb? That was what Keith had thought. The youngest son of the wolf pack's alpha had gone missing right about the same time. The only reason Keith hadn't called already was because he didn't need an alpha throwing a fit about his boy being trapped in an animal hospital. That and he wasn't sure how well the alpha would take a lynx calling but not being able to tell him anything about what happened to his son.

"It's okay. You're safe now. Tell me who to call and I'll let you sleep, though you should shift back before you do. Having a hurt human in here would be a little hard to explain."

Caleb nodded and flashed a small smile before he rattled off a phone number. He then settled back against the couch and shifted back to the small brown wolf Keith had first met. Caleb then fell asleep—more like passed out, but Keith wouldn't point that out to Caleb. No need to wound his pride any more than it already was.

LATER THAT day Keith pulled up in front of a large log cabin in the woods to the east of Seattle. The long gravel drive appeared to have been freshly raked and was tidier than he would have expected. He knew this was Alpha Hunter's home, though he'd never been there before, but somehow the level of care made Keith wonder if Liam Hunter simply took pride in his home or if it was just for show.

Shaking off his curiosity, Keith took a deep breath as he swung his leg over his bike. As he stood beside his Harley, he thought about what he was there for and tried to ignore the worry and doubt. He wished now that he'd thought to call Vance or Chance or Kelley. They were his best friends and confidants. They were also strong and would defend him no matter what. But as he hadn't called before, it was too late, since Keith was already at the Hunter home.

Before he could get bogged down in any more worries, the front door of the cabin opened to reveal a petite older woman, her lips pulled down into a frown so tight the edges of her lips were white. "Alpha Heir Skyler?" she asked, her voice as worry-tinged as her face.

Keith approached slowly, his hands open and facing forward as he moved. "I am."

"Good, good. Liam's waiting on you inside. Please come in."

"Thank you, ma'am," he replied as he stepped past her into the large home.

The inside of the log cabin had an open floorplan with tall windows, lots of light, and rustic wooden furniture placed around the main room. There was a grouping of men, all wolves from the scent of them, clustered around a man that was much larger and more imposing—Liam Hunter, Alpha of the Everet Wolf Pack.

One of the men turned to face Keith, his brows raised so high they were almost hidden behind his bangs. "Alpha Heir Skyler? You come alone?"

"I come to bring word of Caleb to his father, not as the heir to my tribe. Is there a reason I shouldn't be here alone?" If he'd been there in an official tribe capacity, he would have had others with him, at least for the first meeting, but he'd come as a vet, not as a shifter.

"Don't mind Jacob, son. He's just a little too stuck on formalities." Liam motioned Keith to approach. Once Keith was closer, he tipped his head ever so slightly to Liam. He would show the wolf alpha respect in his home, but as heir to his own tribe, he would not subjugate himself too much.

Liam nodded and held his hand out to Keith. They shook hands; then Liam offered Keith a seat before sitting on the couch himself.

"Thank you."

The woman that had let Keith in joined Liam where he sat. He curled one arm around her protectively, then asked, "You said you had word of Caleb when you called before."

"Yes, sir. He was shot while hunting in one of the national park areas on the southern side." The woman gasped, as did many of the others there, but they all held their tongues. "I was called in to help calm and treat an injured wolf. What I found was Caleb severely injured but holding his own. He's currently resting at the animal clinic I help run for the parks here."

"He's not an animal," the woman snapped.

"No, ma'am."

"Jazabel, calm down and let the boy explain." Liam's words were kind, but there was a steel behind them that would have made a lesser cat cringe. "Continue."

"Please understand, I hold no grievance with wolf shifters. Caleb is at the animal hospital because he was in wolf form when I brought him in and treated his injuries. I can't have him sitting around in his human skin there, as I'm the only shifter on staff.

"However, what I have done is remove two bullets, stitch lacerations, and provide plenty of protein and fluids. I've also alerted the park rangers and the game wardens to the idea that we have poachers hunting with guns and dogs. If it hadn't been for the guns, I have no doubt Caleb would have been fine. As it is, Caleb is safe and knows not to shift unless I'm there and we are secluded from the prying eyes of humans."

"How long will he have to stay there?" Jazabel asked, her tone holding curiosity and a little sadness instead of the hostility it had held before.

"A few more days. He's healing well, but I have to be able to justify releasing a wolf back into the wild. I know he's not a wild wolf, but the others don't. Plus, as well as Caleb is doing, I want him as healed as possible before he returns. He's already been hurt by hunters. I don't want him hurt by returning home before he can do so proud and tall." The poor man's ego was battered enough already.

"Can we visit him? Or...." Jazabel looked up at Liam as she bit her bottom lip.

"Maybe you can arrange for a call?" Liam scrunched his brows as he paused a moment. "If you're taking him someplace safe for him to shift between his skins, perhaps he could call home during one of those times?"

"That I can do. He hasn't stayed awake long enough while I've been able to sneak him away so far, but I work nights starting late tonight, so I can arrange a call. I know you're worried, but Caleb is strong and a fighter."

"That he is, son. That he is."

Keith didn't stay long after that, wanting to get home to Jason before his next shift at the clinic. Alpha Liam hadn't been anything like Keith had heard: strong, kind, and caring instead of abusive, cruel, and ignorant, as Keith's father claimed. Truthfully, Keith had heard only good things from the few wolves he'd had dealings with over the years, but it was still good to know Caleb would be going home to a place where he would be cared for, not shunned or hurt for falling prey to human hunters.

TWO WEEKS later, Jason still wasn't 100 percent on board with the whole mating thing, but he was as far as dating and sleeping with Keith. They'd slept together—just slept, or at least sleep was in there somewhere—more nights than not, much to Keith's pleasure, if all the smiles and purring was anything to go by. And if he were honest with himself, he was just as happy, though he didn't purr nearly as well as Keith did.

The only things that overly bothered him, other than the idea he was sleeping with a cat, was that Keith seemed to be spending an awful lot of time with a wolf shifter he'd met through work. Keith meeting a normal wolf wouldn't seem weird to Jason—Keith was a vet for the national parks in and around Seattle, specializing in wildlife rehabilitation. But the fact his boyfriend was hanging out with a shifter—wolf, cat, or otherwise—had Jason quietly seething.

Fears and worries brought on by long misadventures in dating had him about to strangle a man he'd only met once. Caleb Hunter seemed to be a nice, if quiet, guy. Cute in a little-boy-lost kind of way, but the fact he could share hunting and fur time with Keith bothered Jason more than he wanted to admit.

When the knock on the back door came, startling him out of his worries, he nearly tripped over his coffee table trying to go to the door. No one other than Keith came to his back door, so he was doubly shocked when he saw Keith standing there along with the very man-slash-wolf Jason had just been obsessing over.

Jason pulled open the door, bemused at why Caleb was there, though glad to see Keith. "Hello?"

"Hey, Jay. Can Caleb and I come in?"

Caleb's smile was only a shy twitch of his lips as he said hello as well.

Jason stepped aside, allowing both men to enter his kitchen. "You need drinks or food?" He'd learned quickly that Keith was always hungry, even more so after he shifted—not that it made that much sense to Jason, as Keith said he always hunted and ate as a lynx too.

"No thanks. I brought Caleb over because he needs to get to know you some. His father has decided that since I rescued and helped Caleb when those poachers were hunting wolves, Caleb should act as a sort of liaison between his pack and me. The hope is that we can open the way for peace and cooperation between the wolves and lynx here."

"Something the current alpha cat won't ever try to do," Caleb added softly.

"And I fit into this how, exactly?" Jason looked to Keith. "I'm not a shifter of any kind, so I'm not sure how I can help."

"You're the mate of the lynx tribe's heir," Caleb said matter-of-factly. "So courting your input and favor is the logical next step."

"Huh. But…." Jason glanced at Caleb, then returned his gaze to Keith. "But I'm not. I m-mean, we haven't completed or sealed or whatever it's called, this m-mating thing."

"That's a technicality that Alpha Liam Hunter is choosing to ignore." Keith pulled Jason into the warmth of his arms, but didn't kiss him, making Jason wonder again about Keith's interest in the wolf. "I'm not the leader of my tribe yet, either, but he hopes that by working with me now, we can become allies in the future. It makes perfect sense from that standpoint. And since Caleb here isn't overtly alpha-wolf in his attitudes and beliefs, Liam believes he would be the best choice to work with me. With us."

"I…."

"Should I call you Mr. Grant or Jason or something else?" Caleb said in his soft yet masculine voice. "I don't wish to offend by using the wrong name."

"J-just Jason, please."

"Jason." Caleb smiled wider, more genuine this time. "You don't need to worry about me. I'm not interested in guys, no matter what race they are."

Jason frowned, trying to figure out why he needed to be told the wolf was straight. Most people were, after all. "Um, okay. Not sure why th-that's important, but what are y-you expecting from me? I'm not a shifter, and I don't know the politics or anything."

"I think Caleb was trying to reassure you that he isn't after me—as a mate, I mean." Keith bent down and dropped a small kiss on Jason's lips. "Though pointing out someone's feelings that you've gained from their scent is tacky."

Caleb ducked his head. "Sorry, I just wanted him to know I'm no threat to your mating. Even if I was gay, I would never go after someone that's already mated, cat, wolf, or otherwise."

Jason still wasn't sure he liked this whole thing of others reading him by scent, or that everyone liked to point out how he felt—like he didn't already know.

"Baby, I told you, when we mate, it's for life. Another shifter trying to come between mates is obscene and a violation of so many things it's not even something I want to contemplate. However, Caleb's right. I have no interest in him or anyone else, not like I do you. So relax, please. This is really important to me and to Caleb's pack. I'd love to see a stop to the hostilities between our people. My helping Caleb, knowing he was a shifter and not just a regular wolf, has opened communication lines I never thought to breach."

Jason had never thought that his dating Keith would put him in such a situation. He did like hearing Keith claim him in front of Caleb, like he had when Jason had finally met Keith's sister and nephew. But he hadn't given much thought to the fact Keith was the heir of his tribe. His head snapped up as he tried to get the words out, though his tongue didn't seem to overly care what he wanted. "I-I-I…."

"Shh, baby." Keith smoothed his hands up and down Jason's back, lending his strength and support. "I know this isn't part of what you expected to do in your life, especially not so soon. You'll do great, though, and Caleb is quiet and patient, so you don't have to worry about too much yet. Just get to know him right now. That's the biggest part. You'll learn the rest as you need."

"I've never been a liaison before, if that makes you feel any better," Caleb added. The fact he wasn't the only one being shoved into the deep end felt oddly comforting.

"Th-thank you. But," Jason said as he considered how to word this right, "are you sure I'm the right person to work with? I mean, I stutter and don't know anything about shifter society and needs, and my best friend is a vampire." He really hoped that last piece would help him get out of this. And while he didn't want to let Keith down, half the reason he did freelance IT work and design was because he stuttered when nervous. Over the phone, he was fine. When on a job, he did great. But in an office environment? Yeah, no. Then his speech issues were a menace.

"I knew all that up front, and yes, my father, Alpha Hunter, thinks this is important. He wants a bridge between the wolves and the lynx in the area, and so Keith, as the heir of the Glacier Rim Tribe, is the best choice to court. And um, the alpha's mate is often the diplomat, the calming force. The alpha is the more active and aggressive part of the pairing. It's not like how things are in the human world. Being able to speak well in front of the masses isn't a need. Having a good heart and a level head is."

Jason looked up at Keith, hoping he would have some great insight, but no such luck.

"You will do fine, Jay. And once we've completed our bond, no one will ever see you as anything but my mate. The fact you're human or that you stutter when nervous won't matter."

"And the fact you are friends with Prince Aleksandr Tolstoi is actually a bonus," Caleb added. "Had I not scented the vampire as having been here, often, I wouldn't have believed that such a powerful vampire would befriend a human. I didn't know that vampires even thought of humans as anything other than food."

Jason turned and scowled at Caleb. "Sasha is a kind man, fangs or no fangs, and they aren't like that! In fact, there's no killing of humans even allowed here."

Caleb made an odd sort of whining sound in the back of his throat as he hunched in on himself and took a couple of steps back. "I'm sorry. I didn't mean to offend."

He hated hearing others make hurtful assumptions about his best friend and the only family he had. The only family he counted, at least. It took him a moment to realize Keith was trying to calm Caleb down.

"It's okay, Caleb. He's just touchy about how others see his friend. It's no different than how you'd feel if someone spoke derogatory words about your father or your closest friends."

Caleb nodded, though he still stood with his shoulders drooped like a child on their way to the principal's office. "I am sorry. I've never actually met a vampire. Not here. I did once when visiting another pack out east, and they were not like your friend. They did kill and hurt humans. They also actively hunted shifters that came into the cities."

"I didn't mean to snap at you." Jason had tried to give Caleb a reassuring smile when his thoughts caught on the rest of what he'd said.

"Oh, so Sasha's attitudes are un-unusual?" he asked, looking from Caleb to Keith.

"Yes and no," Keith replied.

"That's oh so helpful," Jason grumbled, rolling his eyes at Keith even as Caleb snickered softly.

"Sorry, baby. Not all vampires hunt and prey on humans, but too many do. On top of that, some of the covens do actively seek fights with shifters. But then, so do some packs, tribes, and nests." Keith ran his hands through his hair as he sighed. "Unlike shifters, vampires don't exactly have a larger council, so they only answer to others of their kind if the covens come into contact or conflict, usually."

"Oh. Sasha didn't tell me all that much about other covens, just a little about his own. Sorry, Caleb, for snapping at you. I just…. Sasha is my friend. I know to you he's this prince thing, but to me he's just Sasha. Ya know?"

"It's so weird to hear Prince Tolstoi referred to so casually, but yes, I understand. Or I think I do. I can't imagine being on such close terms with a vampire, a nice one or not. We don't mix with blood drinkers."

"Yeah, he said something about bad blood between your kinds and his, well, between cats and vampires. He didn't say much about wolves, but then I didn't ask, either."

"I understand. Since you're the mate of a lynx, you would most likely only discuss cats with him." Caleb shivered as he spoke, but his tone wasn't hostile.

"Why do you keep doing that when you mention Sasha?"

"Do what?"

"Shiver. Is it th-the discussion of vampires or are you cold? I know you were hurt, so do you need to sit?"

"Apologies, Jason. I'm still trying to wrap my head around the idea of being friends with a vampire. I understand from Keith that your friend isn't like what I was raised to believe they are, so I'm trying." Caleb gave him a little lopsided smile. "Be patient with me?"

"Only if you do the same for me about all things wolf and shifter. Deal?" Jason held his hand out.

"Deal." Caleb clasped his hand at the wrist.

Jason quickly turned his hand to do the same, curious if the gesture was a shifter or a Caleb thing, but not wanting to ask. "Now that we have that all worked out, what was it you specifically needed from me today?"

"Just to officially introduce myself in my new role and to let you have time to warn your… to let your friend know I might be around some. So he's not worried that I'd try to hurt you or something," Caleb explained, his cheeks pinking as he shrugged.

"Oh yeah, that makes sense." It did. Sasha would be worried about a wolf being around, probably.

"And see," Keith added. "You're already comfortable enough with Caleb that your stutter is gone."

Huh, guess so. "Nice to know."

Once all that was settled, Jason found he actually liked being around the young man. Caleb was younger than he, barely eighteen, with a quick wit and a big laugh when he was comfortable with those around him.

KEITH SHOULDER-BUMPED Caleb as they walked back to his home. "I told you you'd like Jason once you had a chance to get to know him a little."

"You did, and you're right. He's very sweet, though a little overly protective of your bond. Doesn't he get that the bite aside, you're already mated?"

"Sadly, no. I've told him. Prince Sasha has told him. But it seems his past boyfriends weren't the kind of men he should have been dating." Keith frowned. He didn't like to think of Jason's past with others, both because Jason was *his* now and because he hated anything that would cause his mate pain. "None of them took their dating seriously."

Caleb nodded. "That would make it harder for him, especially since he's human. I don't know how they tolerate all the uncertainty and broken matings." Caleb paused after he stepped inside the house after Keith. "Isn't that hard on you too, though? The idea that Jason won't be as invested in the mate-bond as you?"

He shook his head as he turned to face Caleb. "No. Not if you could see Jason as I do. One, he's made loyal. Two, he's… I don't know how to explain it, but I think humans do feel the pull, though maybe not as strongly as we do. And three, I think if a human gets to the point of willingly allowing us to give them the mating bite, they're pretty much set on what they want and will be true to their mate."

"Yeah, that would be a big thing for a human to agree to. Can you do that with him without risking his life?"

The explosive breath that burst from Keith said more about his worry than any words could. "There has to be a way, but I don't know what it is yet. I can't go to my father about Jason," he explained and trembled for a moment as he thought of how well his father was going to react once he found out about Jason. "He considers humans to be dangerous and to be lesser creatures. Kind of like how many humans view wild animals."

"Sure, but that's so limited. Humans don't know better about wolves and such, but we know better about humans. I mean, I know he's your dad, but…." Caleb shifted from foot to foot.

"I'm not upset with you, and you're right. It is a very limited and messed-up attitude to have. I've yet to win that argument with my father, though. He doesn't approve of Taylor and me living here for that very reason." Well, that was part of it. He didn't want to tell Caleb how manipulative and controlling his father was. That would go from working behind the scenes in hope to change things in the future to outright disrespect of his alpha—a line he wouldn't cross if he could help it.

"Glad. I don't want to offend, just understand. And thank you for inviting me into your home. Many others wouldn't do that, especially with their young around. I appreciate the faith."

"Zeke likes you, as does Taylor. I'd trust their opinions before most anyone else's. Now how about if you let me check your injuries, just to make sure everything is all healed as it should be? I know you have your own pack healer, but you were my patient first."

Keith couldn't help his concern. When he'd first found Caleb holding off the humans Keith worked with, he'd known immediately that the wolf was a shifter. The humans wouldn't have hurt Caleb, but Caleb hadn't known that at the time. His first concern was if the small shifter would let him near. Some wolves hated other shifters on principle, while others simply lashed out in pain. Thankfully, Caleb was neither. He'd calmed and let Keith close, allowed him to move him and care for his injuries without fighting.

By that time he'd had a good idea of who the little wolf was. Even as a lynx he'd heard that one of the wolves was missing from the local pack. Of course, the situation had turned into formal recognition from Alpha Liam Hunter and this new partnership for Caleb and Jason.

Keith just hoped Jason could swallow his fears and embrace all of Keith and all that being the alpha heir's mate meant.

CHAPTER FOURTEEN

JASON SAT at his desk, hours deep in code, almost done with his latest project. Done in that he would still need to run all the checks and double checks for the new server and programs, but barring some cataclysmic failure in his coding, he would be ready to ship.

It took until he finally sat back, arching against his chair and hearing the loud, satisfying pops, for him to realize Sasha sat perched in the window. "Argh!" Jason screamed, jumping so hard he managed to wind up on the floor next to his chair. "Don't do that!"

"Sorry, hon, but you were so deep in your work and I didn't want to disturb you."

Sasha did look sorry, so Jason decided not to yell again, though his butt didn't agree with him. "Fine, but at least give me a hand up?"

"Sure." Sasha took Jason's hand and tugged him up to standing, showing a great deal more strength than he had before he'd been forced to reveal his fangs. Once Jason was up, Sasha looked him over and nodded. "Okay, now that your dignity is restored, I would like to remind you that you knew I was coming over today."

"Yeah, I know, I just didn't hear you. You know how I am when working."

"That's why I sat over here, nice and quiet. I didn't want to interrupt. But, um, want to tell me about the wolf that was over?"

"You can relax, Sasha. You remember, I told you about Caleb. He's the wolf shifter Keith helped a couple of weeks ago."

"Yes, I know that part, but what was he doing inside your home? I don't have any better relations with the wolves in the area than I do the cats, sadly. I tried once, but...." Sasha stared into the distance, his eyes unfocused and his voice sad. "It didn't work out well."

"I'm sorry."

"No need. So tell me, what was the fuzzy one here for? I'm assuming it's a good thing since you're not upset."

"Yeah, it's a good thing." Jason thought on that a moment and clarified. "Well, I think it is. Caleb's father, the wolf alpha, has decided to make his younger son work with Keith in the hopes of some kind of cooperation and stopping of hostilities. I'm in the middle because they recognize me as Keith's mate, even though he hasn't done the claiming-bite thing."

Sasha leaned in, his head cocked as he asked, "And they know you're human and my friend?"

"Caleb does. I'm not sure if his father knows or not. But is it a problem that he was here? You're not going to go all scary like you did the first time with Keith, right?"

"No, hon." Sasha sighed, waving one slender hand at the thought. "I was simply curious. You've never been one to surround yourself with nonhumans—other than me, of course."

"True, but until recently, I didn't have a reason to. I'm not sure I like this 'role of the mate' thing, especially since we aren't mated yet. But aren't we supposed to be going out tonight?" Jason really wanted to have a "fangs and fur free" evening, even if he spent it out with one of the fanged.

Sasha's light laugh made him smile. "That we are. You wanted to go see the last Hobbit movie. Again. And I want to try a new restaurant I heard about."

"You are such a food snob, which is funny considering most wouldn't believe you even capable of eating."

"Ha-ha. Yes, some misinformation is useful, such as the belief we can't eat food. However, I love to eat and drink, no blood needed. Though...."

"Ewww. Can we not? I'm trying to be good with all this, but seeing you drink blood is not on my life's list of must-dos. Really." Jason couldn't help the shiver that went up his spine. If anyone but Sasha had told him this, he was certain he wouldn't do even this well, but still, he had his limits. And he was certain blood was one of those.

"You're going to have to get past that, hon, if you plan to be the fully bonded mate of the next kitty alpha."

"Yeah, I know."

"Look, talk while you get ready. I've seen you in various stages of undress and won't think anything different now than I did before."

With Sasha shooing him to his bedroom, and following right behind, Jason gave in. "Fine. Look, I'm trying to be okay with all of this, I just...." He pulled out the deep blue dress shirt and black pants he'd already decided on. "Keith keeps saying it's permanent. The mating is, I mean, and that they never cheat. I know you said they can't, but what if he gets bored of me and regrets mating with me?"

"Do you really think he'd do something so permanent if he wasn't sure he wanted you?" Sasha gave him the same pitying look he had when

Jason had claimed he couldn't make it going freelance. "That Keith would go into this against his will?"

"Well, no." *Not against his will, but what if the taboo against gay couples causes trouble later and—?*

"You know, unlike what the media likes to claim, we can't really read the minds of the humans around us. I can't at least. So I need all that thinking to be out loud, hon. Please?"

"Fine, but take your hands off your hips. Oh, which shoes?" Jason had managed to get his pants and socks on, but not his shirt or to decide between shoes or low boots.

"The black chunky boots to your left." Sasha sighed, dramatically. "What was all that rambling in your head?"

"You both said it's like a taboo or something for a shifter to mate a human. What if his tribe does not accept him or they try to convince him it's not a real mating? What if—?"

"See, that's your problem, Jason." Sasha using his name in that hard tone got his attention fast. He hadn't heard Sasha talk like that since his grandy died. "You fixate on *what if* instead of *what is*. Shifters don't cheat. They also can't be talked out of a mating after it's sealed. That's not possible, and while I don't know Keith that well, he doesn't strike me as ignorant of his own nature. Nor does he seem the kind to let others dictate what his heart decides."

"But how can he know his heart so soon?"

"Answer this instead." Sasha fussed with Jason's shirt, unbuttoning and rebuttoning it. "What do you feel for Keith? Is it enough for you to believe it could be love, even if it's not already?"

He hadn't thought of it from his heart's side of things. "I care about him. Want him all the time," Jason added, knowing he was now bright red and not caring.

"Yes, but not worrying about if he feels, if he cares, if he fill-in-the-blanks. Only base this on what you feel. If there were no tribe or other concerns, would you let him complete the mate-bond today? Your feelings only."

Jason sat down hard on the edge of his bed as he thought it all through. What did he feel? He felt like and lust, but he felt a great deal more as well. Would he let Keith bite him and take a chance on his boyfriend, mate, whatever, growing to love him, not just lust him? When the answer came to him, he was glad he was already sitting. Looking up, he stared at Sasha but only really saw the truth of his feelings. "How the hell did that happen?"

Sasha giggled. "Just now figured it out, did ya?"

Nodding, Jason replied, "I did. I would let him, if I wasn't worried about Keith's feelings and his standing in the tribe. How in the hell did I fall for him and not know?"

"Fear. But as much as I should try to talk you out of such things, him being a cat and all, I think you're making a huge mistake by not completing the mating."

"Huh. But—" Jason started to speak, but Sasha put his fingers against Jason's lips, stilling his words.

"Would you rather go talk to Keith than go out with me now?"

He shook his head and mumbled around Sasha's fingers, "Wanna let me answer?" Sasha moved his hand and smiled, motioning for Jason to continue. "Thanks. Can't. Keith's at work until something awful like three a.m. or some such. But whether I'm ready or not, he's still worried he'll hurt me. The bite is one thing I'm really not looking forward to feeling."

"Pishposh. The fact you take in his blood during the mating makes it so you're in no danger. Not really." Sasha gripped Jason's chin, forcing their gazes to meet. "Do you honestly believe I would encourage this if I thought you'd be hurt? That it could endanger your life?"

Jason shook his head as best he could. "No, but he said he has to bite through skin and muscle. That it leaves a huge scar on a shifter, much less a human."

"It does. I've seen the scar. But do you remember me saying your grandy once dated a wolf? The beta's son—at the time—of the very pack you have now managed to befriend."

"Yeah, what of it?"

"Drew considered mating with the wolf boy, so I did all my research into how and what happened and everything between a shifter and a human back then. I somehow doubt that the span of a few decades has changed how mating with a shifter works."

"Oh. I, uh, you didn't say all that before." Jason thought about it, and yeah, that made sense, especially if Grandy and Sasha really had been friends. "Why didn't they?" He'd wanted to ask it, but had been a little afraid to know the answer.

"I had thought to let you explore your relationship with Keith without me having to meddle. Most creatures, be they shifter or vampire, don't like the idea of an outsider in the middle of their mating. As for your grandy's issue, it would have been a mating by choice, but the boy was too immature and had sex with someone else. He didn't take their courtship as seriously as he should, and Drew left him."

"But you said they can't cheat."

"No, I said once mated, *mated,* that they can't. Drew and the pup weren't yet mated. Had they been, that would have never happened. But I also said *chosen.* What you and Keith have is fated. Even now, Keith will have no desire for any but you. What happened to Drew can't happen to you. The only way would be for Keith to sever the mating bond before it's completed. Something no shifter would do. No vampire would, either."

"Vampires have mates as well?"

"Not like shifters. Though a few have fated hearts. It's similar to fated mates for shifters, but it's so rare, many no longer believe in such bonds. My parents were, but I don't know of another pair." Sasha took on that sad, lost look again. "You're really very lucky, even if Keith is a kitty."

COMING OUT of the theater later that night, Jason was startled when two huge men approached him. Well, maybe hurtled toward him would be a better description. Just as he stepped back, hoping they would keep right on going, somewhere else far, far away, Jason bumped into Sasha.

Sasha screeched, and the sound thrummed painfully up and down Jason's spine, making him want to run. He would have, if he could have gotten his feet to cooperate.

"Grab the human," the bigger one snapped as he changed directions and went after Sasha.

The smaller man, though still quite a bit bigger than Jason, managed to get a hold of him, but even as his hands—tipped in claws!—wrapped around Jason's arms, Sasha was suddenly in front of Jason, forcing both men to back up.

They'd gone to the latest showing, so there weren't many people around, most having left before he and Sasha made it outside.

Jason couldn't follow what happened in the next few moments, but somehow they managed to move the grab-and-run-slash-fight down the alley beside the theater. Sasha stayed in front of Jason, blocking both from getting a hand on him again.

"Move, Little Fangs. It's not you we were sent to fetch. You can find your food elsewhere," the bigger one rumbled.

"I would suggest you turn around and leave. Now," Sasha demanded, his hands curving into long, talon-like blades. Jason was certain Sasha had his fangs out and was wearing the same scowl he'd had the morning he first met Keith.

He didn't want the men's attention, but he didn't want his friend hurt, either. Unfortunately, he still couldn't move, not even his mouth.

"Not without the human filth hiding behind you," the smaller one growled. He stepped closer to Sasha. A stupid move in Jason's opinion.

Sasha's hand flashed out and gripped the smaller thug around the neck. The man suddenly dangled from Sasha's grip, even though Sasha shouldn't have been able to manage it, even if he had superior strength, because of the man's size. When Jason looked harder, he realized Sasha's feet weren't touching the ground.

"I will repeat myself only once, cat," Sasha spat. "Leave now or suffer the consequences. This human is under my protection."

"And just who are you?" the bigger one demanded even as the smaller one scrabbled for purchase with his feet and with his hands. He wound up clutching Sasha's wrist as he slowly turned a strange color and his eyes seemed to bulge.

Before Sasha answered, three more men appeared out of the shadows. "Prince Sasha!" one yelled as he sprinted toward Sasha and Jason.

The one suffocating in Sasha's hand made an odd gurgling sound and went limp. The other backed up for the first time. "P-prince? You're the fuckin' fanged prince?"

"Stop," Sasha said, his voice oddly calm. He dropped the shorter attacker, the man landing in a crumpled pile beneath Sasha. Sasha hovered closer to Jason, who finally managed to move, flattening himself against the wall. "Who sent you, cat?"

"The alpha," the bigger one replied in a strange, flat voice.

"Why?"

"Prince Sasha," the vampire—Jason could clearly see the man had fangs—interjected again.

Sasha ignored him and asked again, "Why?"

The huge man trembled even as he spoke. "Alpha says he's corrupting the heir."

"Take your companion with you and return to your alpha. But give him a message from Aleksandr Tolstoi, Prince of the Konstantin Coven. Jason Grant is under my personal protection, as are all he considers family. Unless he wants the entirety of the Konstantin Coven brought to his door, he will watch himself and stay where he belongs."

The unmistakable scent of urine spilled into the air, strong enough that even Jason noticed. The only cat moving gave a slight nod, his eyes so wide Jason couldn't figure out how they were still in his head. "Y-yes, Prince Tolstoi."

"Good. Now take your *friend* and go!"

Only moments later, both cats were gone, the smaller one thrown over the larger one's shoulder. Jason looked around and was finally able to take in the other faces around him. The three men—well, vampires—stood before Sasha, all suddenly appearing as if nothing strange had happened. All in stylish but dark clothes.

"Prince Sasha," the same vampire from earlier again entreated. "What was all this? Since when do the cats go around kidnapping humans?"

"Jalin, I'd love to know the answer to that myself. You know who Jason is. Jason," Sasha said, moving to stand beside Jason, his hand touching softly on his lower back. "This is Jalin, my assistant. The other two are Dimka," he added, motioning to the shorter, blond man, "and Summer," he finished gesturing to a tall, thin, but handsome man with dark red hair. "Dimka and Summer are my personal guards and have helped me keep you safe."

"Uh, hi," Jason said weakly. "Th-thanks? Wh-wh-what w-was—?"

"What was all that about?" Sasha said for him. "That, I believe, is Keith's father realizing that you have some kind of relationship with his son and heir."

"Yes, one he obviously doesn't approve of," Jalin added.

"Quite."

Chapter Fifteen

Keith read the text for the third time as he exited the vet center on the southeast side of the park he was working that night. The fact it was from Sasha, not Jason, didn't make him any happier than the message. All it said, still, was that he needed to get to Jason's as soon as he could and that everything would be explained. The follow-up text said not to worry about the extra vampires at Jason's, but again, there was no further explanation.

He hadn't even known Sasha had his number, though the small, mostly still-logical part of his brain that wasn't panicking pointed out that Sasha could have easily gotten the number from Jason. He just hoped Jason was okay.

No, Jason is okay. He refused to believe any differently until he could see for himself.

Throwing his backpack on, he rushed the last few feet to his bike, and in seconds, he was street bound, hoping he'd miss any cops on the road as he wasn't certain he'd be able to convince his cat that stopping before he got to his mate was a logical idea. Right about then, he was siding with his cat.

At one light he was forced to stop for—why did they always have to go slow when he needed them fast?—he remembered he had a Bluetooth. He pulled off his helmet long enough to put it in his ear, then redonned his helmet. The light turned green just as the call was answered.

"Keith," Sasha's melodious voice rang through the line.

"What's wrong with Jason? I'm almost home. You meant his house, right? Not one of the hospitals?" *Oh Gods! He isn't in the hospital, is he?*

"Hello to you too, Keith. No, Jason's at home. He's resting at the moment, actually. But you do need to get here as soon as you can *safely.* You getting injured won't help Jason."

He knew the vampire was right and forced himself to slow down and pay better attention. Wrecking on his bike would hurt and just slow him down. "Right. Now, what's going on? You understand, getting a message from a vampire, the prince no less, is bound to worry me."

"Yes, Jalin said something about that as well. But I was a little pressed for time, as Jason needed to be calmed down a little. He's fine, just freaked out. But there are issues you need to know about or you, your sister, mate, and nephew are all going to have problems."

Keith made the last turn before he entered his neighborhood, thrilled to see he was nearly there. "I'm almost home. I'll come straight to Jason's. Make sure your friends don't get too upset." He didn't overly care about their feelings but figured not fighting with vampires would be ideal right then.

"That would be best, and actually, Summer is outside guarding but knows to let you past. No worries."

No worries. The vampire *doesn't want me to worry. Yeah, right!* "As long as he, she, whatever doesn't slow me down, we're good."

"Summer is a male."

"Don't care. I'm here."

Keith cut the connection and parked his bike next to Jason's Toyota. He immediately noticed three new vampire scents. He just hoped they were all Sasha's people, as he was in no mood to deal with anyone getting in his way.

He jogged up the three steps and grasped the knob, happy when it turned easily. When he stepped inside he wasn't quite certain what to do. Jason was stretched out on the couch, sleeping. Sasha was in the large, comfy chair beside the couch. And another vampire was walking in from the kitchen area with what was—*sniff*—tea?

"Hello again, Keith." Sasha's voice was soft, the same way his or Taylor's was when they were trying not to wake Zeke.

Keith froze, looking between the three men, then decided to ignore the two vampires and headed straight for Jason. "What's wrong with him?"

"Nothing. He's just a little upset. It's the why that's our main worry. You need to sit and let me explain, as this is important for Jason, you, and your little family next door."

It was hard, but Keith sat, on the coffee table, and once he had one hand on Jason, he was able to calm down enough to really focus on Sasha. "What happened? Wait—" Keith sniffed again, startled by the scents that hit him. "Why do you smell of cats? And urine?"

The other vampire frowned as he set the tea tray down on the side table instead of the longer one he had been angling for.

"Thank you, Jalin. Jalin, this is Keith, Jason's mate. Keith, this is Jalin, my assistant, though he seems to prefer butler at the moment." Sasha accepted the cup Jalin handed him. "The point at the moment is that the scent of cat, the urine, and your sleeping mate all are interconnected. Jason and I went out tonight—he mentioned that you knew that. Things were fine until we left the late movie, when a pair of cats—I believe your father's elite guard—tried to snatch Jason off the street."

Keith fought the need to scream even as he wrestled his inner cat to stay down and listen—running off to kill their father was not advised. Yet. "Obviously you stopped them," he forced out. "Why would they try to take Jason? That makes no sense."

"Well, one of the two couldn't answer my questions as he's the one that kept trying to put claw to Jason. He will be lucky if he can ever speak or meow again."

"If he wakes up," Jalin added with a snort.

"Yes, I fear I may have done more damage than I intended, but he was pissing me off." Sasha spoke calmly between sips of one of the flowery teas Jason liked. "The issue here is what the bigger one said."

"And that would be?" *Come on, fang boy, out with it!*

"Patience. It boils down to the fact, or well the claim, that your father sent them to retrieve Jason, believing he was corrupting you somehow. Considering how they intended to take him and the fact they had claws out from the beginning, I do not believe they planned to bring him unharmed to their alpha."

Keith was up, pacing, before Sasha was more than halfway through the explanation. He hadn't even known his father knew about Jason yet. He'd been holding off telling him until he could convince Jason to complete their bond, that way no one could question the validity of their mating. "Dammit!" he hissed. "Trying to snatch a human off the streets is unconscionable. To touch *my* mate is…." He couldn't even form words for a moment, all his worry and anger boiling into one emotion.

"Keith?" Jason's groggy voice broke through his agitation and panic.

He shoved the table out of his way and was on his knees and beside Jason in seconds. "Jason? Baby?"

"Hey, calm d-down. I'm okay. See?" Jason added, sitting up and patting the cushion beside him.

Keith took a moment to run his hands over Jason, breathing him in, making sure he really was all right. "You're okay?"

"Yeah, Sasha and his f-friends stopped the two from g-getting to me. But, um, why would your f-father try to have me kidnapped?"

"That's a great question. I don't know, but I intend to find out."

"Sasha?" Jason said, looking away from Keith and to his friend. "If Keith's here, all your friends don't have to be."

"I know Keith'll protect you, hon. I just didn't want any surprises while we waited for him to arrive. I'll let Summer and Dimka know they can relax and go back to whatever they were doing before."

"Thanks," Jason and Keith said together. Jason giggled when he realized they had.

Sasha stepped out of the room, and a short time later, he was back, but without the extras.

"Better?" he asked.

"Sorry. I didn't mean it to come off as antivamp or something. I just don't know them and your message freaked me out more than a little."

"Had I my own mate, I wouldn't hesitate to change the setting to better fit my comfort if someone had tried to harm mine. No worries. For now, the issue is that your father knows of Jason and obviously does not approve. I'm not sure what he thinks Jason is doing to corrupt you. If it's the fact he's human, he's gay, or if your father realizes Jason is your mate. But whatever it is, he's in danger. I'm also worried for your sister and her kitten."

"I didn't.... Don't.... I'm not sure at the moment. I can call some friends that live on tribe lands, but I think they would have called me already if they'd heard anything."

"Unless your father convinced them you really are being corrupted somehow and they worry you don't see the danger. His reasons don't have to be real, just sound logical enough to wrap fear and uncertainty in."

Yeah, that's what worried Keith. What would make his friends not call him? Either they didn't know or his father had gotten to them. He hoped it was the former. "One way to find out. Call."

"I don't want you hurt because of me," Jason interjected. "Why would they think I was corrupting you? Is it that I'm human or is it that I'm gay? I mean, I knew he wouldn't approve no matter what, but to have me kidnapped when you and Sasha both say that's forbidden...."

"If he realizes I've been dating you, maybe. I just don't know. He's gotten more controlling and narrow-minded, not that I know what to do about it. I'm not yet of age to challenge him for control of the tribe."

"Of age? But you're older than me." Jason looked so confused.

"Until I'm thirty, I'm not old enough, by our laws, to inherit the tribe or challenge the alpha for leadership," Keith explained. "I'm the eldest and male, so he's stuck with me as his heir. If he tries to denounce me, with no backup, he'd be opening himself up to any other alpha or alpha wannabe to challenge him. He can't be that stupid."

"Perhaps he thinks of your nephew as your backup heir?" Jason glanced from Keith to the window that looked out onto the home Keith shared with Taylor and Zeke.

"Shit. I didn't call Taylor." Keith grabbed his cell but was startled when Sasha stayed his hand.

"I checked on her and the young one, Zeke. Dimka was with her until I released him and Summer. She knows about the attempted attack. She would be over here, but she didn't want to scare Zeke."

"Oh. That makes sense. Can't believe I didn't think to check on her."

"Until I told you about the cats your father sent, you had no reason to worry for her. But what are we going to do about this? I sent a message back to your father that he shouldn't try this again and that Jason and those he considers family are under my protection. For a sane shifter, that would be enough, but I'm not certain what's going on in your tribe or with your father."

"Yeah, neither am I." Keith debated what to do, not liking his options. "Jason, you sure you're okay?"

"Not a scratch on me, though my shirt can't say the same." Keith noticed Jason was in a long-sleeved T-shirt, not the kind he would normally go out to dinner with a friend in. Jason pushed up the sleeves, and yes, his skin was unscratched.

"How about you sit in my lap instead of beside me and I'll make a few calls and see what I can find out? I can't have people coming after you like this. I never thought they would," he added, more to himself. He'd known his father would have a fit, but kidnapping Jason? That he hadn't expected.

When Jason was settled, Keith was able to take a full breath, finally. If he never got a text like that from anyone, vampire or not, again, it would still be too early. After debating a moment, he called one of his friends, Vance, whom he suspected was gay or at least bi. "Van?"

"Hey, man. How are things in your new house?"

"House is good, but have you heard anything weird from the alpha about me? Or those I'm around?" He hoped he wasn't tipping his hand, but of any of his friends that lived on tribe land, Vance was the last one he'd worry about his father getting to.

"He's been, well, you know, humans are bad, different is bad, even more than usual, but no, nothing about you. Why?"

"Couple of cats attacked a human. I'm just worried about what's going on."

"A human? What the hell? No, no way would I know about that and not tell you. You really think your dad knew about it?"

"Don't know, but can you keep your ears up for me? I'm not there like I was, so I can't do my own snooping real well."

"Yeah, not a problem. Wish you were old enough to take over," Vance mumbled. Keith only barely caught the words.

"Thanks. Be careful, 'kay? I don't want you in the middle of something if there really is a problem."

"No worries."

They hung up, and Keith was no closer to an answer now. Would his father have done this? Or was the attack meant to drive a wedge between alpha and heir?

"I heard most of that," Jason said, his head on Keith's shoulder. "How likely is this Vance friend of yours to know and tell you the truth?"

"If I had to call a friend to come protect you, it would be Vance, Chance, or Kelley. Vance would be my first call. He's actually who I plan to have as my second when the time comes."

"Second? Like in *Star Trek*?" Jason asked, chuckling.

"Sorta. We don't use the same designations as the wolves do. Second is like a wolf's beta. But yeah, same idea. What bothers me the most is that we are still an incomplete mating. If those cats had hurt you, I wouldn't be able to help you heal like I could if we were." That was a huge part of Keith's anxiety, the part he still couldn't get a grip on completely. What if Jason hadn't been out with the lethal little vamp?

"Now see, that's why I don't understand why you two aren't already mated. You know you can heal him, you even defended that point when we were fighting, yet you haven't claimed your mate, leaving him vulnerable." Sasha's words were true enough, a point Keith was going to ignore if possible, but his voice was dripping with sarcasm.

"One, Vamp Boy, he has to agree. Two, I'm still worried about the pain it will cause, even if I can heal him. Three, he's not real agreeable to the part where he'd have to ingest my blood. Oh yeah, and four, since you love being nosy, he hasn't said *yes* yet!" By the last word, Keith was panting. Why couldn't anyone get that he wasn't going to claim his mate against his will? Jason had to agree or it wouldn't take and would likely destroy any hope for them being mates ever.

"What if my a-answer was y-yes?" Jason asked, his voice barely above a whisper.

Keith stopped moving, barely thinking. He blinked rapidly as he tried to figure out if he'd heard Jason right. "Baby?"

"Are you su—?"

Keith placed one finger lightly over Jason's lips. "I've never been more sure of anything in my life. The real question," he continued, pulling his finger away, "is are you certain? This is forever, baby. Shifters don't do divorce."

Jason nodded. "I am."

"You have no idea how happy that makes me."

Before Jason could think of anything more to say, Keith dipped his head and pressed his lips to Jason's. This kiss was different from any they'd shared before. Keith's lips were coaxing, gentle, but with a demanding undercurrent. Jason clung to Keith, hungry for every touch. He parted his lips, thrilling in Keith's taste as his tongue swept in, claiming everything it touched.

As the kiss continued and deepened, Keith lowered him to the bed, somehow managing to remove his sleep pants in the process. When Keith finally pulled back, his normally vivid blue eyes were instead bright hazel with technicolor blue outlining the slit pupils. As Keith's lynx heritage came through so clearly, Jason was certain he'd never seen anything as beautiful or hot in his life.

"I want to take my time, Jay, but…." Letting out a small roar, Keith grabbed Jason, then flipped him over and lifted his hips into the air.

Jason scrambled to get his knees under himself, already panting from a mixture of fear and desire. "Wha'?"

"I need." Keith's voice was more guttural, primal, as he demanded instead of enticing.

Keith's hands smoothed up and down Jason's back, and when he turned his head to look over his shoulder, Jason jolted at what he saw. Lust. Need. Keith's hands and fingers were thicker and tipped with long, sharp claws. His face seemed wider somehow, and his eyes faintly glowed in the low light of the room.

Teeth! Jason closed his eyes, not ready to face the reality of what he saw in Keith's mouth. Keith's jaw was longer, and filled with huge cat teeth where his normally flat, human teeth had been. Jason sighed as Keith draped himself over Jason's superheated body and rubbed his hard cock against his ass.

"T-t-touch me, p-please," Jason begged, his own need ramping up as never before. The tease of Keith's cock against his skin, but not in him, was almost painful.

Keith slid down Jason's trembling form until he knelt behind him again. When Keith's hands massaged Jason's cheeks, pulling them apart again and again, Jason thrust back, needing so much more. Keith's tongue touched his taint, then slowly flicked up, over his needy hole, to the top of his ass, then back again. Over and over until he finally zeroed in on the point Jason wanted, needed Keith to fill.

The rough muscle teased and swirled around Jason's opening, making him tremble so much he lowered his chest to the bed. Moments or maybe hours later, he couldn't tell anymore, Keith pushed his long tongue through Jason's fluttering muscles over and over again.

When Keith reached under Jason and gripped his leaking and neglected cock, Jason almost came. He bit the inside of his cheek, trying to stifle the whimpers and *ohmygod*s that kept trying to come out.

Keith pulled back and growled, "No, I want your sounds as much as your body and heart."

He followed the demand up with a sharp nip to Jason's hip. Letting himself go, he cried and chanted "Oh my God!" and "More!" and "Fuck me, dammit!" until Keith gave him what he wanted.

Keith moved off Jason for a moment but was back almost before Jason realized he'd gone. Cool liquid hit his throbbing hole, and the knowledge of what Keith was finally going to do made Jason cry out again.

"I can't open you up like normal," Keith growled, his sharp claws scratching at Jason's skin. "Push out for me, baby. I don't want to hurt you."

Jason did as asked, thrilling at the pressure and stretch as Keith's cock slowly forced its way inside. It burned yet felt so fucking good! Jason trembled with the effort to stay calm and not come yet. He wasn't going to lose it so soon, dammit.

Eventually, Keith slid in all the way, and Jason was certain Keith was bigger than he normally was. He felt so full, so filled, as if every point inside was being pressed on and stroked at the same time. Keith pulled back slowly, and the drag on Jason's opening was delicious. Then Keith snapped his hips forward, slamming in all the way, forcing cries from both of them.

He set a hard, demanding pace, in-out, pull-push, empty-full. Keith's sharp claws dug into Jason's hips, and the pain was welcome instead of detracting from the moment, as it had their first time together. Now that he understood, he found the pain made the pleasure sharper, more overwhelming.

"More, more, more...." He needed the pain, the pleasure, everything that was Keith. He needed more, but he couldn't quite find it. Then Keith's claws slid up to Jason's shoulders and he again dug into the flesh there. The angle changed, forcing another keening cry from Jason. He was positive he was either going to come or die any moment now, but he knew if he didn't get something, he would come apart. Unfortunately, he didn't know what the something was. The only thing keeping him together by that point was Keith and the pleasure-pain in every nerve from head to toe.

Keith pulled Jason up so they were both kneeling. He was so far inside Jason that Jason thought he ought to split in two. A moment later, Keith's wrist appeared in front of Jason, a long, thin cut seeping blood along it. "Drink so I can claim you! Now," Keith demanded, his voice more cat that human.

Jason didn't think, he just did as Keith wanted. He latched onto the cut, sucking and licking the skin, taking in the small trickle of blood there. The moment the blood touched his tongue, his body bucked back against Keith, and he bit down harder on Keith's wrist, making more blood flow into his mouth.

The roar above him should have scared him, he knew that, but instead it made him even more desperate for Keith. Then the pain hit. Keith's cat teeth sank into Jason where his shoulder met his neck. Those long fangs slid through skin, muscle, and bone, he was sure. The pain was incredible, but even as his mind shut down, his body convulsed as his orgasm hit and the excruciating pain merged with unbelievable pleasure. His world shifted back and forth between the two as he felt muscles tear and bones break.

Just as he blacked out, he heard Keith's roar and knew Keith had found his release. Then the world went dark.

KEITH THRUST into Jason's welcoming body, unable to get deep enough no matter what he did. He moved his clawed hands to Jason's shoulders, trying to find the angle he needed. He needed to fucking be inside Jason's skin, not just his tight channel.

Jason keened, his body trembling as his mate met him thrust for thrust. Never in his life had he needed anyone like he did Jason, and the sweet cries his mate kept making had him swelling even more, his body shifting even more as he slammed into Jason's clenching body.

His cat demanded he complete their mating. Demanded the bite, every instinct in him screamed bite! But his human side held on enough to remind his cat that Jason had to drink first or the bite could kill him.

Yanking Jason up so they both were on their knees, Keith kept moving inside his mate, the drive to fuck and claim all there was. He managed to make a small cut on his wrist, then dug his free hand back into Jason's shoulder, holding him even as he demanded Jason drink so he could bite.

The first touch of Jason's tongue to the cut sent shock waves through his body and soul, the pleasure so sharp he nearly cried at the joy of it. But when Jason groaned and bit down, his human teeth managing to break skin, Keith lost what little hold his human side still had. He sank his teeth into Jason's shoulder and neck, piercing skin, muscle, and bone as he claimed his mate, body and soul.

As his fangs sank that last inch, his orgasm roared through him, along with joy, bliss, and *ohmyfuckinggod*s. His ecstasy and euphoria blending with Jason's as their spirits met and merged for a moment, forever locking them together as one soul, only with two bodies and minds.

When Jason went limp in Keith's arms, he panicked, but the loud panting and strong heartbeat soothed his worry. It took a moment for him to realize Jason had simply passed out. Pulling out of his mate was physically painful, but he needed to make sure Jason had taken in enough of his blood to heal. He'd bitten harder and farther into Jason's shoulder and neck than he'd thought he would and had felt muscle tear and bone snap. At the time, his cat had reveled in the knowledge that Jason was theirs. Now, however, Keith worried if he'd hurt his mate too much to heal.

Keith laid Jason down on his side, then checked the deep wound, but as he watched, he witnessed something he'd never seen anyone but a shifter do. Jason's body knitted itself back together, and the bleeding stopped and the entry points healed over. Even as he continued to watch, his cat demanded they help, and before he thought it through, he bent and gave long licks to the trickles of blood and to the torn skin.

Each lick caused Jason to moan, and as Keith watched, Jason's cock hardened as though he was licking it instead. Unable to do otherwise, he wrapped one hand around Jason's cock and started stroking it as he continued to bathe Jason's bite.

Jason's eyelids fluttered open. His beautiful hazel eyes were unfocused as he thrust into Keith's hand.

"I need more of you," Keith murmured, rolling Jason onto his back. Jason continued to thrust, but touching wasn't enough for Keith. He needed more.

Gripping the base, he bent and licked Jason's spend from his cock and abs. The taste overwhelmed him for a moment. He then licked from crown to balls, up one side and down the other, before making another trip up, nipping the thick vein on the underside as he went. He teased his mate's cock, stabbing his tongue into the tip, searching for every drop, then around the head, before finally diving down, taking him all the way in. Keith had always been thankful for having no gag reflex—no cat did, really—but being able to deep-throat Jason, sucking and licking, was one of the great joys of having his mate.

"Keith!" Jason yelled as his hands wound into and clutched Keith's hair, his hips snapping up as he fucked Keith's mouth.

Keith used his other hand, now that he could keep his claws in, to tease Jason's opening, dipping into him and then rubbing pressure on the rim again, over and over, loving how his mate came undone below him.

By the time he had three fingers in Jason, and was gently squeezing his balls and sucking his cock, Jason was mindless, unintelligible sounds falling from his lips continuously. He added a fourth finger, making sure to tag Jason's gland on every couple of thrusts, loving that his come and not the lube was making things so slippery. Jason suddenly gripped harder, nearly sitting up as he thrashed while coming hard. Again.

Keith panted with the need to be back inside his mate. The tight pulsing of Jason's ass around his fingers was almost enough to send him over the edge. Thankfully, he managed to hold on, because when Jason opened his eyes and motioned Keith to him, he quickly knelt and pushed back inside his mate, reveling in how tight Jason was as his muscles contracted.

He slowly, gently thrust, rolling his hips as he sank inside.

"Oh God," Jason moaned. "You feel so good."

"It's not too much, being back inside you after you've come? Twice?"

"No, please. You feel amazing." He sighed as Keith curled his body over Jason's, continuing his lazy pace, allowing his orgasm to slowly build as they shared soft kisses and touches. By the time his orgasm finally rolled through him, all he felt was bliss, and all he knew was that Jason was his.

He stayed inside Jason as long as he could, and both men sighed as Keith finally slipped out of his mate.

"Be still, baby. Let me clean you up a little, and then you can rest."

Jason merely nodded, his eyes barely open and a small smile on his lips.

Keith hurried to clean himself up, then turned on the hot water before dampening a washcloth. He grabbed a dry towel, then returned to Jason so he could clean and dry his skin. He lay the towel over the wet spot, then curled around Jason, spooning with Jason as he felt his mate finally give in to sleep.

Jason would sleep for a long while, he knew that. The mate that was bled always needed time to recuperate after. He didn't join Jason in sleep, choosing instead to lie next to his mate, holding him. He'd felt the moment their bond clicked; the sensation was unmistakable. He could feel Jason now; feel him inside him, as if he were merely an extension of Keith. Keith knew Jason wasn't, he was his own person, but the connection was so strong, so overwhelming that Keith sent up a thank-you to Baast for blessing him with such a wonderful mate.

Eventually sleep managed to claim Keith as well. The scent and feel of his mate was too much to resist, so he welcomed the rest, knowing Jason was safe in his arms, as he would be always.

CHAPTER SEVENTEEN

THE RINGING was the first thing Jason noticed, then the deep lethargy throughout his body. As he fought his way back to consciousness, he tried to remember why he was so tired. About the same time he came fully awake, memories of the night before slammed into him.

Keith!

Opening one eye, he was dismayed to find Keith wasn't in bed with him. Of course, he knew Keith might just be getting a drink or checking on his sister and nephew. Still, it didn't sit right with him that he was alone after everything that had happened the night before.

The sudden restart of the loud ringing startled him, but at least reminded him why he was awake. Jason scooped up his cell and checked the ID, then answered. "Hi, Sasha. Didn't you have enough of me last night?"

Light laughter rang through the line. "No, hon, I think that was Keith that had you last night."

"Brat! Now what has you calling me at—" Jason checked his alarm and was surprised to see the time. "Is that right? It's after ten?"

"Yes, it is. I thought you'd be up by now, but it seems your kitty is really a tiger… in bed."

"Boo…. That's bad, even for you."

"I'm always bad. So how are you doing this morning? I was about to come over and check on you since you weren't answering your phone."

"Sorry, only just woke up. I'm fine." He paused and truly considered how he felt. "Tired, but I don't hurt. Wait, that can't be right. I know he tore muscle, and I *know* I heard something in my shoulder snap. How do I not hurt?"

"Snap? Nothing's supposed to snap!" Sasha barked just before the line went dead.

Jason tried to call him back, but the phone kept ringing and then going to voice mail. He switched to text, but that didn't get him any kind of response either. Giving up—guessing that Sasha was probably on his way over, as no other ideas made any kind of Sasha-sense—he flipped the sheet off, intending to get up and find clothing. He paused when he moved his other arm and again didn't feel any pain.

A minute later, he stood in his master bath, jeans forgotten in one hand as he stared at the huge scar on his neck and shoulder. He'd known it would be bad, but what he saw was much bigger and nastier-looking than he'd imagined. It looked weeks, not hours old, but damn, he didn't remember Keith's mouth even being that big.

When he heard Sasha's voice call out, he tore his gaze away and hopped into his pants quickly. Sasha had seen him naked before, but he didn't know if his friend had brought his assistant or his scary bodyguards with him again. And them? Yeah, he had no interest in them seeing him nude.

"Jason!" Sasha's strident voice rang through the house, and his head.

"In here, you loudmouthed harpy. Damn! Dial it down a few, would ya?"

Sasha was alone this time, but he was loud enough for ten men. "What the hell is that on your shoulder? And neck? And oh my Gods! What did he try to do? Eat you?"

Sasha pulled Jason around to face him, even as he continued grumbling, though Jason no longer understood a word he said. Sasha lightly touched the scar, his pale blue eyes squinting hard as he did.

"You want to calm down and use English? You know I don't know Russian. Well, I'm assuming all that was in Russian. The point is, I am alive and moving just fine, so calm down and talk to me like a normal person, please."

Sasha closed his eyes a moment, then took a deep breath before releasing it slowly. "Jason, that's… that huge fucking scar is much bigger and nastier than any claiming bite I've ever seen, and trust me, I've been around long enough to have seen a goodly number. Are you sure you're okay? You should be in the hospital, or morgue, from the looks of it."

"Ha-ha, very funny. I know it's a little worse-looking than I expected, and I'm pretty certain I remember something snap, but I feel fine, as you can see. Don't know where Keith is yet, but it's okay." He took a couple of breaths, making them loud and showy, to prove his point. "See?"

"No, what I see is that your mate can't control himself and hurt you. Bones snapping isn't normal, nor is the mating mark supposed to be that big."

"Look, let me get something to eat and drink, then we can find Keith. I'm sure he can explain everything. I mean, he's supposed to be the heir to his tribe, right? Maybe their alphas make bigger marks than regular cats?" He wasn't sure that made sense, but if it would get Sasha to calm down, he was all for the excuse. Until he located his mate, it was all conjecture anyway.

Sasha humphed but agreed. By the time Jason made it out of his bedroom, deciding that dressing was important after all, Sasha's irritation seemed to have settled some, and he had a plate of chips and sandwiches waiting for Jason.

"You're feeding me now?" he teased, a little surprised by Sasha's attitude.

"Humor me, okay? First you don't answer your phone, well after you should have been up, and after the attack last night, I was worried the idiots had tried again. Then, of course, you start talking about snapped bones, so sue me if I'm worried. Now eat."

"Yes, Daddy." Jason took a huge bite of his sandwich, pleased when he realized it was turkey and bacon on potato bread. "Mmm…. Dis iz gud."

"Don't talk with your mouth full," Sasha said, smiling finally.

Sasha fiddled with his cell while Jason finished both sandwiches and all the chips. Jason surprised himself by eating so much. He considered making another, something he never did, but decided against it in the end. "Now that I feel a little less tired, you want to tell me why you were calling in the first place? I mean, you know I'm always up for chatting with you."

"Unless you're writing code."

"True. And I get that you panicked about the scar and all, but what'd you need to begin with?"

"Oh, um, I was just wanting to make sure things were okay with you and cat boy. When I left last night, you had agreed to finish the mating. Just wanted to make sure you were still all right with everything."

"Well," Jason said, thinking about what all had happened from before Sasha left until he fell asleep in Keith's arms. "I extracted his promise to marry me."

"Really?" Sasha squealed. "You asked and he said yes?"

"Well, I more said I wanted to do this the human way, not just the shifter way, but he said yes. That's the important part. What came after, I'm not telling you." Jason stuck his tongue out, loving that Keith was his. His…. "Oh my God, Keith said yes!" he suddenly yelled. He couldn't believe Keith wanted him, not just as someone to have sex with but forever. Jason reached up and touched the mark again, wishing he could mark Keith somehow. Not violently like Keith had marked him but some way the other shifters would recognize.

The deep chuckle that boomed through the room startled Jason, as it wasn't Sasha's. He turned and smiled wide.

"Keith!" Jason was up and out of his seat before his brain caught up to his actions.

Keith opened his arms and let Jason slam into him. "Hi, Jay. Miss me?"

"Mmm-hmm. Where'd you go?" he asked, not lifting his head from Keith's shoulder.

"To make a few calls and to check on Taylor and Zeke." Keith kept one arm around Jason, as he ran the other hand up and down Jason's back. "The fact you were attacked has Taylor a bit freaked out. For you, not for herself or Zeke. She's certain Father won't do anything to them."

The almost dainty snort behind him made Jason turn, finally, though Keith didn't let him go. "What was that for?" he asked Sasha.

"No offense to your sister, Keith, but I don't agree with her assessment. I'm worried about him trying to get Jason again, but I'd also be worried about her and your young one, if I were you. Your father's not known for being fair or level-headed. But then, considering what Jason looks like today, I'm not so sure you are, either."

"I'm very fair and level-head…. What do you mean about how Jason looks?" Keith stepped back, his gaze sweeping Jason from head to toe and back again. "He looks damn fine this morning."

Jason knew his face was bright red. If the heat hadn't given away his embarrassment, Sasha's giggle would have.

"I meant under his clothes."

Keith made a strange, low growling noise and snapped, "Mine."

"Oh good grief." Sasha's sigh was loud and pointed. "Really? I meant his shoulder, you Neanderthal. Not his personal bits."

"I knew that."

"No worries, Sasha's just a little concerned about me today. The scar is a *little* bigger than you said it would be is all."

"Yeah, I knew it was and I don't know why. I mean, I do, but I don't." Keith sighed as he ran his fingers through his hair, making it stand on end like it had been on the day they'd met. "It's hard to explain."

"Humor me, cat. Try, because that looks worse than even a wolf makes, and lynx are supposed to be smaller."

Keith motioned for Jason to let him see. Jason pulled his T-shirt off over his head, still amazed he could even move his one arm. "Oh, baby. I'd hoped it would be more healed by now." Keith traced the outline, his face a mixture of worry and fascination. "But I guess it's not going to go down more."

"It shouldn't be that huge," Sasha countered. "And no, that's not going to go down much more." His gaze shifted from Keith to the bite. "Did your mouth grow or something? Because it's too big."

"Before he bit me, I noticed all of him seemed bigger. His face was wider sort of... I don't know, more flattened, and his eyes were different too. I didn't focus on it too much, though." Jason looked away, unsure how either man would take his admission. "I didn't want to panic or anything, so I tried to focus on the fact it was Keith, not how the changes made him look."

"I know, baby. And yeah, I've never partially changed like that. Claws out, eyes shifted, or even teeth dropping isn't unusual, but if such a thing as a true movie-type were-creature was possible, I swear that's what was happening. I had claws, teeth, even a thin version of my lynx fur on my mostly human body. That's part of why I wanted to talk to Taylor. She was mated, so I'd hoped she'd know what the hell happened."

"Any l-luck?" Jason didn't like that Keith was asking others about something that should have been special between them, but then, he'd let Sasha look at his scar too, so he guessed he couldn't complain.

"No."

"A few more syllables would be nice." Sasha's tone was only slightly less cold than the glare he had fixed on Keith.

"No, she doesn't know. I've never heard of something like that happening, but I've also never spoken to any cats from outside our tribe, so I don't know if it's happened before."

"Wait, you're telling me you don't know why you partially shifted? And you didn't know that was possible? Have you never been to your council or the pack alphas' get-togethers?" Sasha's eyes were huge and sparking as he stared at Keith. "No, I refuse to believe that the heir has never heard of this before."

"Why? What the hell does a vampire know about being a shifter that I don't?" Keith demanded, his words more a snarl than a question. "And how?"

Watching the two most important men in his life fight with words and body language wasn't much better than watching them go at it physically. "Why d-don't you," Jason said, his voice deliberately soft, "sit with m-me," he continued, tugging Keith over and into the chair Jason had been sitting in a few minutes before. He then sat on Keith's lap, wrapping his arms around Keith as best he could in the odd position. "And Sasha, maybe you c-could stop snapping at K-Keith and tell me what you think Keith ought to know. P-please."

Sasha stomped back to his chair, his attitude and irritation palpable. "I know of only a few times or situations that would cause a shifter to partly shift, and it is extremely rare, but still…. Keith should know his own history."

"If I knew about this, I swear I would admit that. Even if it were something I didn't want to share with a vampire, I would still own up to knowing something."

"I know you would," Jason soothed. "Sasha?"

Instead of answering, or at least answering in a way they could all understand, Sasha let forth a string of harsh-sounding words as he gestured wildly.

"English, dear, please," Jason said when he finally went quiet.

Sasha straightened his clothes and smoothed down his hair before he looked up and met Jason's eyes. "I know because someone I was very close to had it happen when he claimed his mate." He paused again, seemingly to gather his thoughts, or maybe his courage if the loud swallowing was any indicator. "It only happens to a rare few, but they are considered to be the chosen of Baast. They're usually stronger, faster, and more willful than the average cat, even more than a normal alpha. Oh yes, and they never take feline shifters as mates."

Jason turned on Keith's lap so he could see both his lover and his best friend. "Are you faster and stronger?" He chose to leave out the willful part. That was obvious from the fact Keith was a vet, lived away from tribe land, and had even taken a human as a mate. "I've only seen you shift twice, and not seen another shift, not another lynx."

Keith didn't answer for so long, Jason wondered if he was refusing to or if he was too shocked to reply. "Keith? Honey?"

"Sorry, baby. Um, yeah, I've heard of Baast's Chosen. They had huge tribes, and other alphas often chose to live under the… under the special alphas. But the last one died—"

"Almost two hundred years ago, taken down by a rogue band of vampires that my father and his warriors destroyed."

"No," Keith countered. "He lost an alpha challenge to—"

Sasha jumped up, his face taking on a strange darkness and his fangs were out. "No! Orin didn't lose to a damn shifter! He was murdered by vampires. Ones my father destroyed for their crimes against shifter and against—" Sasha's mouth snapped shut, the audible click loud in the suddenly quiet room.

"Oh Gods," Keith moaned, shifting Jason off his lap and standing fast. He moved to Sasha's side too fast for Jason to track. "You know because you were the mate you mentioned?"

"No, my sister was."

"But you're an only child." That's what he'd told Jason when they first met, but then he hadn't mentioned his little fang-and-blood issues, either.

"I had a younger sister," Sasha started, his voice suddenly hollow and chilling at the same time. "Nadia. She was barely eighteen when she met her beloved one. She didn't care that he was a cat, not a vampire. It was an even worse taboo then, to be with one not of your race, but Orin only saw his mate, not that she was a vampire. He loved her, doted on her, even offered to take on any task Father and Mother wished to prove he should have the right to claim her as his mate.

"Mother and Father, having been the vampire equivalent of fated mates, saw the truth of their love and gave their blessing. Not everyone agreed, but none in the coven would speak against their prince and princess. Unfortunately, some outside the bonds of our coven learned of the mating and decided to destroy the *beast* and his *tainted*...."

Jason launched himself at Sasha before quickly wrapping his arms around his friend as he cried. "Shhh, dear. That's not now," he crooned.

"Jay."

He hushed at Keith as Sasha clung to him. Keith was obviously not happy with Jason holding Sasha, but he wasn't about to let his friend hurt alone. His partner, mate, whatever, would just have to deal.

After a few more minutes, Sasha seemed to calm and settled back into his seat. "Sorry. I don't usually lose it like that."

"It's fine. Isn't it fine, Keith?" Not waiting for Keith to answer, Jason continued, "See? It's fine."

"It's not," Keith grunted, still wearing a path in Jason's floor. "An extremely upset vampire and a human should not be mixed." He continued to grumble as Jason turned to gape at him. "Why would the tribe lore be so skewed if rogue vampires were to blame? Why wouldn't Father have used that to vilify vampires more?"

"Excuse me, very much!"

Keith stopped and looked up, seeming to only notice then that Sasha was calmer and Jason was no longer holding him. "Huh?"

"You want to try that whole rant again for the class?" Jason didn't like how Keith seemed to see Sasha and wasn't about to put up with it.

"What? Wait, did I say all that out loud?"

Both men nodded. Sasha patted Jason's hand. "He's just worried I'd lose control and hurt you, hon. Were it anyone but me, I might even agree with him, but I would never endanger you. But," he continued, "that's a good point, about why tribe lore claims it was an alpha challenge. I have no clue as I never concerned myself with the tribe again after we lost Nadia."

"You wouldn't hurt me."

"No, but he's still getting used to me, hon. Shifters and vampires have a long and bloody history between them. Give him a little leeway."

"Fine." Jason wasn't honestly sure he'd be so okay with it if he didn't know Sasha so well, but the idea that shifters lied to their own concerned him. "Maybe to keep all vampires from paying for what the one group did? Especially since your father destroyed the bad ones?"

Keith stopped pacing and stared at Jason. "Maybe. But I'm pretty sure that if Father knew it was a cover, he'd have made sure the record was at least half corrected. He hates vampires. If he wasn't sure we wouldn't win against Sasha's coven, he'd have tried to start a war, I'm certain. But I have no idea why we don't know about the rest."

"And that, right there, is why I make such a point of being the big, bad, scary prince most see me as."

"Sasha, after seeing you take on those two shifters yesterday"—Was it only yesterday?—"I don't think it's an act. Had you not been protecting me, I'd have been terrified of you."

"As well you should," he said, a strange smile spreading across his face. "Some respect power, some only respect those that they fear."

"And if you aren't big, it's even more important to carry the attitude," Keith added.

"But how do we find out what to do about the strange changes?" Jason asked.

"I would suggest your mate contact the lynx council. I would also recommend that the current alpha not be informed of this development until then, as he's already shown his willingness to attack others to get at Keith. So until you speak with the council, neither your mating nor the fact that Keith is one of Baast's Chosen should be revealed to the tribe. For both your safety and that of those next door."

Keith wrapped his arms around Jason again. "Sadly, I agree. I'm reluctant to even confront him about his attack on Jason until I know more.

I am calling in some help, though, so I'll know Taylor, Jason, and Zeke are safe until then. I'll even have them meet with you and your guards if you like," he added, nodding to Sasha.

"I don't need to be guarded." Jason was getting seriously sick of both their attitudes. He wasn't helpless.

"Yes, you do," Keith replied at the same time Sasha said, "You do, hon."

Jason stepped away from both men and threw up his hands. "Fine, now you both want to play Neanderthal boy! Now, if you'll excuse me, I'm going to go get properly ready as I have work to do today. You two can sit in here and plot the overthrow of the evil cats or whatever." With that pronouncement, he stalked from the room, not happy with either man but kind of turned-on by Keith's possessiveness.

CHAPTER EIGHTEEN

KEITH WAITED until his closest friends had all arrived. Taylor was at the house, but Zeke was next door with Jason, much to Jason's irritation and Zeke's fascination. When he'd first seen the scowl on his mate's face, he'd worried Jason didn't like kids, but Jason had informed him—loudly—that the actual issue was that he didn't appreciate being treated like someone that needed rescuing instead of an actual partner. Jason hadn't liked the arguments Keith had given—any of them—but Keith still believed his friends needed to be updated on what was going on before they were faced with his human mate. Keith also hadn't wanted Zeke to overhear, not wishing to speak ill of the child's grandfather in front of him.

As he stood in the center of the living room, Keith looked over his oldest friends and closest allies and hoped his faith in them was justified. He motioned them to sit on the couch, reserving the two chairs for Taylor and himself. Vance was tall and broad shouldered, with short blond hair and almost golden amber eyes. Chance was shorter but also a bit stockier, with thick brown hair cut in a modified mohawk and pale green eyes. And then there was Kelley. He was thinner than either of the other two, yet stronger than Chance. He had shoulder-length auburn hair, dark blue eyes, and a wicked smile all the time.

"Van, Chance, Kelley," he said, nodding to each in turn. "Taylor will be out with us in a moment, and then we can get down to why I called you."

"No need to wait on me, big brother," Taylor singsonged as she entered the living room, a wide smile on her beautiful face for his friends. "Hiya, boys."

They each nodded and gave their various forms of *hi* back.

"So, what's up, man?" Vance asked as he sat forward and rested his elbows on his knees.

Kelley sniffed and then gasped, his gaze snapping up to Keith's. "You mated? Who the hell with?"

"And why do you smell of human?" Chance asked, his nose wrinkling slightly. He looked around the room as if the human in question would suddenly appear.

"You know, it would be easier to answer if you let me talk. Sheesh!" Keith paused, waiting for any other words of great wisdom to come forth. When no one spoke, he continued. "It's all interconnected with what I called Van before to ask about. Though I am surprised it took you this long to notice," he added smugly. "The problem right now is that someone sent two of the tribe's enforcers to attack and retrieve my human mate."

All three men started talking at once, arguing among themselves about mates, scents, and speed of observation. After waiting a full minute, Taylor sighed and gave the ear-piercing whistle they all hated, then smirked at them when they whined about the sound. "You know, you might learn the answers to all those *terribly* important questions, and even a few of the stupid ones I heard you three throwing around, if you shut up and hear the man out."

"Fine," Vance snapped, his scowl the kind that made most shifters back up in fear, though Keith knew it was worry, not anger that fueled his friend's dark look. "But unless it includes an apology for not telling us you found your mate, I'm gonna beat you, alpha or not."

Kelley, Taylor, and Chance all snorted at Van but stayed quiet otherwise.

"Look, we only completed the mating last night, if you must know. And until that happened, I didn't want to risk it getting known because—"

"But—" Vance began. However, Keith cut him off, not wishing to be interrupted yet.

"*Because* my mate is both human and male. Oh yeah, and his best friend is Prince Tolstoi." He waited for more interruptions, but instead of the cacophony he expected, each man's mouth hung open as they stared at him.

"Okay, I'm wondering which of the facts you listed," Taylor said, fighting not to laugh and mostly managing, "is what just fried their brains."

"Guys?" Keith hadn't expected them to all go quiet like that. They were never quiet. "You still with me?"

Kelley managed to get words out first. "A human male? One who's a friend with the vampire prince? *Are you kidding?*"

"Uh, no. Jason is my mate, my very human mate, and his best friend—who knew vampires befriended humans?—is Sasha. Come on, don't tell me you can't handle this," Keith said, his voice pleading, though he didn't care. He didn't know how he'd handle losing his friends if that was the outcome. But as hard as it would be, he'd pick his mate over them.

"Well hell! When you set out to give the old man a heart attack, you go all out." Vance grinned but then sobered, his powerful body suddenly tense. "Is that why the attack on your mate? Wait, how did the alpha know already when even we didn't?"

"Yeah, you see part of the problem? There's more than just that going on, though. Thankfully, Father's not tried again. Yet," he added, and everyone nodded in understanding. "But, um, something happened during the claiming."

"Seriously, man, love you and all, but I don't *love you* love you, ya know? I really don't want to hear about your freaky sex life."

Not appreciating Chance's mouth right then, Keith lost his hold on both his temper and his cat. "Will you grow up and pay attention," he growled, his voice more cat than man. Instantly, all three men and his sister cowered, each tilting their heads, baring their necks.

"S-sorry," Chance managed to get out, choked though his voice was.

"I partly shifted," Keith said instead of responding. His emotions were too close to the surface just then, and he worried he'd only manage to upset or scare them all more if he tried.

"Partly? As in…. Wait," Vance boomed. "You mean like the überalphas of old?"

"Yes, though I'd love to know why you know about that part of the story when I didn't."

"Eh." Vance shrugged. "My mom's family isn't from our tribe, so I probably know a lot of things others don't. My grandparents loved telling stories when I've gone to visit them. But I also knew it wasn't safe to talk about those things under the current alpha. Sorry."

"I'd love to hear some of those stories, later. For now, we need to focus on the fact I am one, as opposed to who did or did not know about that part of the legends."

"That's…." Kelley stared up at Keith. "I'm not sure. Is that great news or more reason to worry?"

"Good questions," Keith replied. "I'm not sure, sadly. I would say great for the tribe, since I'm the heir, but not so much because the current alpha is obviously not going to take any of this well. Hell, I had to get informed by a vampire as to why I'd even changed like that, and yeah, it's a huge mess."

"A vampire?" Kelley asked. "No offense to your mate, who I'm expecting to meet soon," he added with a glare, "but why would he know, much less care? The vampire, I mean."

"Agreed," Vance added. "Vampires here aren't as bad as they are in many other places, mostly thanks to their scary prince, but what would it matter to a vampire if you knew?"

"Guys," Taylor sighed, "if he's the friend of Keith's mate, he would have a really good reason to want to share information with Keith. Besides, he's not vicious like Father claims. When Jason was attacked, his friend sent a guard to watch out for Zeke and me until Keith could be called."

"And before you ask, any of you," Keith said, seeing the hurt flash on all three faces, "I didn't know what was happening until I returned home, so I couldn't call you to watch them for me. And then there was that little issue of finally claiming my mate." He didn't care that his grin was totally out of control. The knowledge of his mark now declaring Jason as his made both his human and his cat happy.

Vance cocked his head as he stared at Keith. "Okay, I get all that. I even understand why you didn't tell us before about your mate, but what are we going to do now? None of us will allow your sister—no offense Taylor, I know you're a strong cat, but Alpha Skyler's guards are lethal and enjoy fighting—your nephew, or your mate to come to harm. There are others in the tribe that will agree with us, I promise you."

"None taken, Van." Taylor looked from Vance to Keith. "And he has a good question. What are we going to do? Because you know I'm with you, as is Zeke. And I know many of the younger lynx wish you were already the tribe leader."

"Some of the older ones too," Kelley added. His parents were more than likely on his list, as his parents and grandparents had often wanted to do more than was allowed: schooling, working, having human friends without having to hide. Well, allowed by their current alpha.

"I know, though I don't know how many will stand with me if it comes to a challenge. I won't allow my mate to be harmed simply because he's male and human." Keith stopped pacing and faced them again. "I'm going to make a call, and probably a trip to Toronto soon, as I think the vamp—" he cut himself off and took a deep breath. "I need to stop thinking like that. I believe Prince Sasha is right, I need the lynx council's resources and possibly their help."

His cell rang, pulling Keith's attention from his friends. He unclipped it and saw his father's number flash across the screen. With a wince, he held one finger up to keep the others from speaking yet. "Hello, Father."

"Hello? That's all you have to say to me?" Adam snapped.

Keith blinked, confused as to what his father expected as a greeting. "How about you tell me what has you so upset, and I'll see if I have a better greeting?"

"You move my daughter and grandson into a vampire-infested area, getting one of the guards I sent to keep an eye on her and the boy nearly killed, and you want to know what I want?" Adam bellowed. Even if they weren't all cats with exceptional hearing, they wouldn't have been able to miss what he said. "I want your disobedient ass home and to stop endangering others for your willful whims! That's what I want!"

Keith's gaze cut to Taylor, who shook her head. He knew she didn't believe Adam, but still felt relief at the verification. When he looked at his friends, each one's face was an odd mix of confused and indignant. Almost in unison, each folded his arms across his chest and glared at the tiny bit of plastic in Keith's hand.

"I will not and have not ever willingly endangered Taylor or Zeke. You, on the other hand…."

The screeching that followed was, for the most part, unintelligible. When Adam finally managed words, he didn't make himself any friends among those gathered. "I will send guards to collect Taylor and Zeke first thing in the morning. And you will be brought before the tribe council for endangering the kit and for consorting with vampires."

"You try to have Zeke and me carted off and you'll regret the day you were born, much less the ones we were," Taylor said, making her voice loud enough for their father to hear and hard enough that he could pick up the threat within. "I stand with my true alpha, not someone that would abuse his power for personal gain and to manipulate others."

Before Keith could manage to unstick his mouth, Taylor having firmly shocked him silent, she hopped up and took his cell before hanging up on their father. She then turned it off as she glared at it.

"Obnoxious old windbag. Does he really think ordering us collected like kits out after curfew will work?" she asked with a huff.

He wasn't sure what to think or how to word it even if he had the right words. Instead, Vance beat him to it. "You can't say shit like that, Taylor! You just declared Keith your alpha."

"Yes," Taylor said, her tone patronizing. "I realize what I said and I spoke true, and don't any of you try to tell me you don't agree with me, because we both know you'd be lying."

"But I'm not the alpha." His mind was still stuck on the fact that his father wanted him brought up on charges before the tribe's council. He

knew his father wasn't happy with his choices, that he'd be even more so
when he found out about Jason, but the only reason for an heir to be brought
before them was to have the heir declared unfit and either imprisoned or
banished. "He wants me stripped and…."

"Shhh, Keith. No one's going to banish or lock you up. We won't
allow it."

Taylor's words were meant to soothe, he knew that, but she'd declared
him their alpha. No, *her* alpha, which meant their father would think he was
setting up his own tribe, something that simply wasn't done. Tribes didn't
split. How was he to protect her and Zeke alone?

She kept going while his mind raced and swirled. "Right now it's a
kind of tiny tribe, I'll give you that. Just six cats and a human, but you have
managed to win yourself allies among both wolves and vampires. Besides,
he wouldn't be foolish enough to try to send his guards and violate the rights
of trial or succession."

"I don't have six cats," he finally managed to say.

"Um, by my count you do," Vance countered. "You, Taylor, Zeke,
me, Kelley, and Chance. Actually, if you count Kelley's parents, his two
sisters, and his grandparents, you have even more. I'm sure there will be
others too."

"What was she talking about wolves? I get the human and the vampires,
since your mate kind of brings the vampires with him. But what wolves?"
Chance asked, looking from Taylor to Keith and back.

"That was part of what I had to tell, but I hadn't gotten to it when this
all blew up. Um, Liam Hunter, the local wolf pack's alpha, decided that
since I helped save and treat his younger son, we should work together.
Caleb and me, I mean. I pointed out that I wasn't the alpha but got some
weird nonsense about inroads before I took over."

"Great! Wolves, humans, vampires, and lynx." Vance clapped his
hands, then rubbed them like some old cartoon villain. "Sounds like a killer
party or the start to your new tribe."

"You have to have a second," Taylor pointed out, ignoring Vance. "If
Father goes through with challenging you, you have to have chosen your
second."

"I know that, I just didn't imagine all this happening so fast or so
soon." Keith knew who his choice of a second would be. He thought his
friends would know as well, but he still worried how Chance and Kelley
would take it.

"Keith, take a breath and relax some." Kelley clapped him on the shoulder. "We all know Van's your second and we're your guard."

"Well, yeah, I mean, if he'll accept."

Vance closed one eye and cocked his head to the side. Unhappy with his view, Keith guessed, he first closed the other eye, opening the first, then shifted his head the other way. Finally, he gave up and opened both eyes wide. "If I'll accept? Man, like I'd let you pick someone else! Now," he continued, standing, then going to one knee, as did Chance and Kelley. "If you will accept my service, I would be honored to be your second."

"And we your guard," Chance and Kelley added together.

Keith wondered if they'd been practicing that for a while to have it so coordinated but decided not to ask. Instead, he clapped Vance on the shoulder, meeting his gaze. "I would be honored, Van, and I couldn't think of two I'd rather have at my back," he added, moving to do the same with Kelley and Chance. "But each of you realizes what you risk? What you are swearing to protect?"

Vance stood, the other two following right behind. "A human, your sister and her kit, and it seems, the bonds you've forged with both wolves and vampires. Not what I expected, but then you never are one for the status quo."

Keith started laughing, and soon all four of them were. Eventually, Taylor asked if she should go get Zeke and Jason, but he still didn't think Zeke needed to know what was happening. The kit was only five and didn't know what his grandfather was really like.

"What about if I go get Zeke while you four get ready to go over to Jason's? I'm sure your mate would like to know what's up, just as I'm sure your friends would like to meet him."

Kelley shook his head. "If our former alpha is really dead set on stopping Keith and on getting you and Zeke back on tribe land, that's not a good idea. Someone should be with each of you for now." He stopped speaking a moment, then he turned wide eyes on Keith. "Is there a chance someone could have gotten to them while we were all over here talking?"

"No. No! Calm down. Sasha, you remember, the vampire prince? Yeah, he didn't like the idea of Jason and Zeke being alone, either. He's over there now, and I'm willing to bet that at least one of his guards is in the area. I don't know how they do it, but I couldn't sense Sasha or his men until I was almost to them. It's actually pretty terrifying to consider."

"Luckily, he's on Jason's side, and since that's Keith's, we're fine." Taylor grinned and took off out the side door, heading straight for Jason's house.

Keith still needed to talk to Jason about their living arrangements; he didn't intend to continue going back to Taylor's when he ought to live with his mate. With that thought in mind, he followed his desire back to Jason, happy when his friends followed right behind.

CHAPTER NINETEEN

JASON SAT at his desk, trying to catch up on his work. He didn't mind part of the reason he'd gotten a little behind: spending time with Keith was always high on his list of things to do. However, the drama with hateful cat men, meeting Keith's second and guards—he still wasn't sure he liked the idea he needed guards—and the worry about Keith forming his own tribe had been more than he could manage while still working as he normally did.

Thankfully, he always worked with the idea that he should be done well before the actual deadline, so he wasn't truly behind, per se. But he didn't like cutting it too close, either, so he worked while Keith was with his cats or at his human job and helped as much as he could the rest of the time.

Right then, Jason was struggling to keep his mind on the coding instead of worrying about later that night, and more importantly, what would happen the next morning. Keith was going to Toronto to see the lynx council. Jason had argued that the council could send a representative to Seattle, but Keith insisted that wasn't how it was done. They would only do that for an alpha challenge.

He didn't like the idea of Keith being gone. They hadn't even known each other that long, but the thought of being without his partner didn't sit well with him at all. He felt better since Keith had moved in. Simple things like seeing Keith's wallet and keys on top of his dresser thrilled him more than he'd ever admit outside his own head. But part of it, he knew, was that he still hadn't found a way to mark Keith. His being with all those cats, without Jason there, had Jason's fear of loss working overtime.

"Hi, baby."

Jason jumped, nearly falling out of his chair. He turned after catching himself to see Keith leaning against the doorjamb to his office. "Uh, h-hello?"

"Sorry, I didn't mean to startle you, but I wanted to let you know I'm back." Keith moved into the room, not stopping until he was close enough to touch Jason's face. He cupped Jason's cheek, a soft smile on his lips. "Missed you."

"Missed you too. I thought you wouldn't be home until later. I'm sorry."

Keith frowned, his forehead wrinkling as he looked Jason over. "What for? There's nothing for you to be sorry for, but something has you all worked up. Want to share?"

With a sigh he decided to try to talk Keith into letting him go to Toronto with him. He just hoped Keith would understand his worries and wants. "C-can we go to the couch to t-talk?"

"Sure." Keith took his hand and squeezed it slightly before pulling him to stand.

They walked together to the living room and both sat close on the couch. Unfortunately Jason wasn't sure how to explain his issues. "I... I don't l-like you going a-alone."

"Um, I'll have Van and Kelley with me. Chance is staying here to watch over Taylor and Zeke. And I know you don't like the idea of being guarded or of not going to the council with me, but you don't have claws or preternatural senses to help you fight others off. What if someone tried to hurt you?"

The fact Keith was right didn't make Jason any less unhappy about the trip, the guarding, or the marking. "Wh-what if you find s-some nice c-cute kitty there?" he mumbled. He knew Keith claimed he would never stray, but they'd only known each other a short time, and, as Keith and his friends had pointed out, he wasn't a lynx and couldn't hope to keep up with one.

Keith stared at Jason for what seemed an eternity before he finally spoke. "Um, there are so many things wrong with that that I'm not entirely certain where to begin. First off, you're my mate. Cute or not, there's no one else for me. Ever. Hell, it's not even possible to have sex with someone else after you've been mated. I've told you that, as has your friend Sasha. Secondly, you're who I'll be going back to at the hotel between meetings with them. And—"

"What hotel? Why w-would I be at the hotel there if y-you're insisting on leaving me here?"

"Oh hell no." Keith jumped up, his increased volume seeming to match his increased height. "There's no way I'd leave you here while I go all the way to Toronto. Not gonna happen. What the hell conversation were you in on earlier? Taylor, Zeke, and Chance are staying. You, Van, Kelley, and me are all going to Toronto. I'll leave you at the hotel while I go to the council headquarters, at least until I know their official stance on my mating with a human. Where in all that did you get the idea you're not going too?"

Nothing Keith said made sense to Jason. But he'd heard his partner, mate, whatever, say he'd be left behind. That meant Jason would be here, right? "But, y-you…. Didn't you say I'd be s-staying and working while you w-went off and did the lynx-tribe thing?"

"Well, as you work from home," Keith said, settling back onto the couch before he turned and tugged Jason until he rested against Keith's strong body. "I figured you'd be able to take at least some of it with you. You didn't say anything when we were all discussing things, so I assumed that meant you were good with working from the hotel. I figured when I'm not at the council and you're not working, we could explore all the positions you can handle and all the noises I can make you make." The leer in Keith's voice left Jason unable to miss his intentions that time—or to wish they could get to the latter part of Keith's list.

Swallowing hard, Jason tried to work out how to explain the rest of what he needed to say, hopefully before all his thoughts were scrambled. Not that he minded how often or well Keith could reduce him to incoherent sounds and a lust-slash-pleasure-addled mind.

"Something else bothering you, baby? Your body is still way too tense." Keith rubbed his cheek along Jason's temple as he tightened his hold.

"Wish there was a way for m-me to m-mark you," he mumbled. In light of everything else, it seemed a stupid issue to have, but he didn't like the idea of others thinking Keith was still on the market. Keith was his!

"Baby, you can't give me the mate mark like I did you." Keith bared his one wrist to Jason. "I know you bit me hard enough when we mated to break skin, but I'll always heal. It's just how it works. That doesn't mean other shifters—lynx, wolf, or anything else out there—won't know I'm mated just by scent alone."

"They will?"

Keith nodded against the top of Jason's hair. "Mine changed when we mated, and that isn't something that will wear off, no matter how long ago that night was or how much I bathe. It's a fundamental part of shifter makeup. We change when we mate and it's for life. I know lynx don't mate like that in the wild, but then they don't usually form tribes, either. That's the human in us coming through."

Oh, huh. "I like the idea of you smelling like me, even if I d-don't like the idea of everyone scenting you."

The deep rumble behind him was one he both felt and heard. "Gods, but I do adore you. How 'bout if we go get you packed, as I'm guessing you didn't do that while I was out tending to things so we could go?"

Jason shook his head. He hadn't packed because, well, because he was a twit who needed to ask for clarification instead of being quietly upset, obviously.

"Then that's what we'll do now. And just maybe I'll show you a few more sounds you can make after."

Worries and thoughts of packing gone, all Jason wanted right then was for Keith to teach him everything. He'd never wanted anyone like he did Keith, and it both surprised and thrilled Jason that Keith seemed to feel the same for him.

"P-please?" he panted, his body hot and needy just that fast.

"You're right," Keith growled between nibbles to Jason's neck. "Pack later. Right now, I think I need to taste my mate again."

JASON ROLLED over, confused as to why the light was coming from the wrong area of his bedroom. He felt the heat of his lover's body and curled against it, seeking both Keith's warmth and the connection they shared. After cracking one eye open, he didn't realize where he was for a moment, but then the previous night—and the mad dash to the airport earlier that morning long before anything living should have been up—slammed into him.

Right, they were in the hotel in Toronto. Jason peeked at the bedside clock and bit back a groan. He'd been asleep for four hours, but it didn't feel like that much. Still, a warm, naked Keith wasn't something to ignore or pass up.

Spooning tighter against him, Jason ran one hand up Keith's side, across his hip, and down his thigh. Keith stretched out somewhat, a soft moan slipping from his sensual lips, but he didn't stir otherwise. Well, other than his quickly hardening cock.

Not wanting to wake him yet, Jason resisted the urge to dive in and pounce. Instead, he decided to explore a little, taste, and see how much he could do before Keith's mind kicked in and Jason found himself filled and panting. Though that was always a good thing to aim for, he wanted more right then.

Carefully shifting and touching, he managed to get Keith to lie on his back. Kneeling beside him, Jason took in how toned and handsome his man was. Keith had such pale skin, with a lightly fuzzy chest, the hair tapering down to a thin line as it met his belly button, then descending lower until it met the soft, short curls that surrounded the most delicious cock he'd ever seen, much less tasted. Oddly, Keith usually seemed to prefer giving the blowjob to receiving, but Jason wasn't about to give up tasting Keith.

After careful thought, Jason bent and began kissing up Keith's body, starting at his left hip. He kissed and tasted the soft skin along the prominent bone there, then up across Keith's abs, teasing along each ridge, up until he found a tight little nipple, just begging for his attention. Giving in, he flicked his tongue across the pebbled flesh before lightly nipping it and sucking it into his mouth.

A loud moan sounded through the room as Keith bucked up against Jason's body. "Holy hell, baby!"

Grinning to himself, Jason continued his torture on that nipple until Keith was writhing beneath him, moaning nonstop. Jason then kissed across to the other, giving it the same torture and attention.

Keith slipped his hands into Jason's hair and gripped tight as he thrust his chest up against Jason's mouth. Jason bit down hard without thinking, something he would never have done before Keith, but instead of being shoved away or yelled at, Keith roared, and moments later, Jason found himself facedown, ass up, with Keith towering over him.

"By the Gods, baby," Keith growled as he kneaded Jason's ass hard. "You have any idea what biting me like that does to me?"

If it made Keith react like that, Jason would have to remember to bite more often. "N-no," he managed to get out, though his attempt at innocence failed thanks to his hated stutter.

"The fact I know you're stuttering because you're so turned on right now is almost as hot as you biting me. Never thought I'd like being bitten, but damn!"

A moment later, Keith nipped Jason's cheeks, following the curve where ass met thigh, before returning to his massaging. "I want to fill that ass of yours again, feel how tight and hot you are, but...," he said, confusing and frustrating Jason. He wanted Keith in him—now!

Jason looked over his shoulder as he pushed up enough to partially turn over. "Wh-what's wrong?"

Instead of answering, Keith tugged on Jason until he lay flat on his back, and then Keith settled between his legs. Their cocks slid together, eliciting moans from both men, but Jason wanted Keith in him, not to rub off against each other. That felt damn good, and was a lot of fun, but his body ached with the need to have Keith back inside.

Hoping to encourage Keith, Jason wrapped his legs around Keith's hips and thrust up. "P-please, Keith," he begged.

"Better," Keith murmured against Jason's neck as he left a tingling trail of kisses from shoulder to ear. The sudden shock of Keith biting him caused Jason to buck and shout. Keith hadn't used his fangs, only his human teeth, but *ohmygod* did it feel wonderful.

"Again!"

"With pleasure." True to his word, Keith bit hard again and again, leaving bruises, Jason was sure, but he loved the hot flares of pain that quickly morphed into bliss.

He was so caught up in pleasure he didn't notice when or how Keith managed to snag the bottle of lube, but when a slippery digit circled his needy hole before slowly pushing in, Jason pushed his chest harder against Keith's bites, and his ass down to get more of Keith inside him. The sudden shock of penetration rocketed through him, overwhelming his senses. Keith's progression of one to four fingers in Jason's ass was faster than normal but was still too long at the same time. "Dammit, Keith. Stop p-playing and fuck me!"

"Your wish...."

Keith's cock pushed against Jason's opening, and as Jason bore down, Keith popped inside, the shock of how large Keith was still just as amazing as their first time. Both men groaned, but Keith didn't pause until his hips sat flush against Jason's butt.

He dipped his head before he took Jason's lips in a searing kiss. Keith's tongue missed nothing as he explored and plundered Jason's mouth. His thrusts matched the need and urgency of the kisses, each building the longer the kiss went on.

Jason moaned into Keith's mouth as he used his legs for leverage to make Keith go deeper and harder. He dug his fingers into Keith's back, overwhelmed with how unbelievable Keith made him feel, how deep he was inside Jason, and with how much he seemed to want Jason.

As the thrusts became more powerful, Keith tore his mouth away and shifted from Jason's mouth to his neck. Excitement thrummed through Jason, and a moment later his thin control shattered as Keith thrust so hard and deep Jason arched up off the bed. Keith then bit down hard on his neck, right over the mating bite, catapulting Jason into an orgasm only outshone by the one when Keith had given him the mark initially.

His world zeroed in until there was nothing but Keith and pleasure, until his mind shut down completely. Moments, or hours, later—he no longer could tell and didn't care—Keith roared out his completion above him.

Each man clung to the other as they calmed, panting into each other's necks as Keith lay draped over Jason. Keith chuckled, and the sounds and motion did interesting things to Jason. "Damn, baby. You sure know how to wake a man up."

That pronouncement was too much, so Jason quickly joined Keith in his laughter. "Ass," he managed, swatting Keith on said ass. "Now get off me."

"Fine, fine." Keith moved over and sat up. "I need to get up and get ready, anyway. I wish I didn't have to go. I really don't like leaving you here alone, but I won't risk your safety, either."

"You really think they'd attack me for being human?" Jason wasn't certain if that was a real or imagined threat, as his experience with shifters was a bit of a toss-up. The wolf, Caleb, liked him and was nice. Keith's friends seemed to think Jason was fine. But then the attack and the knowledge of how Keith's own father had ordered it flashed through his mind.

"I'd rather not find out the hard way. There will be more shifters there than I'll have with me, so protecting you, if needed, would be hard, bordering on impossible." Keith ran one hand through his hair and frowned. "Just stay in for now, please. I'll know better what to expect when I get back."

Jason didn't like being effectively grounded, but he didn't relish the thought of what could have happened the other night if Sasha hadn't been with him. "I'll be here, working. If I need a break, they have a gym, restaurant, and even shopping right here in the hotel. So go figure out what's going on so we can move forward."

"In some of that downtime, why don't you think about what you want for the human wedding you want us to do? They've had gay marriage here a lot longer than we have in the States, so there might be some places we could check out to find out more about all the ins and outs of a wedding when I get back. I've never been to a wedding, so I'm not sure what all goes into one."

Jason had only been to one, a het one, but he'd always wanted what his grandparents had, only with two grooms. It was one thing he'd never thought he'd have, and he still wasn't certain Keith really wanted one with him, but he pushed the doubt and questions aside for another time.

"I will."

Keith bounced up from the bed and sauntered into the bath. Jason wanted to join him, but after a quick check of the clock, he knew that wouldn't be the best idea. He had no interest in having Keith's friends walk in on them. Or rather, he had no desire for that to happen again. The first time had been horrible enough and they hadn't even been naked then.

Trying to forget about when the three men had shown up the night before so Keith and he could get on the road with Van and Kelley, Jason pulled on a pair of jeans and went in search of the room-service menu as he listened to his lover sing in the shower.

CHAPTER TWENTY

KEITH SAT in the car and stared at the innocuous building in front of him. This shouldn't be his first time here, but as per his father's wishes, he'd never accompanied him to any of the council meetings. Now he wondered why his father hadn't wanted him there. At the time, he'd claimed he wasn't needed there yet, and that Taylor and the rest of the tribe needed him at home instead.

"Come on, Keith," Vance said, slapping his shoulder. "It's not that big a thing, and I'm betting they will be more interested in the fact you partially shifted when you mated than in the fact your mate is human."

"Easy for you to say—you don't have to wonder if your next move is to return to your mate to spend the evening enjoying your mating or back to your mate to protect him from the council and their enforcers."

"True, but either way, we need to know what we're facing. Now get out of the car and be the leader you're meant to be."

"It won't be so bad," Kelley added. "And then you can go read or play chess with your mate."

That got Keith's attention. He turned to stare at his friend, seriously wondering if the stress was already messing with his mind. "Read or play chess? What the hell are you talking about?"

"Well," Kelley drawled, "as I do not ever want to see you two doing sex-type things again—seriously, I still need brain bleach—I'm going with you two playing chess or reading or maybe watching a movie… on opposite sides of the couch."

"Dork, and I mean that with the utmost respect." *Well, mostly.* Keith turned away from his friends, shaking his head, and opted for facing the council instead of his friends' insanity. "Come on."

"Right behind you, boss," the two cats said together.

"SO LET me get this straight. You're here because you're forming your own tribe instead of succeeding your father as leader of the tribe you were born to and are the heir of?" Johnson, the small lynx he was meeting with, asked, both brows raised so high Keith couldn't see them through the man's inky-black bangs. "I'm curious why you would do that instead of simply taking over your tribe."

"Agreed," Bruce said.

Both cats were smaller in their human skins than Keith, but he knew never to make assumptions based on size. He'd learned that lesson young, thanks to his sister. "That is correct. I am no longer the heir of the Glacier Rim Tribe." He hated how the words tasted on his tongue almost as much as the truth to them. "Alpha Adam Skyler has deemed me unfit based on my mating a human and my insistence on working with beings other than lynx."

Vance shifted behind Keith slightly, as did Kelley, as they waited for a response. Keith fought his need to fidget, not wanting to show his nervousness, though he knew both men before him at the table could scent his worry and stress.

Bruce cleared his throat and looked from Keith to Vance and Kelley, then back. "What creatures are you associating with that he objects to strenuously enough to remove you? And what does your mate being human have to do with anything?"

"Alpha Hunter of the Everet Wolf Pack of Seattle. The alpha decided I should work with Caleb, his youngest son, acting as a sort of diplomat, after I rescued the boy and helped heal him."

"Cooperation with other shifters is important to foster, so that doesn't make sense." Johnson stared at Keith as if he knew there was more. Which was correct. Keith just didn't know how they would view the next part.

"Also, my mate is friends with the vampire prince in our area, and with Jason comes Sasha's friendship." Keith ignored the hiss from both men, instead forcing out the rest of his explanation. "Prince Tolstoi has been amenable to interspecies cooperation and even protected my mate when enforcers from my old tribe attacked him."

"Wait." Bruce turned to Johnson and asked, "Did he say 'him'? As in a male mate?"

Instead of answering, Johnson looked back to Keith. "I assume that you didn't leave your mate where the enforcers might try again while you came here, correct?"

"No, he said 'him,'" Bruce insisted. "You did say *he*."

"Yes, I did." Keith squared his shoulders, expecting a fit, if not an outright attack. "Jason is both male and human."

Bruce bounced slightly in his chair. "And did you half shift when you claimed him?"

"Yes, did you partially shift? That's far more important than new tribes or princes and wolves." Johnson's grin wasn't quite as out of control as Bruce's, but it was close.

"Uh, yes."

Johnson clapped, startling Keith—and his friends too, if their jumps were anything to go by. "Wonderful! We haven't had one like you born in so long, not here at least, that many wondered if Baast would never forgive how our last one was killed."

"You know it wasn't an alpha challenge, right?" Keith asked.

Both Johnson and Bruce gave him curious looks. "Um, why would you think that?" Johnson asked. "He was murdered for taking a vampi…. Oh… my…. You said Prince Tolstoi is your mate's friend? It was his sister that Alpha Orin Green mated."

"And it was the previous Prince Tolstoi that destroyed the whole of the band that attacked and killed both of them," Bruce finished.

"I thought that because that's what we have been taught. All of the tribe was taught that the supposedly powerful Alpha Orin died in a challenge with another alpha. It was, in fact, Prince Tolstoi that informed me of the facts about Orin and of what I am." He wondered what else he would soon find to be a lie, but Bruce's scowl brought him out of his worries.

"A mere alpha win against one such as you? Never! If your father realizes what you are, he may well not wish to challenge you."

"That would be my hope, sirs. I do not wish to make any live within my tribe that do not want me to be their alpha, but I will defend to the death any who choose me and mine."

"As well you should, son. As well you should." Johnson shook his head. "I would like to see your shift, the half shift, so we may verify you as an Alpha King. Regardless of that, you and your mate are welcome here, as are your second and guard."

Bruce hopped up from his seat at the long table, grin still firmly in place. "Once verified, we will have to contact your father and make him aware of our decisions. But please, shift. I've always hoped to one day see the were-shift."

"In a moment, if you don't mind. First, why did you assume I might be one of Baast's Chosen when you learned about Jason being male?"

Bruce smirked. "That's easy. Those like you never mate with those that can bear them children. I don't know why. As far as our histories show, that's simply how it's done. But the other part of why I hoped is because your old tribe is the very one Orin led. To have a new Chosen of Baast appear in the same tribe means she has to have forgiven Orin's loss."

Huh. "Okay, I guess that makes sense." Sort of.

"Now, will you shift, please?" Johnson asked.

"Wait," Vance said, and both councilors turned to stare at him. "If it's really as big a deal as you say, is shifting for you enough or will others have to see too? I only ask so others will not doubt my alpha's claims."

Keith hoped the audience of two would suffice, at least for now. He'd only shifted during his mating and then once to show his friends and his sister, never for others. Well, he'd also shifted while alone a couple of times, before he'd shown Taylor and the others, nervous he might not be able to on command. However, like his regular shift, it was innate once triggered. And while he no longer doubted his shift, he didn't like the idea of being put on display, either.

"Duncan Greer, the council leader, should also be shown. But other than that, please, enjoy Toronto, the council site, and don't worry about your mate. No Alpha King in history ever took a lynx shifter as a mate. It's not what Baast chooses for them—you."

"And the issue of Jason's gender?"

"I have no idea why you're so concerned with that point," Johnson replied. "It's not overly common, but gay shifters happen. We are much more interested in your half shift than in the gender of your mate."

The next couple of hours were intense and enough to drive Keith slightly insane. He had to meet everyone on the council, shake their hands, and answer so many questions his head throbbed, and of course, he also had to show Duncan, Johnson, and Bruce his shift.

That had been the strangest thing. Before, when he'd done the partial shift it had felt odd, or maybe just seeing fur on his human-like body had been too startling for him to notice the rest. This time, however, he thought of the half-lynx, half-human form and felt his body bulk up some. His face felt odd, though he didn't have a way to determine how it was specifically different. His hands had elongated and shifted into paw-like talons, his feet did the same, and the swirling of short lynx hair all along his skin was.... He wasn't certain how he felt about it. It felt almost like a mild itch all over before the fur spread across his body.

"Oh. My. Goddess!" Duncan shouted when he faced Keith in his Alpha King, or Beloved of Baast, form, as the few others like him had been called. "Can you be still a moment?"

Keith wasn't sure why Duncan asked but stayed where he was. He tracked every movement in the area made, itching to move instead of allowing the others to be behind him—even if they were his own men.

"Hurry up," Keith snarled, then paused, taken aback at how animalistic he sounded and how odd talking around his fangs felt. He'd spoken many times before with his teeth dropped, but this was entirely different. Curious, he decided he'd have to change back in their hotel suite in front of the full-length mirror on the back of the bathroom door.

"Simply stunning," Duncan murmured, coming back into Keith's sight. "I've seen paintings and read descriptions, but never have I seen one like you."

"Peachy." If there was one thing he hated about all the attention—well, he didn't like a lot to do with this trip—it was how the council members spoke of him as if he were a fascinating piece of art instead of a living, breathing person. "Done?" The deep rasping of his voice was something else. He wondered if it sounded as strange to Jason during their mating as it now did to himself.

"Oh, my apologies. Please return to your human skin, and you may get dressed if you like," Duncan replied.

The council members in attendance all huddled together, despite the fact he could hear them. Keith was just thankful they all seemed enamored of his shift and supportive of him forming a separate tribe.

Keith returned to where Vance and Kelley stood and took his clothes from Kelley. He slipped into them quickly and felt better once he was covered, though he knew that was silly as the bits of denim and cotton were hardly a shield of any kind.

"What do you think?" Kelley asked, fighting not to stare at the council, even as he alternated between looking furious and a little in awe.

"I think I want to get back to the hotel and make sure Jason is okay. Then I want to tour the city a little, but mostly I want to be back home where I can make sure Taylor, Zeke, and Jason are all safe."

"They are. Chance would call if anything was wrong, and Jason is fine. He's not stupid. He'll stay where it's safe until we get back." Vance spoke to Keith, but he never stopped watching the council. Keith couldn't decide if that was out of awe, curiosity, or concern.

Before they could worry too much, Duncan, Bruce, and Johnson approached.

"I'd like to send someone with you to monitor how your new tribe progresses," Duncan said. "We don't usually have breakaway tribes like the one you're proposing, nor do we usually support one tribe over another. However, we will look into your allegations, and as we have come to full agreement that you are, in fact, one of Baast's Chosen, we wish to see how your unusual partnerships and friendships with wolves and vampires alike go."

"You're not upset about the vampire?" Keith asked, wanting to make sure his working with and trying to befriend Sasha wasn't going to bite him in the ass.

"No. It's more than a bit unorthodox, but Prince Sasha has a history of treating us fairly, including in how he and his father avenged Orin and his mate. The fact she was a vampire is of no import to us, only that she was his mate. It's the same as with your human. He is your mate. Period."

Keith couldn't believe what he was hearing, but readily agreed to have one of their number stay with his newly forming tribe. He hoped the new cat would even be a resource for his tribe now that he knew how much—at least in part—his father had kept from him.

By the time they were allowed to leave, Keith had met his new cat, a male named Trace, and if anyone tripped his "gaydar," it was Trace. They'd arranged a time to pick him up before they left to go home. The only negative, or odd, thing the council had told him was that his having a male mate did not, in fact, relieve him of the obligation to have an heir.

That was the only part he worried over. He couldn't have sex with a female. Not only was he 110 percent gay, but it was literally impossible for him now that he'd sealed his mating with Jason. He wasn't sure how that would work out, but he was thankful he didn't have to figure it out right away.

When they pulled away from the site, Keith sighed loud enough to cause both his friends to laugh.

"A bit tense, are you?" Vance teased. "And is it just me, or is the cat we're taking with us gay, or was I totally misreading the man?"

"Oh, I think he's gay," Keith agreed. "But that isn't a problem. Right?"

"No, no problem. I'm just going to love watching the girls pout when they figure out they can't turn his head with their charms."

"Eh, you're just hoping the ones who will be disappointed are your exes," Kelley teased.

They laughed most of the way back to the hotel about one thing or another. The closer they got, the antsier Keith became. Until he saw Jason, made sure he was fine, he couldn't let go of his worry that his father had somehow found his mate while he was away. He knew it was ridiculous, but that didn't make the worry any less real.

As soon as he parked, Keith hopped out of the car and took off straight for their suite, not stopping other than to wait for the damnably slow elevator and to open the door.

"Jason?"

"In here," Jason replied, a moment later, stepping out of the bathroom freshly showered, in nothing but a towel. "Th-things go o-okay?" he asked between nibbles to his bottom lip.

Keith took the three long strides needed to reach him, then wrapped his arms around his mate and buried his face in Jason's shoulder, inhaling. He calmed as the scent of his and Jason's intermingled mate scent seeped in. "You stuttering because you're worried or is something else wrong?"

"J-just worried about you and what that c-council of yours might do to you. Now d-did it go well?"

"Yeah, just missed you, baby."

"Um, m-missed you too. You s-sure you're okay?"

"I'm fine. Now. I didn't like not knowing how you were, but the council recognized me and my claim on you. You're welcome at tribal things now, so I won't have to leave you like this again."

"Good. So… how 'bout you show me how happy you are to see me," Jason said, his voice playful yet completely alluring at the same time.

Deciding to take Jason up on his suggestion, Keith dropped his hands to Jason's towel-covered butt and lifted. Jason wrapped his long legs around Keith's hips, and they devoured each other as he carried Jason to bed, intending to take advantage of not having anyone around for a while.

It would be hours before he let Jason up from the bed, and then only to refuel before taking him again against the shower wall. To his surprise and joy, Jason became even more wanton when Keith partially shifted.

By the time they fell asleep, he'd devoured his mate repeatedly, falling for Jason a little more each time. It wasn't the sex but how Jason reacted, never seeming afraid or repulsed by Keith's obvious inhumanness. He'd never thought he'd have a mate, yet Baast had gifted him with one better than he ever could have imagined.

CHAPTER TWENTY-ONE

BY THE time they'd gotten back to their—Keith still thrilled inside over living with Jason—home, Keith had been too tired to do more than strip and curl up around Jason. Some day he wanted to take Jason back to Toronto and simply explore the city and the country around it, but that would have to wait.

At least he hadn't had to take the new cat with them. Five men, plus baggage, in one car would have been awful. As it was, Trace would be joining them sometime in the next week, as he needed time to deal with work and home issues.

When the alarm buzzed, rudely breaking him out of his dreams of Jason—naked and wet—Keith groaned. He didn't want to get up, but considering he'd taken the impromptu trip, leaving the other vet to take up the slack for him, he knew he had to get up and get to work. Later that day he had to sit down and truly work on his new tribe.

Some from his old tribe had already left messages with Chance about petitioning to join his new tribe. That had been a true shock. He had only just returned from the council and he had six additional cats, and in two cases, their families as well, wishing to move and join him.

Pushing thoughts of his new tribe out of his mind, Keith carefully slid out of bed, not wishing to disturb Jason. After a quick shower and shave, he quietly dressed and left the bedroom with his shoes in hand so he wouldn't wake Jason. In a few minutes, Keith was on his bike, heading toward work and a very long day.

A STRANGE knocking sound pulled Jason from a deep sleep, and while he knew it had been a good dream, he couldn't remember anything about it after sitting up in bed. He looked around, confused as to why he was awake. For the last week he'd woken alone, as Keith was spending longer than usual at work, both playing catch up and having to deal with emergencies.

Just as Jason decided he'd dreamed the noise, it came again. Someone—or someones—was at the front door, again. Ever since he and

Keith had returned from Toronto, cats who wanted to join the tribe had constantly interrupted them. If it had been any other reason, Jason would have thrown a fit, but how could he complain that so many people wanted to support and be with Keith?

Then again, he had mixed feelings about that last point. There were two females who definitely had designs on his lover. He'd overheard one saying that Keith would tire of Jason and want to be with someone who could understand and accept both sides of him. That had gotten Jason thinking of a way to show Keith that he wanted Keith's cat, half-cat, and man.

Before he could ponder too much, the knock repeated, more forcefully. With a loud sigh, not caring that no one was there to hear him, he got up, threw on a pair of jeans, and grabbed a T-shirt on his way out of the room. He'd managed to pull it on before he opened the door.

Jason stared blankly at the strange man standing there. He suspected the man was another cat, but as his senses were human, not lynx, he couldn't be certain. "Hello?"

"Hello, Jason. May I come in?" the man asked, his voice almost a purr. Jason took his time looking the man over, not sure about having strangers inside when he was alone. He was handsome, at about six feet with pale blond hair and light jade-green eyes. He wore skintight black jeans, a slim-fitting turtleneck sweater, and more bracelets on his arm than even Sasha did.

"M-mind if I know who you are f-first?" he replied, looking past the man to the sleek silver car parked on the street. Jason knew that one of Keith's cats was around, so this guy shouldn't be a danger, but still.

"Oh, my apologies. My name is Trace Wilson and I'm here to see Keith. He knows to expect me."

Trace? Oh! "N-no, no. That's fine. He told me y-you would be here sometime this week. C-come in."

Stepping out of the way, Jason wondered what he was supposed to do with the man until Keith got home. It was barely eight in the morning, so Keith would most likely not be back anytime soon.

"Thank you." Trace walked—more sauntered, really—into the living room and looked around.

"Would you l-like something to drink? I'm not s-sure when Keith will return. He's at w-work right now."

"I figured as much as his scent isn't too recent. I'd love some water, though. Mostly, I'd really wanted to meet you and find out a little about you and the area. My hope is to find an apartment close by, quickly, but I don't like deciding such things based on images from online. Too much of a chance that the site isn't really like the pictures."

Even though his work and business were online, Jason knew that people also liked to pick and choose what they showed you. He'd done the insane driving all over with his Realtor before deciding on the house he now lived in. So what Trace said made sense to Jason, as he felt the same way, and he said as much as he left to grab a bottled water for Trace.

"Thanks. So…," Trace said before taking a sip.

"So?"

"Well, I'm not certain what to ask you, honestly. The council thought it important for someone to accompany Keith as he set up the new tribe, and as I don't have a family of my own to worry about uprooting, I was chosen. But I've honestly never dealt with a human mate before. A wolf mate, once, and even one that found their mate in a true lynx, oddly enough."

"That h-happens? Mating with the animal kind of lynx? I th-thought lynx didn't mate in the wild. The permanent b-bond type, I mean." Since he'd found out what Keith was, Jason had done a lot of Internet research on lynx and had learned that, unlike many other wild creatures, lynx males never stuck around after mating.

"Only know of one," Trace said with a shrug. "He swears she's his mate. Who am I to judge? It's no stranger to me than the thought of Alpha Skyler having a human mate. You can't shift between forms, so it's not much different. Always stuck in only one skin."

"Nothing wrong with being human," Jason snapped, thrilled when his stutter didn't show up.

He'd about had it with cats thinking he was lacking something based on the fact he was human. And of stuttering every time he met a new lynx.

"Didn't mean to imply there was. It's just a fact that makes his mating similar to yours, though in the opposite fashion. I happen to like humans. Shorter lived than we tend to be and the whole divorce thing still baffles me, but I went to a human college and befriended many." His voice dropped to a whisper, and he leaned forward. "I even dated one once."

Jason couldn't help it. He giggled until his sides hurt.

Trace seemed confused as he tilted his head to one side and stared at Jason blankly for a minute before he joined in, laughing loudly. "Yeah," he managed once he'd calmed some. "I guess saying that to a human isn't like saying it to some of the uptight cats I'm often around."

Shaking his head, Jason grinned. "You said that to not only a human, but a human whose best friend is a vampire. So yeah, that's *so* not a concern for me."

"Okay, so I'm not always the brightest." He flashed that wide grin again, making Jason think that maybe he knew a vampire Trace should meet. He was just Sasha's type, well, other than the whole being-a-lynx thing.

"We can't all have brains and beauty," Keith's voice cut in.

Startled, Jason jumped up and turned, shocked at the thunderous look on Keith's face. It confused and worried Jason. "Wh-what's wrong?"

"You have a stranger in our home and you ask that? The fact I know who he is doesn't change the fact that you wouldn't have known."

Something didn't seem right about that. Keith had told him that Trace was coming, so why be weird when Trace actually arrived? The fact Keith's knuckles were scuffed didn't make any more or less sense to him, either. "Keith? Dear? What happened to you?" he asked instead of responding to Keith's paranoid ramblings.

"Dad's cats aren't at all amused with me 'stealing' from his *chain*," Keith sneered when he ground out the word. "Two jumped me outside the little eatery I stopped at to grab us breakfast." He held up the bag he clutched in one hand.

"Is this common?" Trace asked as Jason went over to Keith. He took the bag from Keith and set it down before he lifted each hand in turn to his lips, leaving a soft kiss on the bruised and cut skin. Jason knew the wounds wouldn't last long, the ones on Keith's skin at least.

"It's the third time since Taylor announced to him that I was her alpha. That's in addition to the attack on Jason before we left for the council meeting."

"It's okay, Keith. Sasha was with me, so no one was hurt but the one that tried to hurt me," Jason soothed. He didn't want Keith fixating on his past outing with Sasha or on why ever he was upset over Trace being there.

"It's not, actually," Trace said the same time Keith growled, "Like hell it is."

Jason couldn't help it, he laughed at both men's indignant faces. "Well, at least that you two can agree upon."

"Baby," Keith grumbled. "I don't like you alone with cats I don't know well yet."

"And that's my fault. I knew you weren't home, Alpha Skyler. I wanted to get a feel for how Jason was with you being a lynx and with all the upheaval. My most sincere apologies for making you worry. However," Trace continued, waving one hand slightly, "the only issues I see with your mate is that he's too sweet."

"He is that," Keith said, tugging Jason into his arms for a tight hug. After a moment, Keith released him, and they moved to the couch together. "I've made sure all those petitioning to join my tribe know that Jason is human and male and that I won't tolerate prejudice against anyone: human, gay, or any nonlynx shifter. I've also let it be known that I have a tentative pact with Prince Tolstoi, so hunting or hurting vampires isn't allowed unless they are actually trying to kidnap, torture, or kill."

"Thank you," Jason said, thrilling at how Keith leaned into him as they sat together.

"Nothing to thank me for. I won't tolerate that kind of hate. Now, anyone want to tell me why you, my mate, were giggling with the new man and why your stutter was gone?"

Ah, that's what the issue was. Huh. "It left when he ticked me off, and then he made a joke that I found funny."

"To be fair, I didn't mean it as a joke." Trace smiled softly as his gaze shifted from Keith to Jason and back. "Though, I do agree, saying that to a human was a touch ridiculous."

Jason nodded. "I've dated humans too," he added with a wink.

"Oh, I see." Keith tightened his hold on Jason. "You're one that doesn't limit your search for your mate by species." He nodded. "That makes sense."

"In what way?" Trace asked.

"Why the council wanted you to stay with us here. You wouldn't see Jason being a human as an issue."

"Actually, no cat should. He's your mate. Period. Nothing else matters. Though," Trace continued, his gaze dropping slightly, "if he showed the mating mark, it might make others trust it more."

"Trust?" *Why wouldn't they trust in my being Keith's mate?*

"You're mated to the most rare kind of lynx shifter there is, and it's not like there's tons of us to begin with. It's been so long since one of Baast's Chosen has been among us that some doubt that they're real. Well, on this continent, that is. Europe has two, Asia one, and I've heard there's even one in Africa." Trace leaned back in his chair, a wicked grin on his face. "I can't wait to see how the lynx here react the first time they all see him take his Chosen form."

"We'll know soon enough. I'm holding to the traditions I grew up with for the most part, only without the hate and bigotry. So that means we will have our monthly gathering soon. I've already reserved one of the large camping areas in the national park here so we can shift, hunt, and play without worry of humans finding us."

"That's a good thing, but, um…." Trace tugged at his sleeves and cleared his throat. "Is that safe? For Jason, I mean."

"Why wouldn't it be?" Keith asked, his voice oddly resonant and low. "No one would dare harm him with me there."

"Oh, uh…." Trace's gaze flicked to Jason's, the apology clear on his face. "I didn't realize you'd be at the gathering. My apologies."

"No offense taken. When Keith first mentioned it to me, I didn't realize he meant for me to go, but as he wants it to be like an—" Jason looked at Keith. "—engagement party of sorts?"

"Yes, exactly. I'll stay close to the camp since Jason can't shift and run with us. But we're going to start with a party welcoming the new cats and announcing both our mating and our upcoming nuptials."

"Actually, that makes sense. Mating in both the lynx and human ways. Have you decided on what to do since Keith can't wear rings? No male shifter ever does."

Yeah, that had been a sore point for Jason since Keith had explained why he never wore jewelry. He had to be able to change at any given time, now even more so, which made wedding bands impossible for him to wear. Jason had been looking forward to putting one on his lover, wanting to mark him somehow, but sadly none of his ideas had panned out yet.

"Did I say something wrong again?" Trace look so confused, but even how nice the man was being didn't help Jason's annoyance any.

"I wanted some way to mark Keith as mine. He left the huge scar on me, a mark that the cats I've met, the wolf that stops by, and even Sasha and his guards recognize and respect. But there's no way for me to put any kind of mark on him to show others that he's mine too. Besides, you say shifters, especially male lynx, don't wear jewelry, yet here you sit with…." Jason squinted as he tried to count. "What is that? Six bracelets?"

"Well, that was actually—" Trace ducked his head and blushed. "I didn't think I'd need to shift while with you, a human, and I've always loved the look myself. I didn't think you'd mind."

"I don't mind, though it seems odd because of what you just said about the rings."

"Is that all?" Trace shrugged one shoulder again, making Jason want to grind his teeth. "Go get a mates' tattoo. There are—"

"Wait! A what?" Jason barked out.

"If all you want is to mark your mate, why not go get a mate tattoo? There are—"

"Calm, baby. Let the man explain. What tattoo, Trace?"

"There's a tattoo that some mates get—usually because the female demands her mark be put on her mate, since most of the time it's the female marked, not the male. We don't stray, can't, but some of us tend to get territorial even knowing that. It's also done for interspecies matings, like yours, because the other mate can't mark the dominant partner." Trace beamed. "You just have to find a tattoo artist that works with shifters."

Keith stared at Trace. "I knew there were ways to tattoo us. Taylor has one in memory of her mate that died. But—" Keith twitched as if he wanted to pace, but he didn't let go of Jason or stand up. "But I've never heard of it for mating."

"Why not?" Trace again cocked his head to the side. It reminded Jason of how Keith acted in cat form, making him smile. "If it can be done for memorials or because some wish to mark themselves like humans do, why not use it in lieu of rings?"

That decided, the three men chatted and Keith and Jason ate. Jason offered to make something for Trace, but he insisted he'd eaten before he arrived. Before long, they had Trace, Vance, Chance, and Kelley all piled in the living room, talking and debating the best ways to do different things as far as running the tribe, admitting new members and families, and even picking safe land to use.

Jason loved listening in, as he was able to learn a great deal about shifters, lynx in particular. The more he heard, the more comfortable he became with the idea that Keith really wouldn't ever tire of him or want to leave. He still wasn't sure he believed Keith loved him rather than just lusted after him, but he hoped that would come in time.

Love wasn't a word they usually used with each other, and honestly the only reason he cared to hear it was to know for certain that Keith was happy with him as a partner, rather than just being influenced by the mating drive. He also wondered if Keith had the same worries in the opposite form—if he worried Jason would leave, as humans so often did.

Resolved to do his best to show Keith he did want him, not only because he knew Keith wouldn't cheat, he sat back and listened. His mind spun as he contemplated exactly how to show Keith that he respected, accepted, and loved both of Keith's sides.

He'd find a way to show him that the cat and the man were part of his heart.

Chapter Twenty-Two

Jason had spent the last two weeks meeting new people—all lynx—working, or helping to plan his wedding to Keith. He didn't want anything big. Just something simple and in front of friends and family. Keith had offered to keep it small and do a "justice of the peace" type wedding, but Jason didn't want that, either.

A wedding with a JOP seemed less somehow, though he knew he was in the minority on that opinion. Keith didn't care; he said the wedding could be whatever Jason wanted. That lack of interest, or at least that's how Jason perceived it, irritated him even more. He knew that in Keith's mind, they were already bonded, so this was a mere formality. But for Jason, the legal wedding truly marked their bonding, even if the legal one was easier to dissolve than the mating.

Now he was preparing to attend Keith's first tribe gathering and party. Where he'd be the only human. And one of only three gay men. And… and… and….

"You know, if you keep scowling like that, your face will stick that way," Sasha teased from behind him.

"Yeah, so I've heard." Jason sighed, not sure why all this bothered him so much. Well, no, he knew why, he just didn't know what to do about it.

"Why so sad? You're planning your wedding and getting ready for a shifter party. You should be excited, not scowling at the computer."

"I don't… I wish Keith would give more input about the wedding. I know it's not a big deal to him, but it is to me." He'd never thought he'd have one, after all.

Sasha came over and perched one hip on Jason's desk. "Instead of worrying about things like that, why don't you figure out what would make this special for you both? He's a vet and a lynx. Maybe an outdoor wedding would be more meaningful and comfortable. Talk to his second and guards. Maybe they would have ideas about where to hold it. As for the wedding itself, hon, the only important part is that you both agree to love, honor, and cherish, not the when, where, or whys of it."

"Outdoors?" Jason could do outdoors. Maybe at the same national park they were holding the gathering and party? Keith didn't have tribe land yet, something that frustrated him, though he refused to admit that out loud, so maybe that would help him feel more comfortable.

"Sweetie, you're marrying a shifter. Outside is a huge thing to them."

"Yeah." Jason sighed, thinking of all the times Keith had come in from the woods out back, still in his lynx form. Keith made a handsome cat, though he always scowled when Jason said things like that. "I think I'll do that. I know all his people there will be lynx, but I still want you to stand with me, shifter-slash-vampire issues be damned."

Sasha leaned over and kissed Jason on the cheek. "Of course I will, hon. Does Keith know you want me as your best man?"

"Yeah, he said you were my family and that you and your guards would be welcome."

"Wonderful. I know Dimka would like to go. I know you only recently met him, but he's been guarding you for years now. I know he'd enjoy seeing you happy. And believe me, he's wanted to protect you from more than a few humans, but I forbade him."

"From humans?" *Why would he want to do that?*

"From your exes, hon." Sasha patted Jason's hand. "Now are we inviting the wolves and have we picked out the mating tattoos yet? Oh, and just where are you planning to have them placed?"

My exes? Wait.... "Did you say wolves? I only know Caleb, though I did intend to invite him. I think it would be good for the lynx to see Caleb there, and I know it would make Caleb happy. He thinks it's cool that the Gods picked me for Keith. I'm still not sure about all these Gods and Goddesses of the shifters, but Grandy raised me to be open to what all's out there." He shrugged, not caring what Keith believed, just that he was true to whatever it was.

"Which is a good way to look at the world. I liked Drew a great deal, always thought he had a good head on his shoulders. I even offered to bestow immortality upon him, but he wanted to spend his life with Lily and then move on when you were ready. I think he intended to stay a little longer than he did, but I'm sure he's happy wherever he is."

"You d-did? But I thought vampires were b-born. You said your parents and sister were all v-vampires too."

"Calm down. Most vampires are born. We're a race, just as much as humans or shifters are, but unlike shifters, we can 'turn,' for the lack of a better word, a human into a vampire. We can't do it often, and only the stronger lines can manage it at all. I've never done it, though I do know how." Sasha waved off the words as he sat up straighter. "But you didn't tell me about the tattoo…."

Sasha stayed, even managing to get him away from his computers and plans for a bit. Jason was sad to see Sasha go, but he was thrilled that Keith would be home soon. He hurried to the utility room and grabbed the bags of things he'd bought that morning. Everything needed to be in place when Keith arrived.

JASON FOUGHT not to grin when he heard Keith open the front door. He tried to bury himself in the code he needed to finish but couldn't do it. Instead, he got up and went out to meet his partner, hopeful he'd be there when Keith saw the new addition to the guest bath.

"Hey, baby, how was your day?" Keith stepped over to Jason and wrapped one arm around his shoulders.

"Fine. Sasha was here earlier, and I've packed everything I should need for tonight." When he noticed Keith's nose wrinkle as he scanned the area, it became harder to keep a straight face. "What's the matter?"

"Um…." Keith turned, releasing Jason. He kept sniffing and twitching his nose. After a few moments, he wandered toward the guest bath. When he stepped just inside the door, he froze, his mouth opening and closing, but no words came out.

"Keith?"

Keith cleared his throat, though his voice was still a strange mix of rumble and croaking. "What's this?" he asked, pointing to the brand-new litter box, neatly set up with fresh litter and a liner.

"A l-litter b-box." Stupid stutter. Now wasn't the time for it to reappear.

"And why do we have one?" Keith's tone was mild, yet curious, thankfully.

"W-well, I w-wanted you to know that I ack-accept all of you, not just the human side. P-plus, it makes any que-questions about cats seen c-coming and g-going less of a w-worry."

The choking sound from Keith worried him until he realized Keith was laughing so hard he could barely breathe.

Jason joined in; thankful Keith had seen the humor in the gift. He'd thought Keith would, but he wasn't positive. "You don't mind, do you?" he managed eventually.

"No, baby, I don't. But what on earth prompted this?"

"Well, I've o-overheard some of your friends and tribe members make c-comments about the fact I'm human, that I can't sh-shift, and that I wouldn't be a-able to accept both parts of you. I just…." Jason shrugged, his face hot as he stammered out the rest. "I j-just wanted you t-to know that a-all of you is l-loved and im-important to m-me."

Keith wrapped Jason up in his arms and warmth, burying his face in Jason's hair. "I'm sorry they upset you. I'll talk to them, but thank you. You don't know how much this means to me."

"You d-don't have to d-do that and th-thank you."

"I do, actually. They can't make you doubt yourself or us like that. I won't allow it. But as long as you don't actually intend for me to use it, I think the litter box is great." Keith kissed Jason's temple before he let go. "For now, how about if we finish getting ready and then head out? It will be a small gathering, sorry about that, but I can't wait to show you off."

JASON HAD been to the park a few times as a teen but hadn't been back in ages. As he pulled the car into the parking area, knowing they'd have to lug all their stuff to the site, he swallowed hard. Once in park, Jason looked over and smiled at how eager Keith seemed. His beaming and twitching reminded Jason of watching a kid at Christmas.

"Eager, dear?"

"I am. Can't wait to show you off and to run and play with the others as a group. It's one thing I wish I could share with you that I can't, but I'll make sure not to stray too far from the site."

"I'm not worried about you running off to play. I have my laptop, cell—though I doubt I'll get much coverage out here—and my trusty Kindle." He'd also made sure to bring his own blanket and pillow but didn't feel the need to point that out as Keith had been the one to load them into the car.

Taylor and Zeke climbed out of Taylor's car, Zeke bouncing worse than his uncle. "Can we go play now?" he pleaded as he tugged on Taylor's hand.

"Not yet, love. We have to tend to our things first. And remember, you won't go running with Keith and me tonight."

"I know." Zeke sighed as he rolled his eyes. "I have to stay with the other kits, close to the camp."

"Exactly. Besides, Jason will need you to help him. It's his first gathering," Taylor whispered, like it was some great secret. "He'll need you to help him once all the other adults run off."

"So I stay behind to take care of Jason?" Zeke grinned wide. "Yay!"

"Yep, so for now, grab your bag and follow me while they get all the heavy stuff."

Moments later, it was only the two of them again, and Jason was finally able to let out his laugh at how earnest Zeke had seemed when told to help Jason. "He's too cute, ya know."

"I do. Sadly, so does he." Keith pulled off his overshirt, fussing about how it was too hot already.

Jason collected the discarded shirt and tossed it back into the car. "Since you love showing off those muscles of yours so much—" Jason took a moment to admire Keith in his biceps-baring tank. "—you can be the one to carry the coolers you brought." Honestly, Jason had been shocked when he'd seen them. The things were huge.

"No worries, baby. You tend to your electronics and I'll get the rest. Now—" Keith paused and inhaled deeply. "Let's head out." With that announcement, he turned down one of the long paths and strode purposefully with one large cooler on his shoulder and another rolling along behind him.

Hurrying, Jason hitched his laptop bag higher on his shoulder and grabbed his backpack before jogging to catch up with Keith. "You think all the new members will show?"

"Everyone knows where and when. I imagine they will all be there. Just don't be disappointed at the small numbers. We'll grow as a tribe and fill out in time."

"Ha! I have no basis of comparison, plus I know why it's smaller than you'd like it to be. Maybe we can look into buying some property that abuts the park?" He could do that for Keith. Jason knew how much he chafed at not having tribal land, but they could work on building up money and land. They both made good money, well, decent at least, so it wouldn't be too hard to manage.

Keith froze and turned his head to stare at Jason with wide eyes. The movement was so abrupt, Jason nearly collided with Keith. "You'd-you'd do that? You would help me buy land, build my land up?"

"Well, yeah. I mean, you're my mate and my soon-to-be husband, right? Why wouldn't I?"

"I…. It just never occurred to me that you would want to be that invested in the tribe. I'm sorry."

Jason puzzled out what Keith said, not liking what he came up with. "Why wouldn't I? If it's important to you, then it's important to me." He shrugged, though it probably looked a bit odd with the messenger bag hanging off one side. "This is a partnership, and just because I can't do certain things shouldn't make you think I'm not just as invested as you are."

"Hey," Keith said softly as he set down the one cooler. "Come here, baby." He tugged Jason into a tight hug, burying his face in Jason's shoulder and inhaling as he so often did. "I didn't mean to question you like that. I'm sorry. I guess I'm still working out what being with you truly means. If you were a lynx, I would expect you to be eager for the gathering and all, but as a human, I'm never sure what interests you and what you put up with because of me."

"I don't 'put up with,' Keith. I told you, I want a partner. I want to be your husband. That kind of means that we do things like building a family or helping grow your tribe together. I know there's a lot I can't do, but there's a lot I can. Please let me help."

Keith nodded against Jason's neck as he tightened his hold for a moment. When he stepped back, he was all smiles. "That's what you were trying to show me with the pan earlier, weren't you? That this side of me is important to you, not just the me I am now."

"Yeah, it was. Now how about if we hurry up and get things moved? I'm sure there are a few people that would appreciate us getting the grill going."

It wasn't long before they had the food set up, burgers and brats on the grill, and people mingling. Someone had brought a stereo, and so music was soon playing, though thankfully it was low and whoever was in charge had good taste.

Jason and Keith sat on one of the long picnic tables, eating and chatting, enjoying the company and the festive mood. Jason had been surprised when a few people stopped by to thank Keith for letting them join him, to welcome Jason, and even to drop off gifts. The gifts confused him at first, but Keith leaned in and reminded him that this was like an engagement party or reception. That they were happy to see their alpha happy and mated, so the gifts were merely a physical show of their respect for him and them as a mated couple.

He hadn't expected to be so warmly embraced by the tribe. The only ones cool to him were the same women he'd overheard discussing how Keith would eventually want a real mate. The fact Keith never left Jason's side for long seemed to irk them, but he found their behavior amusing instead.

Things didn't change from the festive atmosphere to one of anticipation until dusk. Many of the people—though there were not quite thirty, and that included the children—were in various stages of dress, though nothing too risqué was showing. As soon as night fell, though, a few of the older members moved the young ones, including Zeke, toward the cabins while the rest of the adults headed toward the woods. They stripped as soon as they hit the wood line.

"Jason!" Zeke yelled, slipping past one of the grandmothers he'd met earlier.

When Zeke reached him, he scooped the boy up so they could more easily talk. "What's up, little man?"

"Not that little," Zeke pouted.

"Uh-huh." Jason settled Zeke on his hip like he'd seen the moms do, then fluffed his hair with the other hand. "But big or small, what do you need?" Jason walked to where the other children were, noticing how the older women seemed nervous around him when Keith wasn't there.

"They said I couldn't call you Uncle Jason, that you weren't really my uncle." Zeke glared at one of the women and a couple of the kids, and Jason assumed they were the offenders in question.

"I'm your uncle too. Some people just have trouble with change, remember? Just know that I love you and want the best for you."

"Uh-huh," Zeke said and nodded, so Jason set him back on the ground. But then Zeke turned and stuck his tongue out at the others. "He's my uncle too."

"Behave, Zeke," he chastised gently. "You want to make your mom and uncle proud, right?"

Zeke looked up at Jason. "Yeah, but they were being mean."

"No, what did I say? They're just not used to me yet, and some people, human and cat alike, take time to change how they think." Jason leaned down and whispered, knowing the others could still hear every word. "The only thing that matters is that you know who I am and that we all love you."

Zeke ran off to the other side of the large circle the cabins made. One of the women he'd known Zeke was upset with came over to where he sat reading—or more accurately pretending to read rather than actually doing it.

"That was nice of you, sweetie. You didn't have to defend us. We shouldn't have argued with him."

He set his Kindle down and looked her in the eye. "No, y-you shouldn't, but not b-because you shouldn't correct a child who's wrong, b-but because you shouldn't l-let your biases affect how you t-teach and raise y-your children." God, but he hated his stutter. With Zeke or others he knew, he was usually fine, but faced with one little old lady and nope, the stutter was back.

She ducked her head slightly. "You're right about that too. I was raised to believe that humans were gay, sometimes, but never shifters. I've met a few that were when I've been away, visiting, but it still seems so strange to me. However, if you're his true mate, I will do my best to remember that Baast never makes mistakes and that love is love, no matter the race or gender."

"Ma'am—" Jason began, but she held one hand up.

"I'm Anna Heart."

He smiled at her. "Anna, it sh-shouldn't matter if I'm his t-true mate or one he chose for himself. We are m-mates and that's all that should matter. Right?"

Her shoulders slumped. "You're right again. Forgive an old woman her shortsightedness. I chose to join Alpha Keith because he's a good man. He's fair and has never been prone to the ego of other alphas I've met. Also, my grandbaby is half-human." She pointed to one of the little girls in the group.

"She's beautiful." Half-human? He'd not thought to ask Keith if mixing was possible when it came to children.

"Thank you. Why don't I let—?"

Her words were cut off when cats started streaming out of the woods, and the adults with him started screaming and collecting the children.

Chapter Twenty-Three

Jason didn't know what to do. The cats charging toward them obviously weren't friendly. That was obvious both from their behavior and from how the others with him screamed and ran, pushing the children into whichever cabin was closest and slamming the doors closed.

Anna was still near Jason, and both took off toward one group of kids that was a little farther from the cabins—the group with Zeke in it—at a dead run. He was a little stunned to see the elderly woman speed past him but couldn't care about it right then. All he wanted was to get to the kids and then to find Keith.

Terrified didn't begin to touch Jason's feelings as he saw one of the lynx turn and head straight for Zeke. Pushing every ounce of speed he could manage, he got to Zeke just as the intruder did. He found himself sprawled on his back with a lynx standing on top of him. The hook of its claws knifed into Jason, pulling a scream from his lungs even as he fought to keep the cat from getting to Zeke.

He managed to move enough to grab hold of the cat's ears and yanked, hoping it would hurt enough to get the damn thing to back the hell off. To his surprise, the cat mewled and scrambled off him, leaving him panting and bleeding in the dirt.

When he managed to look around, he realized he was the only human, or human-looking, one left. He wasn't certain at first if that was because the others with him had shifted or because they had all made it into the cabins. At least he didn't see any kittens, so he knew Zeke had made it inside. Cats were bashing at the windows and doors with their bodies, but none of them seemed to want to return to their human forms and attack that way.

Jason slowly maneuvered backward toward one of the cabins, hoping to go unnoticed. Not only did he fail, but he also realized with a shock that there was one other person in the vicinity that still looked human—the little one Anna had pointed out to him. Torn between trying to make it to the cabin and wanting to protect the little girl, Jason managed to get to his feet and ran for the little one.

"Bad kitty," the little girl yelled as one hissed at her and swatted her.

He wasn't sure what he could hope to do, other than stall for time, but he made it to the girl and scooped her up, trying to keep his body angled to protect her. Jason then opened his mouth and screamed at the top of his lungs, "Keith!"

Two of the cats lunged at him, one catching him in the hand and biting down hard enough to send fire shooting up his arm before releasing him. The other knocked him on his ass—though he somehow managed to keep his hold on the little girl.

Before he could decide what to do—as thinking through the screaming of the cats, the little girl, and the pain wasn't the easiest—more cats poured into the clearing. Terrified, Jason missed when more humans, or well, mostly human-looking men, showed up. It didn't take long for Jason to realize that the new cats were Keith and his new tribe. He also relaxed when he caught of glimpse of Sasha as he flung a cat so hard it landed somewhere out in the wood line.

Watching all the fighting did little to calm Jason or the little one he guarded, but in a matter of a few minutes, Keith was kneeling beside Jason, naked, shushing him as he tried to get close.

"Shh, baby. Let me see how bad it is." When the words finally sank in, Jason flung himself at Keith while still holding the girl. When someone went to move her from his other arm, Jason yelled and swung himself around, intending to beat whomever it was, even if his hand wasn't in the best shape.

"Hey! It's me," Anna cajoled. "Let me take her, please, so Alpha Keith can help you?"

Oh, Anna.... "'Kay" was all he could manage as he turned back to Keith, and now Sasha as well.

"Oh, baby. I'm so sorry. I'll get you to the hospital as soon as possible." Keith gathered Jason in his arms.

"No," Sasha countered gently, "let my doctor look at him. Mine's had a lot longer to learn and won't report it. You don't want a witch hunt for feral wildcats."

Jason tried to pay attention, but now that Keith and Sasha were there, the pain took center stage and he couldn't seem to focus on much else. Someone carried him and did something to his hand that made it hurt even worse. Then there was a cut wrist shoved into his mouth and he was told to drink. He didn't want to, but he hadn't been able to deny Keith before; this time was no different.

After a few more moments, the pain decreased and there was a collective sigh around him.

"Thank the Gods," Sasha said as Keith thanked Baast specifically. As much as he wanted to find out what had happened and what was going to happen—he knew Keith couldn't ignore an attack like that—he slipped into a half doze and then fell into sleep. The last thing he remembered was Keith brushing his lips across Jason's and telling him to rest.

"WHAT THE hell happened?" Keith snapped once they were outside the cabin Jason lay resting in. He'd left Vance and the vampire doctor in with Jason and then ordered everyone else out.

"That's what I'd like to know," Sasha yelled back. "His hand is all wrong, he lost a ton of blood, and he and that small child were out here all alone! Why?"

Keith turned to look for any of the women left with Jason and the children. "You!" he barked at Clarice, one of the older women. "Why were they out there alone?"

"We didn't realize they were outside until we were completely cut off from them. We wouldn't have left them like that." She seemed so indignant, he would have laughed if he hadn't been so upset. "Jasmine can't turn lynx and run like the rest of us. I thought she was with Anna."

"And Jason was left out here, why?" He wasn't about to let it slide that she'd only defended their leaving Jasmine, the little one Jason had been trying to protect.

Anna stepped up to Keith, bowing her head even as she tilted her neck, baring it. When she righted, he realized tears streaked her face, and her skin was so pale he wondered if she might need a doctor. "He was right behind me, so I thought. Then he took off the other way. I didn't know what he was doing, but I wasn't going to stay out here and get attacked." She sniffled a little before continuing. "'Tweren't until we were inside that I realized he had Jasmine, but I was terrified if I opened the door that those vile idiots attacking us would get to the others." She gulped then rushed to finish. "I was terrified for my grandbaby and for your mate. Will your young man be all right?"

Keith looked around to the cabins and then to where Jason and Jasmine had been when he found them. "That's a long way to run, especially when running into a group of snarling cats," he said instead of answering her. He was barely holding it together as it was, and thinking of how much blood there'd been wouldn't help any of them right then.

"He's fast, Keith," Sasha said from behind him. "You may not realize it, but Jason runs every day. But more than being angry at them for failing to protect your mate and the little one, you need to figure out what to do with the cats we detained," he said with contempt. "And what you want to do about the one that sent them here."

"What I want to do is to rip every one of them to shreds," he growled, his cat itching to take over and hunt down his father. He knew who was ultimately to blame for the attack, but that didn't make him any less in want of blood from those who had actually attacked. The sudden tension behind him only barely penetrated Keith's ire.

"That wouldn't be advised," Trace said from his other side. "Your father, I assume, is the one behind this?" At Keith's nod, he added, "Then might I suggest you stop worrying if he plans to challenge you and you challenge him instead? He endangered kits and humans alike. Neither is acceptable."

"I never wanted all this," he mumbled as he turned to look back at the cabin where Jason lay under the watchful eye of both shifter and vampire. "I wanted to show my mate what family was like for us. Share our gathering with him so he'd be as proud to be associated with them as I am."

"This isn't your fault," Sasha soothed. Never in his life had Keith thought a vampire would try to calm him, but for whatever reason, it worked. "But the one here, whom I do not know the name of yet," Sasha said a little tersely, as if Keith had deliberately not introduced them, "is right. Your former alpha made a move, twice now. This time you need to show your claws, not your connections."

Keith turned his head and bellowed, "Van!"

Almost immediately, Vance stood before him, cowed as everyone else in the area seemed to be. Well, all the shifters at least. "Yes, Alpha?"

"Go find out if my father's second is among those captured. If he is, issue my formal challenge and release him. Only him. If not, take however many cats you deem necessary and deliver the challenge. I will not allow another attack on my mate or my tribe!"

"Yes, Alpha." Vance took off fast enough it managed to startle most of the others. Keith knew how fast Vance was, but not many did.

"I will contact the council as soon as possible," Trace said, his gaze not leaving Sasha's even as he continued to speak to Keith. "I will let them know what is happening. Since I was here, participating in your gathering, I can verify that you did nothing to cause the attack."

"Thank you, Trace."

Trace bobbed his head once and scurried off in the opposite direction.

Keith rubbed his hands over his face hard and sighed. He wanted to go check on Jason, but he needed to interrogate the detained cats. "Gods!"

"No," one of the other vampires with Sasha said, "just vampire."

When Keith looked over, he realized the man was holding up Keith's discarded clothes. "Uh, thanks."

"No problem."

Keith tried for a smile but didn't think he succeeded. Giving up, he pulled on his clothes and returned to Jason, and worried when he didn't wake up. "You sure we don't need to take him to the hospital?" he asked the doctor. That was another position he didn't have filled yet. Well, they had him, but he didn't know how to treat humans, only animals.

"I believe Prince Sasha induced his slumber, Alpha Keith," the vampire said, not looking up from where he poked and manipulated Jason's wounded hand. "I think...," he continued, bending closer as he looked through a strange set of optics similar to what Keith had seen a jeweler wear. "Yes, I believe a small piece of tooth broke off in your mate's hand. Untreated, it could cause all manners of infection and poisoning."

Keith gasped at the word *poisoning*. "You can get it out, right?"

"Yes, yes. Now go hyperventilate over there, please. I don't want you passing out on top of my patient."

BY THE time Keith heard back from Vance, he knew that they had been attacked by fifteen cats in total and that, yes, his father's second had been among them. Sadly, he was one of the ones who had escaped before he, his new tribe, and the vampires could contain them all.

Sasha seemed to be in just as foul a mood as Keith was, though he didn't think it all had to do with Jason. The vampire glared off and on at the spot where Trace had disappeared. He wanted to ask what that was about but didn't have the strength or even the patience to find out right then.

When Vance strode back into the clearing, four men with him, he seemed almost chipper.

"Alpha Keith," he said, baring his neck. "Challenge has been delivered and accepted. The old fool said it would be easy to take back his missing members because you were a"—Vance made air quotes and snickered—"pansy ass that wouldn't be able to even hold his own. He's convinced himself that you being gay somehow makes you less of an Alpha and less of a fighter. Moron."

"Wait, he thinks I'll lose because I'm gay?" Keith wasn't sure how to feel about the slam. "What the hell does my choice in a mate have to do with my strength, training, or, well, anything?"

"I have no idea. He even made reference to your Chosen One of Baast status, but acted as if it meant nothing when compared to you being gay. Oh, and he demanded that the challenge be held as soon as possible and that you return his missing members."

"If I could turn them over to the human police, I would, but as it stands, I'm not certain what to do with them until the time comes."

"That's an easy one," Trace said as he finally reappeared. "I've sent for council enforcers. They will take the ones you caught and deal with them. Then you will defeat your old alpha in the challenge—especially if he chooses to ignore what you truly are—and afterward you have the choice of taking over the old tribe and reintegrating everyone or banishing them and building up your new tribe."

"The only ones I want to banish are those that would attack women, children, and humans. Those I have no interest in ever dealing with again. The others are welcome, always."

"You're a good alpha," Trace replied and smiled. "For now, though, you need to set up for the challenge. Somewhere secure, and I would recommend that you have as many there to witness, though not close enough to be seen as interference, as possible. Don't know that having the vampires there would be advisable, as your association with them is still seen as a possible flaw in your leadership strength. I would, however, recommend that you invite your wolf connection. Again, not close enough to interfere, but close enough to witness who the winner is. You should also have your personal guard, second, and mate there. However, since your mate is human, that might not be the best idea."

"Why not?" Keith asked, turning his irritation over the whole situation on Trace.

"Because it might upset him to see you fighting, naked, in front of a crowd of people. Humans have strange sensibilities about such things."

"Oh." Well, that did make sense, and he wasn't sure how Jason would feel about being there or the fight. "I didn't think of that. We're all raised to know hunting and how fights work; humans aren't. I'll talk to him." Keith turned to stare at Sasha. "When he eventually wakes up."

"You wanted him awake to feel the removal of a tooth from his hand or the stitching or—?"

"I get it. You did it to protect him. I know, really. I just don't like when you do that."

"And I don't like needing to," Sasha said with a dainty snort. "Now instead of fussing at me, why don't you go work out the details for—"

Jason's yell was loud and pained, and before Keith thought about it, he was standing next to his mate, hissing and doing all he could not to rip the vampire's throat out. "Away."

"I was stitching up his hand after removing the tooth fragment when he came to and started yelling." The doctor's gaze shifted from Keith's to Sasha's, who was beside Keith, not looking any happier than Keith felt. "I thought you'd left him under until you returned and would then wake him."

"I did." Sasha reached for Jason, but Keith grabbed his wrist tight. "Keith, let go of me. Jason shouldn't have woken. In fact, I don't think he did." Sasha shook his wrist in Keith's grip. "Now."

It took all Keith's will to release Sasha and to step back. When he did, he realized Sasha was right. Jason wasn't awake. He'd yelled, they'd all heard him, but he looked just as unconscious as he had when Keith had left him earlier. "What happened?"

"I made him sleep but that doesn't mean he can't feel." Sasha brushed his hand along Jason's brow. "The repairs to his hand must have been too much. The fact your healing is working on him means he shouldn't still be in that much pain."

"This would be the likely culprit, Prince Sasha." The vampire doctor held up a jagged bit of tooth, small but dangerous-looking. "This is what I pulled out of his hand just before he started screaming. Maybe if his mate fed him again it would work better now. It's hard to help a wound that still has a foreign object in it, after all."

"Then why don't we all excuse ourselves for a time," Sasha said as he herded the others out.

In a matter of a minute or so, Keith was alone with Jason. The idea of feeding Jason healing blood while he was unconscious sat heavy on his mind and heart, but he'd seen how it healed Jason when they'd mated. He had to believe it would again now.

Cutting his wrist enough to start the trickle, Keith brought it to Jason's mouth and was thrilled when Jason swallowed without help. When the cut healed, Keith sat back and watched as the torn skin knitted itself back together, though scars that wouldn't have been there for a shifter were left behind. Jason's color also improved, as did his breathing.

Satisfied, Keith stood and let Sasha and the doctor back in. He wasn't leaving Jason's side until Sasha woke Jason again and Keith could make sure his mate was really okay.

Chapter Twenty-Four

Even though they were mated—the tribe and council had already accepted Jason as his mate—Keith still didn't want to wait until after the challenge to marry Jason. When Jason had first proposed, odd though it had been, Keith had only said yes to make Jason feel better. It was a human tradition, not a lynx one, so it hadn't meant that much to him.

Now, however, he paced in the room he'd claimed to get changed in, dressed but so nervous he couldn't focus.

"Keith, you need to calm down." Vance was the only one inside the room with him. Chance stood outside, as did Kelley.

"I'm trying. I don't even know why I'm so nervous." He wiped his hands down his pants and again tried to reason with himself and his cat. "It's not like this changes whether we're mates or anything."

"No, but it's a huge thing to Jason. I think you're just picking up on how excited and nervous he is. For a human, a wedding is a huge deal, like claiming our mate is to us. Only this one takes place in front of others and doesn't involve sex."

"That's…. That's probably true. Our bond keeps strengthening, and sometimes his feelings do bleed over."

Vance chuckled. "Man, if you think that's true, then just breathe and try to calm down. It'll probably help your mate to calm down too."

Could that work? "One way to find out." Keith stopped where he was, closed his eyes, and took in a deep breath, held it, then let it go slowly. He repeated the actions a few times and instead of focusing on the wedding, he thought back to that morning, to how content he'd been just to hold his mate as the man slept. How Jason's soothing scent always wrapped around Keith and both calmed and excited him.

As his breathing slowed and his pulse settled down, Keith was finally able to sort his feelings from Jason's. He was thrilled that he could feel Jason like that. He'd heard that many of the older lynx had bonds that strong, but he thought he wouldn't be able to share something like that with Jason because his mate was human. Thrilled to be wrong, he opened his eyes and grinned at Vance. "Damn, Van! Thanks."

"Eh, just glad it helped. Now it's almost time, so you need to put your tux coat on and get out there so you can get all legal."

"Dork," Keith teased as he slid into his jacket.

"Are Prince Tolstoi, Caleb, and Alpha Hunter here already?" Jason and he had sent both men formal invitations. Keith had followed that up in Liam Hunter's case with a phone call to make sure he and any he brought with him understood there would be vampires, as Jason's best man or man of honor or whatever Sasha was would be there, as would his assistant and guards. Jason had made a similar call to Sasha, making sure he realized that at least a few wolves would be in attendance. Thankfully neither side seemed too worried about the other.

"They are already here and seated, so stop stalling and get out there."

Keith took a moment to look in the mirror and smoothed down his lapels and his hair, then stepped over to the door and rested his hand on the knob.

When he looked down, Keith again noticed the tattoo on his left wrist. He and Jason had gotten the tattoos only two days before, but with his increased healing and the added speed if he shifted, his tattoo was already healed. It was a tribal-styled design with a series of tiny human footprints and lynx paw prints wrapped around his left wrist, with a Celtic heart knot on the underside. Jason had the same on his, though his was still a little pink, even with the help of Keith's blood; his healing wasn't quite as strong.

"I'm ready," he whispered as he opened the door.

Only a few short minutes later he stood next to Jason, holding his hand. "You ready, baby?"

"F-for you? Always."

The music started as they walked together down the short aisle between their gathered friends and family. Keith took a moment to look around, again taking in the forest they stood within, the clear azure sky, and the fact both Vance and Prince Sasha stood at the front, along with the priest Jason had found.

They weren't of the same spirituality, and as lynx didn't usually involve themselves in such things as human marriages, he'd left it to Jason to decide how this part would be done. In the end, Jason had spoken to a work contact who also happened to be a pagan priest. The fact the priest intended to invoke their spirit ancestors instead of any specific deity suited Keith and seemed to satisfy Jason as well.

When they made it to the front—which seemed a lot longer trip when done in the ceremony than it had when they'd set up the chairs earlier—they stopped together, and each of their chosen men of honor or best men—he still wasn't certain which term was correct—stepped forward to stand with them.

"Welcome to the joining of Keith Skyler and Jason Grant. Today we join these two in the bonds of marriage and love...."

By the time they got to the "you may kiss" part, Keith couldn't remember most of the beginning of the wedding, his nerves jumping again. But when Jason turned to him and pulled him down into a kiss, Keith forgot anything but his mate.

At the press of Jason's lips, Keith parted his lips and sucked Jason's tongue inside, letting his dance with its mate's as he deepened the kiss. Jason moaned, his hands gripped Keith's shoulders hard, and he gave as good as he got.

The loud applause eventually broke through Keith's lust, and he pulled back. They both panted as he smiled and said, "I love you."

Jason gasped, then beamed as he threw himself into Keith's arms. "I love you too. Thank you," he murmured against Keith's chest.

"Now if the two grooms will separate a moment, I'll happily introduce them." Keith and Jason both stepped back and turned to the priest, Jason a handsome shade of red. "Thank you, boys. Please face the crowd.

"It is my pleasure to introduce the happy couple, Keith and Jason. May your lives be long and your hearts be blessed."

Much to Keith's shock, when Jason took his hand at the end of the wedding, he felt their bond strengthen even more. Jason gasped and looked up at him. "Wh-what was that?" he asked, his voice barely carrying to Keith.

"Our bond, I believe. I can feel you inside," Keith said, placing his hand over his heart.

"I can f-feel you too." Jason turned wide eyes on Keith as their friends surrounded them, doling out hugs and backslaps alike. Eventually they made it to the buffet and through the dancing. By the time they could retire to their own space, Keith was exhausted, but just the happy look on Jason's face made it all worthwhile—as did the joy coming through their bond.

THE BLISS from their wedding was overshadowed by the event the next day. Jason didn't want Keith to have to fight, though he understood—

mostly—why it was necessary. One look at his right hand was all it took to know this was the right thing for Keith, his tribe, and Jason.

Jason looked away from the near-perfect dental impression of the violent creature who had attacked him and Jasmine to see the staging area for the fight. They'd gone much, much deeper into the forest and set guards to make sure no hapless humans stumbled onto the challenge.

They'd cleared the ground in a large area, and the spectators lined the outer portion. There was a large blank space on either side of those gathering, through which the two combatants would enter. Jason knew Keith would win, that Keith would be fine, and if he had to set that as a chant in his head as he tried to stand tall and strong for his mate, none of those gathered would know. Well, Sasha would, as would Keith, which is why he worked so hard to stay calm and show his faith in his husband.

Just thinking the word made his heart skip and his worry fade a little. Keith was his, and he wouldn't have any trouble winning. Jason had seen Keith's were-lynx form and knew that when he was in that form, no one stood a chance. Especially no mere regular cat.

Jason did worry about the fact that Keith's father knew about his being a Chosen of Baast. He feared what Adam would do with that information. Would he cheat? Give in? Fight to the death, convinced no gay cat could be truly powerful? The questions circled through him, though he refused to let anyone see more than his love and faith in Keith.

Trace stood in the middle of the open area, speaking the rules. After he was done, he would move to the side. Because he was the representative from the council, he couldn't stand with either group, though he'd told Jason that he would stand with Keith if he were allowed.

"The alpha challenge only ends when one alpha concedes, in which case he is then banished from the lands and community of the winner, or when only one remains alive. Either alpha may concede at any point and the combat stops immediately. No one besides the alpha challengers may enter the combat, period. In the off chance that the alpha to win does not wish to take over the other tribe, the recorded second of the losing will be allowed to challenge for alpha position and thus become the new alpha of the banished tribe...."

Jason listened to Trace, fighting his nerves and fears when death was mentioned. Eventually the instructions and warnings were done and the two men entered the circle. Adam Skyler was a big man, hard and muscular. He was also radiating anger and ego. He more strutted than walked out, obviously sure of his abilities.

Keith, on the other hand, walked like a king, all power and strength without the same attitude, as he entered from the other side. "I give you this one chance. Concede and release those that wish to join my tribe, and I will allow you to leave in peace. You and those that wish to stay with you."

"You're not fit to lead, you unnatural, perverted monstrosity," Adam snarled. "Defend yourself, if you can."

Jason struggled to watch the match, knowing it was important for Keith to know his mate was there. It was also important for the shifters in attendance to see Jason supporting Keith as a good mate should. He had to stay strong for both groups of cats, as both would look on how he did or did not show faith in Keith as a factor of strength or one of weakness. Being male and gay were already two strikes against him with many of the assembled, so being found weak was not an option.

Keith initially fought in the form Adam took, shifting flawlessly from human to cat and back, much faster and smoother than Adam—or any of the other lynx he'd seen shift. The gasps that ran through the crowd the first time Keith shifted from human to lynx were loud and satisfying. Keith's old tribe had little knowledge of their alpha's son's abilities. The sounds from Keith's own tribe were much more satisfied, and if a sound could be smug, theirs was.

After a time, though, Keith became impatient—Jason could feel the irritation and pain as well—and shifted to his were-lynx form, drawing even more gasps and shouts from the crowd on the opposite side of the clearing. While Adam and his second knew of Keith being a Chosen of Baast—as did Keith's own cats—that news had not spread to the regular cats of the Glacier Rim Tribe. Jason couldn't help but smile at Keith in his were-form, proud to be the husband and mate of such a powerful and loving man.

Even once Keith took his were-cat form, Adam did not yield as Jason had hoped. They continued to battle, Adam screaming out insults and taunts when he was in human form. Jason suspected that could he understand the screeches and mewls of Adam's lynx, he would have heard even more venom.

Keith pinned Adam to the ground at one point and bellowed, "Stop. Yield and swear to never raise paw or word against me and mine again and I will let you leave."

Instead of taking the offer, the bleeding and battered Adam sneered and spat at Keith. "You're not a man or a lynx. You're an abomination! I'll

see you dead before I let you continue to poison real cats!" He then shifted
under Keith and, in his lynx form, managed to escape Keith's grasp.

The next thing Jason knew, Adam stood on the opposite side of the
clearing marked for combat, a gun in hand as he continued to rain down
his hate and vitriol. "Return my daughter and heir, all the cats you stole,
and submit to imprisonment now, or I'll remove you from this life. You are
not a Chosen of Baast! You are a perversion of our kind." Adam seethed,
the gun unsteady in his hand as he kept it mostly pointed at Keith.

"Father, don't do this. I do not wish to kill you. Only to be free of
you and yours." Keith's voice was strong as he beseeched Adam to give
in, but his words were ignored.

"Kill me? You can't kill me, boy. Full gun versus disgusting pathetic
shifter? Right will rule and you will die. Your body will be left for the
crows to pick clean."

The gasps and horrified murmurs that ran through the crowd at
Adam's last words twisted Jason's heart. He knew that such a fate was
blasphemous to shifters. Even Adam's people seemed horrified.

Jason prayed to Baast for Keith's safety and triumph, not having ever
done so before. He wasn't even sure he believed in the feline goddess, but
he hoped that if she was real, she really would look with favor upon Keith,
the Chosen of Baast, and protect him.

"Yield, dammit!" Keith said again. "I do not wish to kill you."

"You were always weak," Adam countered as a bright flash and a
loud bang reverberated through the open space.

What seemed like mere seconds later, Keith stood over the still form
of his father, panting and hissing. When he looked up, Jason gasped. Keith
was still in were form, blood covering much of his short, sparse fur as it
dripped from his claws and fangs.

Keith dropped the body and ran straight at Jason. He felt need and
pain but not anger. Part of him wanted to run, but another, stronger part
stood still other than to raise his arms and wait.

The body that slammed into him would have terrified him not that
long ago, but right then, all he could think to do was hold Keith, stroking
down his back as he comforted his mate and love. Keith purred, his chest
rumbling against Jason's as he clutched Jason tight to him. Jason could
feel Keith's clawed hands against his back but knew Keith would never
use them to hurt unless there was no other option—as there had been to
fight in the challenge.

An eternity later, Trace spoke from next to Jason. "Alpha Keith? You need to come welcome your new tribe. There are many waiting for you."

Jason didn't want to release Keith but knew he needed to. Keith let go and stood tall, shifting back to his human form. "Let me get dressed and I will be right there."

"As you wish" was all Trace said before stepping away.

All of Keith's clothes were beside Jason, though he wasn't certain when they'd been placed there. Instead of worrying about it, he handed them over and waited for Keith to dress.

"Do you need me to do anything?"

"Stand with me as I welcome those that wish to stay." Keith leaned in and inhaled against Jason's temple a few times before he pulled back and gave him a small, brittle smile. "You by my side is all I'll ever need."

KEITH HAD been surprised that nearly all of his old tribe joined him. Only those who had attacked him or Jason before the fight, and parts of their families chose banishment—not that Keith would have welcomed the cats who had sought to hurt his mate, anyway.

He'd also found out where the one round Adam had shot went, as he'd been a little distracted at the time. Thankfully his father had been a horrible shot, as the bullet had embedded in a stump beside where Jason had stood during the challenge.

The weeks after were an endless stream of well-wishers, people wanting to move closer to where Keith and Jason lived, and Keith trying to learn all he could about being a good alpha. In that, Trace was indispensable and a boon he thanked Baast for daily.

Trace was also trying to help Keith piece together what all their tribe was missing as far as lore and history. Sadly, no one had any idea why there was so much missing. Even the older shifters didn't seem to know about Orin or human mates, so it had to be that not only did Adam hide information, but Adam's father had to have suppressed the information as well. Keith wished he could ask why, but there was no one left to ask.

The other thing that bothered him was how much time Jason spent working. He hated how his mate was often tied to his damned computers when Keith was home. Keith knew it wasn't right to feel jealous of bits of plastic and wiring, but sometimes it felt as though Jason was hiding behind the machines more than truly working.

As he again debated whether to go in and insist Jason step away from the computers, Jason called out, "Keith, can you come here for a few?"

That was promising. Jason sounded happy and felt downright giddy through their link. Instead of responding, Keith simply hurried into Jason's office. "What do you need, baby?"

"Other than you?" Jason teased, his voice light as he grinned. "Well… I thought you'd like to hear about what my Realtor friend just sent me."

Keith blinked at Jason, confused. "Why are you getting messages from Realtors? I thought you liked the house."

"I do, but I also promised you that I'd help you build up land for the tribe on this side of the city, remember? And well," Jason explained, then stopped as he turned and pointed to the huge screen before him. "I thought this tract of land would be a good start. It sits right against the national park, so you'd have land you own and the forest to run in without worrying about humans."

It took a moment for Keith to process what he saw and what was on the other screens around the big one.

"You've been working on getting us land and how to afford it?" Keith knew his voice was high, but he didn't care. He was too busy fighting the overwhelming wave of pride and joy in his mate.

"I have." Jason took a deep breath, then started speaking faster than usual, "Taylor told me what I needed to look for, and I think I've worked out the financing so we can buy it. I figured it all with both our finances in mind, but I'll understand if you want to only have your name on it. It's your tribe's land, after all."

Jason paused, but before Keith could get a word in, he continued, "Oh, and there's a building on the edge that used to be an animal hospital, but it closed down a couple of years ago. I don't know if it'll be usable, but I thought you could maybe use that at least part-time as a hospital for both animals and the shifters who get hurt in their animal forms."

"Both our names, baby. It should have both our names. It's your tribe too, I assure you." He kissed Jason hard and fast for a little before pulling back. He beamed as he looked at Jason, not caring how lovestruck he looked. "Did you consider the sale of my father's land? I'm not keeping it. Part is going to be sold to those that wish to continue living there, and the rest I'll sell or invest somehow."

Jason turned back to his computers and typed for a moment as the screen changed. "These are the figures for if you decided to sell. Taylor wasn't sure how much you intended to sell, so this may be a bit conservative. However, if you do, that just means we can buy more land or use it to rehab the vet center on the land."

Keith scooped Jason up, barely noticing the numbers and acreage. "Wrap your legs around me, baby. We're going to go celebrate now."

With that announcement, Keith carried his mate to their bedroom and showed him exactly how happy he was.

EPILOGUE

KEITH LEANED against the kitchen doorway, admiring how his son and nephew looked in their new backyard. He still couldn't have imagined how much their lives had changed in the last five years. When Jason stepped up next to him, Keith smiled and let out a little sigh. The day was perfect, clear and warm, but only pleasantly so. He reached out, then slid one hand down Jason's back before tugging him closer and wrapping one arm around his mate.

Once Jason settled against Keith's side, he nuzzled against Jason's neck, loving how his mate smelled and tasted, that scent that said home to both Keith's human and lynx. Right then, though, Keith had to behave since they *were* outside watching Sean and Zeke play. He loved their son and nephew and was thankful that Zeke didn't mind playing with his cousin, even though Sean was both younger and half-human.

When Taylor had offered to be their surrogate, Keith had been floored but thankful. He'd always wanted his own kit, but never thought to have one. He also knew Jason wanted a family but hadn't believed he could ever have one. They had both poured their love into Zeke, even offering to babysit if Taylor needed a break or chose to date. As of yet, she hadn't taken them up on the latter.

Instead of complaining as he'd expected—what child wants to have a baby hang out with them?—Zeke had embraced Jason and Keith's son. Both parents had to be shifters for the child to be a shifter, but that never fazed Zeke any. Even with the six-year age difference and the fact Sean couldn't shift, the children had been fast friends and playmates since Sean was big enough to play with Zeke.

"Papa," Sean whined to Jason when Zeke outran him, again. "No fair." Sean stomped one foot and pouted, the look even more lethal than Zeke's glare.

"Sean, no whining," Jason corrected. "Zeke's just bigger and older. You're doing fine."

They stood on the back porch of the home they'd built on the land Jason had helped him buy. It had been easier once Keith had taken over his old pack and chose to sell much of the land, though not all of it. Some of the families had chosen to move with Keith, some had stayed on the old tribe land, and some families had chosen to leave the tribe. Those who'd left were ones he wasn't sorry to see gone; xenophobia and homophobia were not things he would tolerate.

Rebuilding had been hard in some ways, Taylor and he both missed their father, even after how horribly he'd behaved near the end. Still, to lose a parent was bad enough, but to lose both and to have been forced to be the instrument of his father's death still bothered him at times, but then Jason would remind him that it was his father's choice, not Keith's.

"Keith?" Jason said as he tugged on Keith's arm. Keith barely noticed as he thought back over all the changes he'd made and how so many cats had moved to the greater Seattle area to join their tribe. "Keith!"

The smack from Jason startled him enough to pay attention. "What?" he asked, irritated at being hit, though it hadn't hurt any.

Instead of responding, Jason pointed to where Zeke had shifted to his lynx form. *Wait! Who the hell is the other kit?* "Um, where's Sean and where did the kitten come from?"

"That's Sean!" Jason forced out, nothing but his lips moving as he stared. "You said he wouldn't ever be able to shift."

"But...." *How could that be Sean?*

He quickly released Jason and strode over to the strange kitten, unable to take his eyes off his son. Once what Jason had said sunk in, he'd felt it. He trusted his senses because they never lied. "Sean?"

The kitten turned and stared up at Keith and mewed.

"Can you shift back to your human, baby?" Now that he knew the kitten was Sean, he worried if his son would be able to return to his human skin, but even as he knelt beside Sean, Sean returned to his human form. "Daddy, I shifteded," he said and grinned. "I kitty too!"

"Yes, baby, you are." He didn't understand how a half-human-slash-half-lynx shifter could take both forms, but that was a concern for another day. "Want to learn how to run as a lynx?"

"Uh-huh. Zeke too, Daddy?"

"Sure, Zeke can come too. Let me just tell your papa what we're doing."

Keith stood and shuffled over to Jason—who was much closer than he'd thought. Mind still spinning, Keith managed to get out, "I'm going to run with the boys a little. We won't go far."

"How did Sean shift?"

"I have no idea, baby. For now, just be happy for him."

"Oh, I am. I know how much shifting means to you and that Sean was bound to feel left out as he got older. I think I'll call Taylor while you take the boys out, but um… don't go too far?"

Jason didn't take his eyes off Sean the entire time he spoke, and he looked so confused. When Keith got back, he'd call the council, or maybe just Trace—he'd officially joined the tribe not long after the alpha challenge, though Keith personally thought being near Sasha had more to do with the choice than anything cat related. Any time Sasha was around, Trace followed him almost to the exclusion of all else.

"Daddy?"

"Sorry, Sean." Keith scooped up his son and hugged him tight. "We can play in our lynx forms, but you have to promise to let me know if you get tired. I don't want you falling because you shift back at the wrong time."

Keith stood and stepped back, allowing Sean to change back on his own. He leaned in and gave Jason a soft kiss, then smiled. "I'll be back shortly, baby."

"I'll be right here, love. Always."

That was all Keith needed to know. He loved Jason more than life itself, and to know that his mate loved him and their family, would stay by their side, was more than he'd ever hoped for but had secretly always wanted. Who knew shopping for a house to escape his father would lead him to his heart and his future?

Happier than he ever thought he'd be, Keith stripped and shifted, then he joined Sean and Zeke in their game of kitty tag. He tumbled and ran with both boys as Sean learned his new body.

He took a moment here and there to look over to where Jason still watched, the soft smile on his mate's lips enough to make his heart swell and his love grow.

Fate, chance, and love….

TEMPESTE O'RILEY is an out and proud pansexual, genderfluid whose best friend growing up had the courage to do what she couldn't—defy the hate and come out. He has been her hero ever since.

Tempe is a hopeless romantic who loves strong relationships and happily-ever-afters. Though new to writing M/M, she has done many things in her life, yet writing has always drawn her back—no matter what else life has thrown her way. She counts her friends, family, and Muse as her greatest blessings in life. She lives in Wisconsin with her children, reading, writing, and enjoying life.

Tempe is also a proud member of Romance Writers of America®, Rainbow Romance Writers, and WisRWA.

Learn more about Tempeste and her writing at tempesteoriley.com or on Facebook.

CAGED SANCTUARY
Tempeste O'Riley

Kaden Thorn, a dental surgeon who lives a quiet life, has no hope of finding the love he craves. A vicious gay bashing cost him the use of his legs and confined him to a wheelchair. He has given up hope of finding a Dom or even a nonkink partner to love him. When his best friend practically forces him to attend a dinner party, the last thing he expects is a strong Dom who can see beyond his wheels.

Deacon James is an architect and a demanding Dom, but he has spent the past couple of years without a sub or partner. When an employee invites him to a dinner party to meet his girlfriend, Deacon smells a setup but agrees anyway. He prides himself on being an excellent judge of character, and when he meets the younger dentist, he sees past the chair and finds a sweet submissive man who more than piques his interest.

Kade's fears and demons continue to haunt him, challenging Deacon to use everything he's learned as a Dom to earn Kade's trust and submission. Deacon's determined, though, willing to battle all of it to have Kade by his side and at his feet.

www.dreamspinnerpress.com

TEMPESTE O'RILEY

DESIGNS of DESIRE

Artist James Bryant has forearm crutches in every color from rainbow for fun to sleek black for business. He even has a pair with more paint splatters than metal. After his family's rejection and abuse from a man he thought loved him, James only just gets through the day by painting. He lives in constant fear that he's not worthy of anything, let alone love.

As CEO of his company, Carrington Enterprises, Seth Burns is a take-charge kind of guy, and he is instantly smitten by the artist helping with his newest project. When he witnesses James suffer a panic attack, a protective instinct he never knew he had kicks in. He truly believes nothing is unobtainable—including James—if he's willing to put in the time and effort.

James is shy and confused by Seth's interest in him as a person. With Seth's support, can he work through his fears to finally find the true love he deserves, or will someone finally land the crushing blow he won't survive?

www.dreamspinnerpress.com

TEMPESTE O'RILEY

BOUND by DESIRE

DESIRES ENTWINED SERIES

A Spin-off of *Designs of Desire*
Desires Entwined: Book 1.75

Despite his past abuse, James has come to terms with his relationship with his Dom and lover Seth. Seth treats James with all the trust and love his sub desires. There is only one thing left to do to make it all complete: Seth needs to put a collar on James.

www.dreamspinnerpress.com

TEMPESTE O'RILEY

ESIRES'
GUARDIAN

DESIRES ENTWINED SERIES

Desires Entwined: Book Two

Most people see Chase Manning as the party-boy twink he seems on the surface. Only James, Chase's BFF, knows the depth of his loyalty and the extent of the wounds Chase carries inside. When Chase meets Rhys Sayer, things don't go well, but he can't shake his attraction to the huge, sexy man.

Rhys is a man of contradictions and fear—a strange combination for a PI and bodyguard. He's in a bad place emotionally when he sets eyes on Chase for the first time. When Chase puts the moves on him, Rhys insults him, thwarting any possibility of a relationship. Rhys doesn't see himself as a complicated man, but he dreads the very kind of connection he desires.

Just as they're trying to overcome their uncertainties, Chase is put in harm's way. Luckily Rhys and their friends have all the right talents to help Rhys save the man of his dreams.

www.dreamspinnerpress.com

TEMPESTE O'RILEY

TEMPTATIONS *of* DESIRE

DESIRES ENTWINED SERIES

Desires Entwined: Book Three

Alexander James Noble is a gender fluid gay man who gave up on finding Mister Right a long time ago. He's not asking for much, though. He just wants a guy who loves all of him and appreciates his feminine form too.

At the local LGBTQ center where Alex regularly volunteers, he meets Dal Sayer, an officer of the Milwaukee PD. Because he's been rejected one too many times, Alex doesn't trust the huge cop and the interest he shows in him, but once Dal sets his mind on something, he goes all out. Pushing aside his preconceived notions, Alex opens up just a little and soon caves.

From their first date—while dealing with his father's failing health and his parents' demands for him to settle down and have children—Dal never takes his eyes off his goal of making Alex his. But proving to Alex he isn't like all the men who couldn't see him for who he truly was and only wanted to hide him away is harder than he thought.

www.dreamspinnerpress.com

TEMPESTE O'RILEY

TRUTH _in_ LACE

DESIRES ENTWINED SERIES

A spin-off of _Temptations of Desire_
Desires Entwined: Book 3.5

When Alexander James Noble looks in the mirror, he sees a freak looking back at him. Despite his high grades and plans for culinary arts school after graduation, his parents would hate him if they really knew him.

Forced on a shopping trip with his twin sister, Lyric, and her friends, Alex eyes the girls jealously, longing to be able to dress like them—to be them. The constant struggle of being "gender fluid," wrestling with an identity that seems to change daily, begins to wear on Alex. But all those questions and fears seem more manageable when his sister gives him his first skirt and lace panties.

www.dreamspinnerpress.com

Read more from this author in

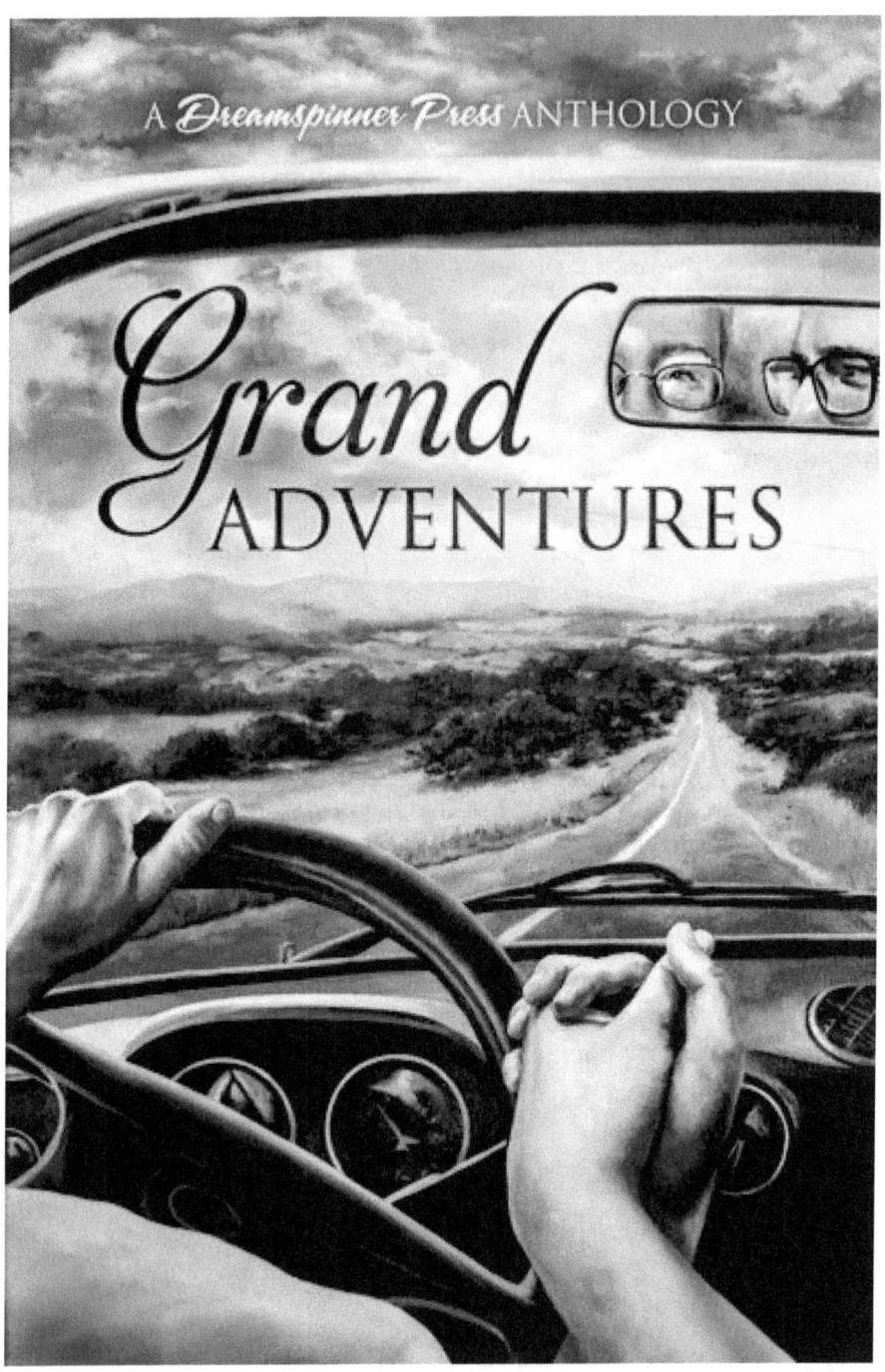

A *Dreamspinner Press* ANTHOLOGY

Grand
ADVENTURES

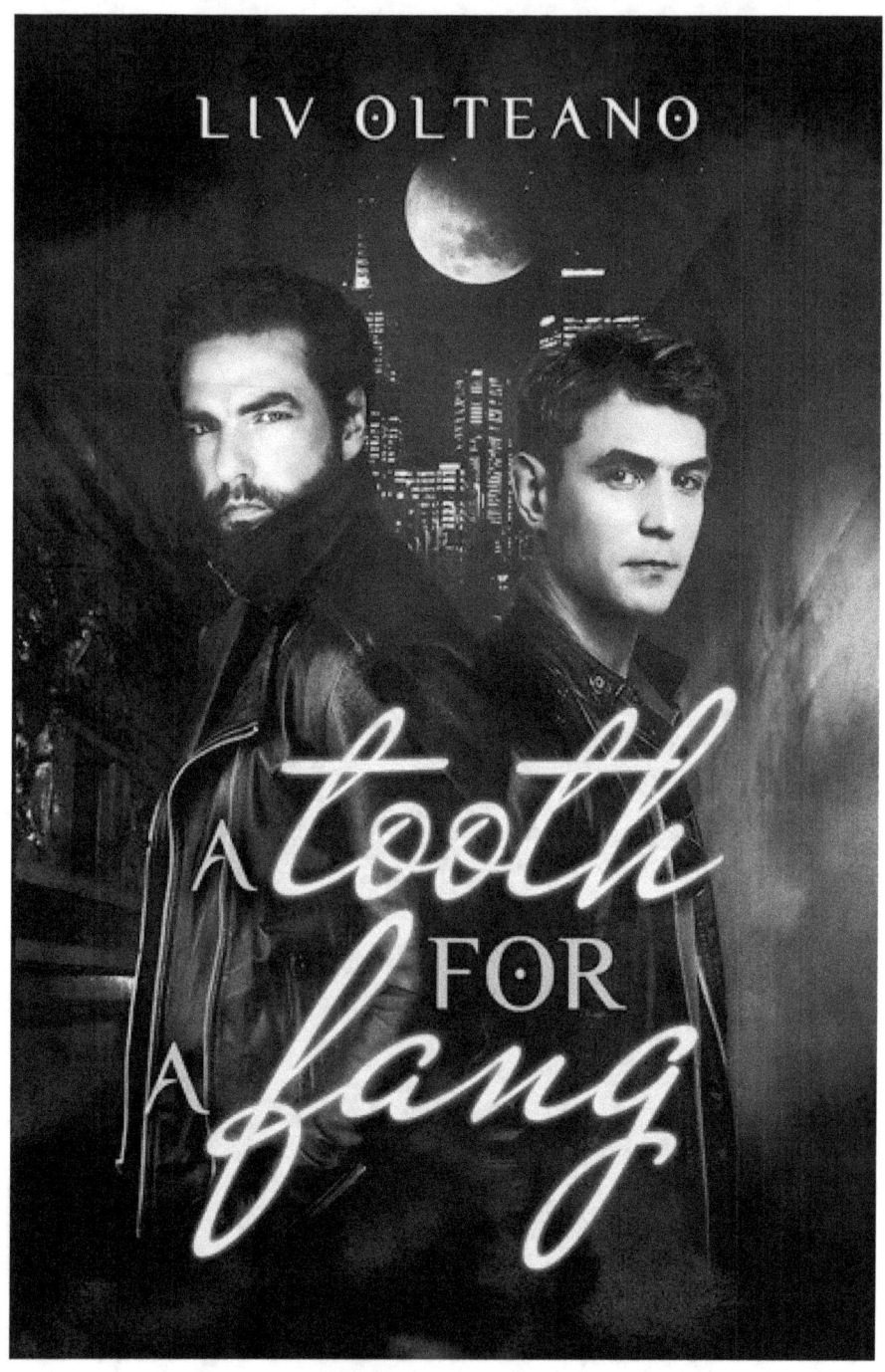

LIV OLTEANO

A tooth
FOR
A fang